**"Did my father know about your affair with Laura?"**

As soon as she'd blurted this out, Jessica belatedly realized she had said something unforgivable.

"How dare you!" James exclaimed, furiously grasping her arms. "I ought to throw you out for a remark like that. Even if you have lost your memory, you're still the same selfish witch Laura says you used to be."

"That's not true!" Jessica was horrified. "I was never selfish!"

"How do you know?" he demanded. "If you *really* don't remember who you are—"

Jessica gulped. "Don't you believe me?" she sobbed, and as if her desperate cry at last struck some sympathetic chord inside him, he released his painful grasp.

Jessica sensed that James had doubts about who she was. She was bewildered about herself, too—and her turbulent feelings for James.

**ANNE MATHER** began her career by writing the kind of book she likes to read—romance. Married, with two teenage children, this Northern England author has become a favorite with readers of romance fiction the world over—her books have been translated into many languages and are read in countless countries. Since her first novel was published in 1970, Anne Mather has written more than eighty romances, with over ninety million copies sold!

## Books by Anne Mather

HARLEQUIN PRESENTS

843—STOLEN SUMMER
869—PALE ORCHID
899—AN ALL-CONSUMING PASSION
1003—NIGHT HEAT
1044—BURNING INHERITANCE
1122—TRIAL OF INNOCENCE

HARLEQUIN ROMANCE

1631—MASQUERADE
1656—AUTUMN OF THE WITCH

# ANNE MATHER

# dark mosaic

Harlequin Books

TORONTO • NEW YORK • LONDON
AMSTERDAM • PARIS • SYDNEY • HAMBURG
STOCKHOLM • ATHENS • TOKYO • MILAN

Harlequin Presents first edition October 1989
ISBN 0-373-11210-6

Original hardcover edition published in 1989
by Mills & Boon Limited



Printed in U.S.A.

# CHAPTER ONE

THE GIRL really was incredibly like her. Sitting opposite her in the railway carriage, Ceci found her eyes straying often to those pale, narrow features facing hers across the narrow expanse of the formica-topped table. The same straight nose; the same mouth—which Ceci had always felt was a little too wide for real beauty; the same eyes, which Gran used to say were like violets put in with a smutty finger; even the same hair, although Ceci's single braid was a contrast to the other girl's loosened waves. But the corn-streaked toffee strands were very similar, and in the same clothes they could almost pass as sisters.

But they weren't, reflected Ceci regretfully, idly speculating on what the other girl's background might be. It was obvious she was not on her way to yet another doubtful interview. No one bent on such an objective would wear such an air of suppressed excitement. Unless it was a first interview, of course. After more than a dozen, Ceci was more blasé. But in any case, no one seeking possible employment would turn up in a coat that was evidently sable. The amazing thing was that the girl should be travelling second class. Dressed like that, Ceci would have expected her to buy a first-class ticket. But then, the train wasn't full, and perhaps the coat was just an indulgence. Who could tell? Gran had always maintained that you should never judge by appearances.

Turning her gaze to the less salubrious suburbs of London through which the train was presently passing, Ceci tried to anticipate her own destination with rather more enthusiasm. But it was difficult to feel enthusiastic about working in the north of England, when everyone and everything she had known all her life were in the south. Her landlady's impressions of living in Yorkshire, like her own, were coloured by images of grimy towns and coal-mines, and inner city deprivation.

Of course, London had its problems too, but London was familiar; Leeds wasn't.

Still, if she had a successful interview, at least it would be a job, doing what she wanted to do most. Since leaving the art college, where she had qualified as a designer in textiles, she had had no luck in finding such employment in London. It was over ten months now since she had been forced to use the small legacy her grandmother had left her to supplement her income, and in spite of living frugally she was finding it increasingly difficult to find the rent for the small bed-sitter where she had lived for the past four years.

While she was alive, her grandmother had done everything she could to support her only daughter's child. Her parents had been killed when Ceci was only four years old, and as she hardly remembered them, her grandmother had been the only family she knew. Things hadn't always been easy, she knew, but Gran had never complained. On the contrary, she used to say that having Ceci to care for had kept her young. Then, four years ago, just as Ceci was entering art college, she had died, too, and since then Ceci had had to support herself.

It hadn't been so bad while she was at college. She had had her grant for expenses, and her days had been fully occupied with the course she was taking. Also, in the holidays, it had been comparatively easy to find casual work. But, since leaving college last July, she had been eager to prove herself in her own field, and she knew if she went on accepting jobs as receptionists and waitresses she would never get to use the qualifications she had worked so hard to obtain. That was why she was on the ten o'clock express out of King's Cross, heading for Leeds and the Ripley Textile Company. She had an interview with the company's personnel manager at half-past three that afternoon; and if all went well—which was by no means a foregone conclusion, she reflected, with rueful irony—she would be moving to West Yorkshire, and a whole new life in the north. It wasn't as if she had any real ties in London any longer, she thought consolingly. Most of her friends from college had either married or moved away themselves, and while until recently she had thought she might be getting married herself, circumstances had proved that this was not to be the case...

'It's warm in here, isn't it?'

For a moment, Ceci didn't respond, not immediately realising that the girl was talking to her. On the contrary, in spite of her grandmother's homilies, she had judged her companion to be plummy-tongued and definitely stand-offish, and it was quite a surprise to hear her actually opening a conversation. In addition to which, her accent was what her grandmother would have described as distinctly 'east of the river', a minor disparagement from someone to whom an accent was definitely not to be encouraged.

In consequence, her 'I beg your pardon?' was also an automatic reflex, so that the girl grimaced ruefully before repeating her question.

'I said it's hot in here, isn't it?' she exclaimed, jerking the sable coat off her shoulders, and tipping it behind her on the seat. 'I expect it's this coat what's to blame. Elegant it may be, but it's too bloody heavy for today.'

Ceci hid a smile. 'It's a beautiful coat,' she said obliquely. 'And yes, it is warm in here. I think the heating's still on. I don't suppose they expected the weather to change so quickly.'

'No,' the girl acknowledged. 'It has been awful, hasn't it? Rain, rain, rain! I thought it'd never stop. Where I live, they thought the bleeding river was going to flood. Cor, that would've caused a stink. Literally, I mean, as well as for the authorities, if you see what I mean.' She grinned.

Ceci grinned, too. 'I can believe it.'

'Anyway, at least the sun has come out now,' continued her companion, nodding at the blue skies that were appearing more frequently as the buildings of London gave way to the cleaner spaces of Hertfordshire. 'Kind of an omen, isn't it? Like you're moving on to better things. Well, I am, anyway; I don't know about you.'

Ceci's smile became a little fixed. 'Let's hope so,' she murmured, not wanting to tempt fate by anticipating it.

'Are you going far?' persisted the other girl, fumbling in an expensive leather handbag and pulling out a pack of equally expensive cigarettes. 'You don't mind, do you? I've got to have a fag. I'm choking!'

Ceci shook her head, and then said reluctantly, 'Leeds,' hoping her companion would not consider it necessary to probe any further. But she was to be disappointed.

'Leeds, eh?' exclaimed the girl, lighting her cigarette with an elaborate gold lighter and then dropping it back into the bag. 'Now, isn't that a coincidence? That's where I'm headed, would you believe that?'

Ceci shook her head. 'No,' she murmured drily, and turned back to look out of the window.

'D'you know Leeds at all?' the girl continued, after a few gulping drags at her cigarette, and sighing, Ceci decided to explain.

'No,' she said briefly. 'It's my first visit. I'm going to attend an interview.'

'Oh, I see.' The girl nodded. 'What are you? A secretary, or something?'

'I'm a textile designer,' said Ceci patiently. 'I design patterns for fabrics, that sort of thing.' She shrugged as the other girl looked confused. 'It's not very interesting to anyone outside the trade.'

'Oh, no. I wasn't thinking that,' her companion assured her quickly. 'I just realised—we look a bit alike, don't we? Same sort of colouring. Same sort of build.'

Ceci pulled a wry face. 'But not the same sort of income, if that coat is any indication,' she remarked impulsively, and then wished she hadn't. Good heavens, the girl might think she was implying something immoral, and that had been the last thought in her mind, until now. 'I mean,' she coloured, 'that is, I didn't mean——'

'I know what you mean,' the girl opposite declared carelessly. 'You're wondering what someone like me is doing wearing clothes like this.' She flicked a hand at the form-fitting jersey silk of her dress and grimaced. 'I dare say I'd be wondering, too, if I was you. Well, I didn't steal the bleeding things, if that's what you're thinking.'

Ceci caught her breath. 'Oh, I never——'

'Didn't you?' The girl regarded her through the haze of her cigarette smoke. 'Well, you might have. Threads like these don't grow on trees, if you take my meaning.'

Ceci licked her lips. 'Honestly, I——'

'I've embarrassed you, haven't I?' Her companion pulled a face. 'I'm always doing that. It's what comes of saying what you mean, instead of mucking about. Where I live—*used* to live,' she corrected herself quickly, 'people don't have time to play with words. And where I'm going, if they don't like it, they're going to have to lump it!'

Ceci couldn't help laughing. 'I'm sorry,' she said, after a moment. 'I'm not laughing at you, really. It's just that—well, when I got on this train, I was feeling pretty depressed, but now—oh, you've made me feel a whole lot better.'

'That's good.' The girl finished her cigarette and, dropping it on to the floor, ground it out beneath her heel. 'So why don't we introduce ourselves, eh? My name's Jessica Devlin. What's yours?'

'Cecily Chambers,' replied Ceci at once, and Jessica smiled.

'Pleased to meet you, Cecily,' she acknowledged, holding out her hand. 'You don't mind if I call you Cecily, do you? As we're never likely to meet one another again, it does seem a waste of time to stand on ceremony.'

'I agree.' Ceci relaxed completely. 'I believe it takes about two hours to get to Leeds. Perhaps we could have some coffee later, to help pass the time.'

'OK.' Jessica nodded, and, shifting the sable coat on to the seat beside her, she settled back to enjoy the journey.

The carriage was fairly empty, Ceci noticed, allowing her gaze to wander. As it was near the front of the train, most people had found seats in the other carriages to save walking the length of the platform, and apart from two men seated near the door, and an elderly lady dozing two rows down, they were the only other passengers.

'Aren't you going to ask me why I'm travelling north?' Jessica enquired suddenly, breaking in to her thoughts, and Ceci blinked and looked back at her.

'Well, I——'

'No. You're not the nosy kind, are you?' Jessica remarked wryly. 'I'd be choked with curiosity, but you're not like that, worse luck!'

'Worse luck?' Ceci frowned. 'What do you mean?'

'Well, here am I dying to tell everybody what I'm doing, and you're not interested, are you?'

Ceci was honest. 'I wouldn't say that.'

'You mean, you would like to know?'

Ceci hesitated. 'If you want to tell me.'

Jessica chuckled. 'Would you believe I'm an heiress?'

Ceci would have believed anything of this extraordinary girl. 'An heiress?'

'Yeah. An heiress. I've inherited my father's business. And his house, and his cars, and his bank balance!'

Ceci stared at her. 'And is that good? I mean—that your father's dead and all?'

'Oh, yes.' Jessica was complacent. 'I never knew him, you see. I was a bastard!' She said the word without bitterness. 'My mother, God rest her soul, would never tell me who he was, but apparently the old devil decided to put the record straight before he snuffed it. I was his only child, it turns out, and rather than leave his money to some nephew or niece, he left it to me. His daughter.'

Ceci shook her head. 'And you knew nothing about him until now?'

'Not until this solicitor wrote to me, asking me to come to his office in Lincoln's Inn. You know, I got one of those letters saying if I'd come at a certain time, I'd hear something to my advantage.' She laughed. 'And I did.'

Ceci was amazed. 'How marvellous!'

'Yeah, isn't it?'

'So—that's why you're travelling to Leeds?'

'That's right. The old man used to live there, or at least, near there. There's a house in a village called Bickersley, or something, and a couple of mills in Wakefield and Bradford.'

Ceci thought it was incredible. 'And you own—everything?'

'Everything.'

'But—didn't your father have a wife?'

'Oh, yes. Mrs Bentley. That was my father's name, you know. Adam Bentley. She—his wife, that is—she still lives at the house in Bickersley. According to the solicitor, I can't put her out.'

Ceci caught her lower lip between her teeth. 'Would you want to?'

'Wouldn't you?'

Ceci thought a minute. 'No. No, I don't think so. I mean, you can hardly blame her for—well, for what your father did.'

Jessica shrugged. 'Maybe. Maybe not. It'll depend how she treats me, I suppose. I don't reckon she'll be too pleased to see me, do you?'

Ceci thought that was probably the understatement of the year. 'So—what do you intend to do?'

'Do?'

Ceci traced a pattern on the table top with her fingertip. 'Do you intend living with her?'

'With Mrs Bentley? No fear.' Jessica grimaced. 'No, I'm only paying them a visit to arrange for the sale of the mills. As soon as I can, I'll be hightailing it back to London, believe me.'

Ceci stared at her. 'But what about your employees? The people who work—*worked*—for your father?'

'What about them?'

'Well—don't you care what happens to them?'

'Did they care what happened to me?' Jessica was indifferent. 'Look—the way I see it, I've had to fend for myself all my life. Now they'll have to do the same. Bloody hell, I'm no bleeding heart! I've spent the past four years behind the tills in the supermarket. You can't expect me to worry about people I don't even know.'

Her logic was unshakeable, but Ceci couldn't help feeling sorry for the Bentleys and their employees.

'Well, I have a bed-sit,' said Ceci reluctantly. 'But I'm finding it difficult to pay its upkeep, actually. That's why I'm applying for this job in the north.'

'Well, I don't envy you,' said Jessica. 'Having to live up north, I mean. Like I say, I can't wait to get back to London.'

'Oh, it might not be so bad.' Ceci found herself defending the prospect. Funnily enough, as soon as Jessica began attacking the idea, she began to feel more hopeful about it.

'Well, it's up to you, of course. It's nothing to do with me really, is it?' Jessica grimaced. 'Me, I'm looking forward to spending some money. Pots and pots of it. The old man wasn't short of a bob or two, I can tell you.'

Ceci couldn't prevent the question that sprang to her lips. 'But what will Mrs Bentley do?'

'Who knows? Who cares?' Jessica evidently wasn't concerned. 'I dare say she's got relatives to support her. I don't. I never have had. I've always been on my own, if you know what I mean.'

Ceci couldn't help thinking that it was rather unfortunate that the Bentleys should have to deal with someone like Jessica. She could see Jessica's point of view. All her life she'd had to struggle for anything she wanted, whereas no doubt this Mrs Bentley had had everything laid on a plate, so to speak. Even so, the unknown Mrs Bentley could hardly be blamed for her husband's indiscretions, and faced with a tough, streetwise individual like Jessica, she might well feel the desire to give up without a fight.

It was nothing to do with her, Ceci told herself, firmly putting her thoughts to other matters. She ought to be considering how she was going to present herself at this interview. Something original, if she could manage it. Something to make her prospective employers believe that she was the ideal person for the position they had in mind. What could she say? What could she tell them? The portfolio on the luggage rack above her head would say it all. If they didn't like her designs, they wouldn't like her. It was as simple as that. She had attended too many interviews not to feel slightly cynical about one more.

The train ploughed on, leaving the crowded south for the more sparsely populated areas of rural England. Conversation had lapsed between the two girls, and Ceci guessed their attitudes of mind were too far apart for there to ever be any real communication between them. She closed her eyes against the glare of the day and let her thoughts drift. What will be, will be, she reflected drowsily, and refused to worry any more.

Jessica woke her some time later, shedding the expensive sable coat on to the seat beside Ceci. 'You've got more room than I have,' she explained, indicating the bag and vanity case beside her with one hand, while setting down a cardboard tray containing two plastic mugs of coffee and two packs of sandwiches on the table with the other. 'Here. I hope you like egg mayonnaise and cheese. I got two packets, and I thought we could share. I'm bleeding starving myself. I suppose it's nerves. I didn't know I had any until now.'

Ceci, in that happy daze between sleeping and waking, was only conscious of the silky hairs of the sable coat brushing her fingers with unfamiliar softness. But then, recovering her senses, she struggled upward in the seat.

'Hmm—I am a bit hungry,' she admitted ruefully, as Jessica subsided into the seat opposite. 'And coffee, too. How lovely! But you must let me pay my share.'

'Don't be daft. It's my treat,' said Jessica, rummaging in her bag for her cigarettes again, and Ceci watched as she lighted one. 'But I had to stand for fifteen bleeding minutes to be served, so I'm going to have to go to the little girls' room before I have mine. Help yourself. I won't be long. Oh, and keep an eye on the skins, will you? It might be a bit difficult taking it with me this time.'

Ceci smiled as Jessica wove her way between the tables to the end of the carriage. The high heels she was wearing caused her to exaggerate the sway of the train, and the lighted cigarette she was carrying skimmed dangerously close to the hair of one of the men seated by the door. Then a light came on to prove she had gained her objective, and Ceci barely hesitated before helping herself to a sandwich.

The sable coat shifted as the train swung into a bend, and its silky folds insinuated themselves across Ceci's lap. Even without its evident beauty, Ceci's love of design and texture would have drawn her eyes to its individuality, and she couldn't resist the opportunity to stroke the satiny pelts. Imagine owning a coat like that, she reflected wistfully. It was the stuff of which dreams were made.

Determinedly putting such thoughts aside, she endeavoured to concentrate on her own destination. Only another hour and she'd be there; in Leeds, anyway. She'd have some time to kill, so she'd probably have some lunch at the station buffet. She might even have time to look around the town itself, although the prospect of carrying her portfolio with her made such an expedition less appealing. It was quite heavy, and there was always the danger that she might lose it. It could even be stolen, although that was less likely, but as a selling point for her talents it was irreplaceable.

She sighed, and picked up a cup of coffee. She wondered how—if she got the job—she would go about finding somewhere to live in Leeds. Were there flats to rent, and were they as exorbitantly expensive as they were in London? If so, she might have to find herself another bed-sitter, and as she knew nothing about the town or the surrounding area, she would have to ask her prospective employers for advice. She supposed there were areas of Leeds that were less salubrious than others, just as there were in London. But that was all in the future. A hypothetical anxiety about a hypothetical situation.

Refusing to be depressed, she turned to stare out of the window again. Everywhere was so green, she thought. At least she was coming north at a time of rejuvenation. It might have been mid-winter, which would have been much worse.

Her thoughts turned irresistibly back to what Jessica had told her. She wondered how the Bentleys intended to treat this newest—and most unexpected—member of the family. Jessica probably had the right idea, after all. They were hardly likely to welcome her. Consequently, she was going in with all guns blazing. No one was going to cripple her with a sniper's bullet.

Ceci shook her head. She couldn't conceive of what it must be like to be Jessica; to be given the kind of news Jessica had been given. To be told you were someone's long-lost daughter—albeit their illegitimate daughter—had all the magic of a fairy-tale. But, like all fairy-tales, there was probably a wicked aunt or uncle in the wings, just waiting to spoil everything. All the same, she had said she was her father's *only* child, which meant there were no jealous siblings trying to stab her in the back. It wasn't unreasonable that Mrs Bentley should consider herself the injured party. Certainly she, more than anyone, had had the most to lose. How had she reacted to the news of her husband's betrayal? Presumably she had been as ignorant as Jessica until the will was read.

The lurch as the train rounded another bend was unexpected, but Ceci's initial thoughts were to prevent the sable coat from sliding on to the floor. It really was too heavy for an unseasonably warm May morning, she mused, but she could understand Jessica's desire not to let it out of her sight.

In consequence, she didn't immediately respond to the sudden rocking and juddering of the carriage, and it was only when her portfolio came tumbling down from the rack above her that she realised something was definitely wrong. The journey had been excessively smooth up until now, with only the occasional hiccup at signals and so on. But all at once it was not smooth at all, and she clutched her seat tightly as the carriage began to tilt.

It all seemed to be happening in a dream, and Ceci wondered if she was still asleep and imagining it all. Things were happening fast, and yet there was an awful slow-motion effect about them, and when she tried to move, the forces of gravity seemed to be holding her in her seat. She remembered someone once telling her that dreams were always in black and white, never in colour. Which seemed to negate the idea that this might be a dream. What was happening now was in colour, terrifyingly so, and the screeching grinding sound of iron on steel was accompanied by a horrible smell of burning.

'We're going to crash, we're going to crash!' she heard someone shrieking behind her, and she guessed it was the elderly woman who had been sitting on her own. For herself, her throat was too tight and her mouth too dry to allow any words to escape. Instead, her eyes turned to the steep embankment at the side of the track with a feeling of total helplessness. The carriage was going to plunge down that embankment. She knew it as surely as she knew there was nothing she could do to stop it.

For some unknown reason, the train had failed to negotiate the bend, and a silent scream rose inside her as she was at last plummeted savagely from her seat . . .

## CHAPTER TWO

'OF COURSE, *she* would survive!' said the woman bitterly, addressing the other occupants of the elegant drawing-room in tense, angry tones. 'Five people killed—including the student who was sitting next to her, no less—but Jessica Devlin lives on to humiliate us all!' She twisted her ringed fingers together and faced the man standing with his back to the screened fireplace. 'Well, I'm right, aren't I? We would all of us have been better off if she was dead!'

'But she's not,' said James Bentley levelly, his low, controlled tones in complete contrast to his dead cousin's wife's heated outburst. 'Apart from these apparently minor injuries to her head, and some cuts and bruising, she's in fairly good shape. At least, that's what Langley says. I haven't spoken to the doctor myself.'

Laura Bentley's mouth compressed. 'You don't care, do you?' she exclaimed, changing her tone. 'You don't care that this—this *brat* of Adam's—is going to put me out of my home!'

'She can't do that.' James Bentley sighed. 'Adam's will distinctly stipulates——'

'Oh, I know, I know. I know what Adam's will says,' Laura interrupted him fiercely. 'I can stay here as long as I like. As long as I'm prepared to humble myself to Jessica Devlin!'

'I doubt if she'll want to share the house with you,' murmured James flatly. 'And you're not exactly destitute, Laura. You have the capital your father left you.'

'And how long will that last?' Laura's mood changed again, and she glanced over her shoulder at the third occupant of the room, a girl seated on the couch behind her. 'Darling,' she mouthed, putting lightly possessive hands on his sleeve, 'I have to see you—*alone*!'

James shook his head. Now was not the time to indulge in personal exchanges, not with Leonie sitting watching them with cool, distrustful eyes. 'Look,' he said, 'I suggest you go and see her. That would be the charitable thing to do. God knows, it can't be much fun being stuck in hospital without a soul to come and visit you.'

'You must be joking!' Laura gasped. 'If you think I'm going to the hospital to see that little——'

'Isn't it time we were leaving, Daddy?'

Leonie chose that moment to intervene, and for once James was glad of his daughter's interruption. He wasn't usually pleased when she chose to show her dislike of her father's cousin so openly, but right now he was grateful for the excuse to leave. In this mood, Laura was impossible, and the last thing he wanted was for her to say something incriminating in front of Leonie. He would explain the situation to his daughter in his own time, not Laura's.

'But you can't,' she exclaimed now, her fingers fastening more securely about his sleeve. 'James, there must be something we can do. Some way we can prevent her from destroying everything Adam ever worked for. I can't believe this is what he would have wanted. Can't you talk to her? Can't you get her to see sense?'

'It's nothing to do with Daddy, is it?' Leonie came to stand beside her father, and James smoothly released himself from Laura's clinging fingers. 'He doesn't want those smelly old mills. He never did. That's why Cousin Adam left *him* out of his will.'

Laura's lips thinned. 'Really, Leonie, I don't think I need to hear your opinion, thank you. Your father knows perfectly well that as nominal head of the family now, it's in his interests, as well as mine, to prevent this girl from selling Bentley property.'

'Well, I don't see——'

'I'll handle it, Lee,' put in James quietly. 'You go and tell Mrs Oates we won't be staying for tea. Oh—and ask Michael to check the oil in the car, will you? I'd like to be sure it's OK, before I take it up to Edinburgh.'

Leonie hesitated, but at fifteen she was still young enough to respect her father's wishes. 'OK,' she muttered, giving Laura a brooding look, and flung herself out of the drawing-room with a definite air of resentment.

'That child——' began Laura, as soon as the door had slammed behind her, but James's expression forbade further comment. So instead she took the opportunity the girl's departure had given her to step closer to her cousin-in-law and grip his forearms tightly, raising her face to his in an open invitation that James, despite his lingering misgivings, was not quite able to overlook.

'Love you,' she breathed, as his mouth brushed the parted softness of her lips, and James had to force himself to remember where and what he was doing. 'James, oh, James, I *need* you! When are you going to admit that you need me just as much?'

Propelling her slim, diminutive frame away from him—albeit not without some reluctance—James took a steadying breath. 'I've never denied it, have I?' he parried tautly, putting the width of the hearth between them. 'But until Adam died, you seemed perfectly capable of living with it.'

'Darling, that's not true——'

'It is true. And in spite of everything else, I won't make a mockery of his death.'

Laura caught her breath. 'But what about me? Hasn't he made a mockery of me?'

James sighed, and regarded his cousin's wife with sudden candour. 'Perhaps you should have asked him for a divorce, as I wanted you to do,' he remarked, bending to pick up a worn leather jacket that had been draped over the arm of the couch. 'Anyway, at least now you're free. That's what you wanted. Or so you said.'

'Free—and penniless,' declared Laura passionately, but James's expression didn't alter.

'Hardly that,' he amended, looping the leather jacket over one broad shoulder and making lithely for the door. 'But you always did like to exaggerate, didn't you, Laura?' He paused, reaching for the handle. 'Give me a ring when you've spoken to the Devlin girl. You know where to reach me.'

'Wait——' Laura came towards him swiftly, teetering a little on her high heels, giving her an excuse, if any excuse was needed, to clutch his arm once again. 'Please, Jamie,' she begged, looking up at him appealingly, 'couldn't you go and see her, darling? I know it's not your problem, but if not for my sake, then for your cousin's.'

'Adam's?' James stared at her grimly, and Laura, sensing an advantage, changed her approach.

'All right—the men who used to work for Adam then, Jamie. Harry Hargreaves, Bob Stobbart, and the rest. Some of them even worked for your grandfather, didn't they? Are you prepared to sit back and let all of them lose their jobs if you could prevent it?'

James's jaw tightened. 'That's blackmail, Laura.'

'No...' Her tongue appeared to circle her full lips. 'Just a teensy-weensy bit of whitemail, darling. Do it. Please! For me—and Adam.'

James was intensely conscious of Leonie's gaze upon him as they pulled away from the house, and his fingers flexed on the wheel of the big estate car, as if subconsciously absolving himself of any responsibility for what he had agreed to do. He knew his daughter would not approve of his actions, and while he could tell himself it was nothing to do with Leonie, his conscience told a different story.

'Why did you do it?' she demanded as soon as the estate car had passed through the gates that gave access to the Harrogate road. 'For heaven's sake, Daddy, you know she doesn't give a—*damn*—about Bentley's employees!' The pause before she used the word 'damn' gave James some indication of what four-letter word she would have really liked to use, but Leonie was too shrewd to give him any reason to turn her protest into a reprimand. 'She only wants some time to try and get the money for herself. I heard her after the funeral, asking Mr Langley if there was any chance of overturning Adam's will——'

'All right, Leonie.' Her father's crisp, cutting tone warned her she had gone too far. 'I think that will do, don't you? When I want your advice, I'll ask for it.'

'But Daddy——'

'I said that's enough, Leonie.'

'But why won't you listen——'

*'Leonie!'*

'Well, it's not fair,' she mumbled, with an unrepentant sniff, and James expelled his breath on a long sigh as he briefly met her sulky gaze.

'You don't understand,' he said at last, slowing and indicating his intention to turn right. 'You're too young, for one thing, and too biased, for another.'

'Biased?' Leonie sniffed again. 'Because I don't like Cousin Laura?'

'Among other things,' agreed her father drily, turning on to the minor road and accelerating into the first bend.

'What other things?'

'As I said, you're too young to understand.'

'No, I'm not.' Leonie hunched her thin shoulders. 'I know about these things. I'm not exactly naïve, Daddy.'

James's lips twitched. 'What is that supposed to mean?'

Leonie's pale cheeks took on a trace of colour. 'You know.'

James shook his head. 'No, I don't. Are you telling me you've had some experience?'

'No, of course not.' Leonie's jaw jutted. 'Oh, all right. You can tease me all you like, but I don't need to be *experienced* to know that Cousin Laura can't keep her claws off you!'

'Leonie!'

'Well, it's true. I just wonder what *you* see in *her*, that's all. She must be incredibly good in bed!'

*'Leonie!'*

This time, James's use of her name was furious, and with a defensive little grimace Leonie's spate of aggression subsided. Instead, she drew as far away from him as she could and, turning her head, devoted her attention to the two golden labradors who occupied the rear seat, and were more than willing to show their appreciation of her affection.

Meanwhile, James endeavoured to concentrate on his driving, aware that once again his relationship with his daughter was in jeopardy. If only Leonie had taken to Laura, he fretted, not for the first time. But from the beginning Leonie had shunned Laura's efforts to be friendly with her, and although James bitterly regretted the fact, he couldn't deny that Laura had never shown any real affection for the child. But then, Laura had never had any children of her own, so perhaps she could be forgiven for not knowing how to handle her rebellious little cousin.

James expelled his breath wearily, permitting himself a brief glance in his daughter's direction. She was such a prickly little thing, he reflected ruefully: tall for her age, but still thin for an adolescent, with a mild case of acne that wouldn't seem to go away. Of course, she was self-conscious, comparing her own straight dark hair and unremarkable features to Laura's blonde beauty. The contrasts between them had only become more pronounced as Leonie had got older, and these days it was almost impossible to get her to be civil when Laura was around. He wondered what Irene would have made of her, but the thought was barely a consideration. Irene had died when Leonie was born—a rare blood infection that had deprived Leonie of her mother and James of his wife in one swift stroke—and therefore she had never known her daughter.

Taking pity on her, James took one hand off the wheel and touched her averted cheek with a gentle finger. 'OK,' he said, conceding that her opinion was valid, 'we'll agree to differ, shall we? Now——' he turned his attention back to the winding country road '—let's consider what we're going to call Minstrel's new foal. Have you had any ideas?'

For a minute, he thought she wasn't going to respond to his overture, but after a pregnant pause she said, 'I haven't thought about it,' in a low voice.

'Then perhaps you should,' James commented with some relief. 'It's due in a matter of days, isn't it? Ted says it should be a winner.'

'Ted would,' responded Leonie, with rather more warmth. 'He thinks all Troubador's foals are winners!'

'Well, you must admit, he hasn't been wrong so far.'

'N—o.' Leonie was grudging. 'Do you think this mare you're going to bring back from Edinburgh will breed well, too?'

'I'm hoping,' agreed James, realising with some misgivings that he would have to put back his trip to Edinburgh if he intended keeping his promise to Laura.

'Can I come with you?' Leonie asked suddenly, and James, whose thoughts had moved to other things, looked vaguely uncomprehending. 'To Edinburgh,' exclaimed Leonie, her eyes moving intuitively over his face. 'Where did you think I meant? The hospital?'

James's mouth tightened. 'I thought we'd agreed——'

'—not to talk about it. I know.' Leonie shrugged. 'Does that mean you *are* going to see this girl?'

James sighed. 'Probably,' he admitted, after a moment's hesitation. Then, rather flatly, 'Someone has to.'

'Why?'

'Why not?'

'Well—she isn't exactly—well, you know.'

'No. You tell me.' James slowed as they approached the back of a tractor and trailer. 'What isn't she? She's family, for a start. Have you thought about that?'

Leonie frowned. 'Do you believe she is?'

'Oh, there's no doubt about it. Adam furnished all the necessary details.'

'But why didn't he acknowledge her before now?'

'Who knows? Perhaps because he was married to Laura and he didn't want to hurt her.'

*'Hurt her?'* Leonie was scathing but, catching her father's eye, she changed her tone. 'Maybe he hoped he'd have a legitimate heir,' she appended instead, and James, who had had the same thought himself, gave her a wry smile.

'You could be right,' he murmured, taking the opportunity to overtake the tractor and trailer. 'Yes, you could be right.'

'Anyway, if she's half as horrible as Laura says she is, I don't think I shall want to meet her,' Leonie declared staunchly. 'Wanting to sell up the Bentley mills and things! She sounds just like Laura!'

James gave her an impatient look. 'You don't give up, do you?'

'Well...' Leonie gazed at him frustratedly. 'I just don't see——'

'That's right. You don't,' James interrupted her flatly. 'Let's change the subject, shall we?'

James went to the hospital the following afternoon. He had spoken to Toby Langley, the family solicitor, in the morning, and ascertained from him the opinion that a visit to see his late cousin's daughter might not come amiss.

'The lass is in quite a state, mentally,' the older man essayed ruefully. 'As if the accident wasn't enough, to lose your memory as well must be pretty scary.'

James's dark brows drew together. 'She's lost her memory?' he echoed.

'Yes. Didn't Laura tell you? Apparently, it's quite a common occurrence in cases like this. A kind of mental block, brought on by some traumatic experience. I expect the crash was pretty traumatic. I heard the girl who was trapped in the toilet was burned beyond recognition. They think she must have been smoking, and——'

'Yes. I'm sure it was pretty horrific.' James had no desire to share Toby's morbid reminiscences. 'So—you think it might help if she sees me; if I tell her who she is, and what she's doing here.'

'Well, you'd have to ask her doctor that, of course,' replied Toby, somewhat put out at being interrupted. 'But you won't need to tell her who she is. She knows that already.'

'She does?'

'Yes.' Toby steepled his fingers. 'They identified her straight away from the photographs and the new passport they found in her handbag. And, if more proof was needed, when they found her she was clutching that sable coat like a lifeline.'

'But she was unconscious, wasn't she?'

'Yes.' Toby nodded. 'Apparently, it's the only thing she remembers. Holding on to the coat.'

James's expression grew a little cynical. 'That figures,' he remarked drily. 'She sounds—charming.'

'I believe she is,' replied Toby surprisingly. 'I've not spoken to her myself, of course. Her doctor—that's Dr Patel, by the way—he advised against any formal discussions of why she was coming here until her memory returns. But I spoke to one of the nurses, and she says she's a very good patient. And you're her father's cousin, after all. She might like to see you. Even if she won't know you from Adam, if you'll forgive the pun!'

In consequence, James approached the coming interview with rather less enthusiasm than he had at first, which was saying something. Confronting a vulnerable amnesiac was not the same as confronting the selfish little gold-digger that Laura had depicted in some detail. Indeed, if he had had doubts about seeing her before, they had now been multiplied ten times over, and half a dozen times after leaving Toby's office he had been tempted to phone Laura and call the whole thing off.

The Infirmary in Leeds was an enormous place, but for all that, James still had a problem finding somewhere to park the estate car. He should have brought Ted Paisley's Mini, he reflected wryly. It would certainly have been easier than parking the Rover.

He eventually found a space next to what appeared to be the kitchens, and, guessing it should properly be reserved for hospital staff, he didn't hang about. He would face any retribution he had to face after the interview was over. Right now, he had more important things to occupy his concentration.

The reception nurse downstairs directed him to the ward where Jessica Devlin was a patient, and after introducing himself to the staff nurse at her station he was shown into the small private ward where the girl was lying. As this was a private ward, at least their conversation would not be overheard by anyone else, James reflected drily, as the nurse admitted him. Although, whether that was an advantage, he had yet to find out. He still hadn't decided how he was going to handle the situation. Maybe Leonie was right. Maybe he should have let Laura handle it herself.

Even so, he couldn't deny an unexpected surge of emotion when he saw the girl lying between the crisp white hospital sheets. In spite of the fact that she was Adam's daughter, he had expected her to look older, tougher, certainly more experienced than the pale-cheeked individual who turned wary eyes in his direction at the sound of the door opening. She wasn't old at all—

twenty-two or three at most, and the brassy blonde his imagination had conjured up had to be quickly revised. Laura had said the police had told her she had blonde hair—probably tinted, in Laura's opinion; blue eyes—although in actual fact, James could see they were more of a purplish colour; and pale, narrow features—which, in Laura's estimation, had to be as hard as nails. In fact, Jessica Devlin was nothing like Laura's description of her, except in so far as a general outline was concerned.

The staff nurse—James thought she had said her name was Jennings—approached the bed first, gently smoothing the sheet as she said soothingly, 'You've got a visitor, Jessica. It's your father's cousin.' She glanced round. 'Did you say—*James* Bentley?'

James nodded briefly, and the nurse turned back to her patient. 'Yes. Your cousin James is here to see you, Jessica. Isn't that nice? Perhaps you'll remember him.'

'Oh, no—I——'

James started to speak, and then decided against it. It would be too complicated to try and explain the situation. Besides, he had no desire for the family's skeletons to become common knowledge in the city. It was bad enough that the will had had to be published. He had little taste for elaborating on their relationship. Consequently, when Staff Nurse Jennings turned enquiring eyes in his direction, he politely raised his hand. 'Um—no,' he said tightly. 'Er—you carry on.' He moistened his dry lips. 'Hello, Jessica. How are you feeling?'

## CHAPTER THREE

A NOT unfamiliar surge of panic rose inside her. It had only been a few days, she knew—strange how she could remember that, and nothing else—and it was going to take considerably longer than that to come to terms with her disability. But the idea that this man—*this total stranger*—could come here and claim to be her father's cousin, filled her with alarm. He could be anyone: a confidence trickster; a media freak, who had read about her story in the papers and had decided to cash in on it; a would-be *murderer*, even! How was she to know? Staff Nurse Jennings said he was her father's cousin James, but when she asked if she should remember him, he had said *no*...

'I'll leave you two alone for a few minutes,' the nurse said, straightening, and ignoring the panicky appeal in Jessica's eyes. 'I'll just be outside,' she added, giving her patient an encouraging smile. 'If you want me, just ring. The button's just by your hand.'

And it was. On the end of a rubber-coated cord that lay easily within Jessica's reach. Swallowing hard, she tried to take a grip on herself and face this man who said he was a relation calmly. Why should he lie? she asked herself impatiently. What did he have to gain? It wasn't as if she was some raving beauty. That was one thing her brain could not disguise. She had spent long enough looking in the mirror to know her features were fairly uniform at best. If only that anxious pale face was familiar to her. But, like the man before her, it offered no reassurance.

'So,' said the man, as the door closed behind Staff Nurse Jennings, 'don't look so scared. I don't bite, I assure you.'

Jessica managed a tentative smile. 'No.'

'No.' James Bentley came to stand at the end of the bed. 'I'm sorry if I've frightened you. That wasn't my intention.'

Jessica's fluttering pulses steadied a little. 'It's all—it's all so strange,' she murmured breathlessly. 'Um—please, won't you sit down?'

He did so, subsiding on to the chair at the foot of the bed with indolent grace. Watching him, trying desperately to see some element of familiarity in his lean, intelligent features, Jessica was struck with the disturbing awareness that he really was a most attractive man. Tall, with unruly, dark hair that persisted in falling over his forehead, and covertly muscular, with the supple economy of movement that usually accompanied physical fitness. His skin was dark, too, as if he didn't spend all his time cased up in some office, and there were fine creases fanning out from his silvery light eyes, that seemed to indicate their narrowing against an outdoor brilliance. He was dressed casually, in narrow-fitting corded trousers and a well-worn leather jacket, and she thought with some inconsequence that he scarcely looked old enough to be her father's cousin. In any event, he was evidently much younger than her father had been, and as his name was different from hers, he must be married to her father's sister.

They—that is, Dr Patel and his staff—had told her that her mother was dead and that her father had died recently, and she had been on the train, apparently coming north to see the other members of the family when the accident happened. Happily, the worst aspects of that journey had been erased along with all her other memories, but she wondered if she shouldn't be feeling grief for the parent she could not remember.

'Your nurse says you're making good progress,' the man who said he was her father's cousin remarked suddenly, and Jessica forced herself to try and act naturally.

'Yes,' she murmured. 'Apart from a few bumps and bruises, and a little shakiness, I'm feeling much better. As a matter of fact, I got up this morning for a couple of hours, and according to Dr Patel, I should be able to leave the hospital within the week.' She contrived to smile. 'Isn't it strange? I know what doctors and hospitals are. I even remember—trains, stuff like that. But I don't remember anything about myself.' Her voice rose a little, and she had to force it down again. 'Silly, isn't it? I really feel such a fraud.'

'It will come back,' said James Bentley reassuringly, regarding her intently from between his thick, stubby lashes. 'As far as I can gather, it's quite commonplace to lose one's memory after some terrible experience. And the accident was pretty terrible. You can take my word for that.'

Jessica expelled her breath a little more easily. 'Do you think so?'

'I know so.'

'But isn't it also true that one doesn't usually forget everything? I mean,' she paused, 'I could understand if I'd just forgotten the accident, and what happened immediately before it. But,' once again her voice rose, 'I don't remember anything. Not *anything*! Isn't that stupid?'

Her voice broke on the final word, and she turned her head aside on the pillow, not wanting him to see the weak tears that overspilled her eyes at the reminder of her helplessness. Heavens, she chided herself impatiently, it wasn't as if she was completely alone in the world or anything. Obviously, she had cousins, and possibly there were other relatives she had yet to meet. Dr Patel had been curiously reluctant to talk about her family to her, encouraging her to try and remember for herself before confronting her with a ready-made biography. But 'Cousin James's' presence seemed to indicate he had given up on that diagnosis, and he had evidently decided she needed some assistance.

If she had been worried that James Bentley might rush to console her, she need not have concerned herself. After scrubbing the treacherous tears away with the heel of her hand, she turned her head again to find him watching her with a distinctly guarded expression on his face, and his apparent lack of sympathy made her ask impulsively, 'Shouldn't I remember you?'

She seemed to have disconcerted him now, for he removed the ankle he had raised to rest negligently across his knee, and, leaning forward with his arms along his thighs, he countered swiftly, 'What do you think?'

Jessica swallowed. 'What—what do I think?' she stammered uncertainly. 'I don't know what you mean.'

'No.' He straightened his spine and regarded her unblinkingly for a moment. And then, as if accepting her word, he nodded. 'No, I see you don't. Well—that is quite a complication, isn't it?' His lips twisted. 'I wonder what Laura will try to make of this!'

'Laura?' Jessica seized on the name eagerly. 'Is that another cousin? Please, won't you tell me about my family? Dr Patel has been so vague, and I really want to know.'

James Bentley drew his lower lip between his teeth for a moment and then frowned. 'What exactly did Patel tell you?' he asked, and Jessica wondered why he was asking. Surely he must *know*?

But he was clearly waiting for her answer, and, circling her lips with her tongue, she said carefully, 'He—he told me that my parents are dead; that my mother died some time ago, but that my father only died recently. You—I suppose you must be related to my grandfather's sister.'

James Bentley's eyes narrowed at this. 'Now, why should you think that?' he enquired suspiciously, as if she had said something wrong.

'Well——' Jessica chose her words with caution. 'As your name's not the same as mine. I mean, Dr Patel told me that my name's Devlin.'

The man who said he was her father's cousin seemed to relax a little. 'Ah,' he said, and nothing more for a little while, so that Jessica began to wish she had never asked the question.

The arrival of Dr Patel didn't resolve anything. Apparently his staff nurse had informed him that his patient had a visitor, and he was evidently eager to speak to anyone who could formally identify her.

'Staff says you're Mr *Bentley*, is that right?' the small, dapper Indian doctor enquired politely. 'I'm very pleased to meet you. Does this mean we will soon be losing our patient?'

James Bentley looked slightly taken aback. 'I beg your pardon...'

'Well, you are a relative, are you not?' Dr Patel commented evenly. 'I understand from my nurse that you're Miss Devlin's father's cousin. I am very glad to see you. Perhaps we can speak together for a few moments before you leave. Was my patient coming to stay with you? If so, I should like to discuss the treatment that will be necessary after she leaves the hospital.'

'Oh, but——'

James Bentley seemed about to say something, but then he met Jessica's anxious gaze and seemed to change his mind.

'Very well,' he essayed instead, and for the remainder of Dr Patel's visit they discussed the less personal aspects of Jessica's condition, treating her, she felt, like the ignorant child she felt herself increasingly to be. If only she could remember, she thought despairingly, staring at this man who was related to her with desperate eyes. Surely she should remember something? Were all amnesiacs so devoid of memories?

The man who claimed to be her father's cousin left with Dr Patel. She was glad he didn't attempt to embrace her or kiss her before he went, even if it left their relationship still in that limbo land between what was real and what wasn't. She would have liked to have asked him more questions, but Dr Patel's arrival and his own strange reticence had precluded all but the most perfunctory of exchanges, and he didn't even say when—or even if—he intended to return.

Two days later, Jessica was well enough to spend most of the day out of bed, and she spent the greater part of that time seated in a chair by the open window. The weather was warm—almost unseasonably so, she knew—although once again how she knew that and not other things was a mystery to her. Nevertheless, it enabled her to wear only the silk négligé that matched the nightie they had found in her suitcase, and although she felt its lace-trimmed sleeves and hem were rather elaborate for a hospital patient, at least she felt some affinity with them as they were hers.

Although, she had to admit, the style of the night-clothes, and the day clothes, too, for that matter, did not seem all that familiar. The sable coat did seem vaguely familiar, or perhaps that was because they had said she was holding the coat when they found her. In any event, the clothes were hers, there was no question about that, and probably once she started wearing them again she would feel differently about them. She certainly hoped so. To believe anything else quickly led to panic.

She was sitting by the window when one of the junior nurses came to tell her she had a visitor.

'Is it James Bentley?' Jessica asked at once, conscious that she was suddenly hoping quite desperately that it was. The forty-eight hours since his first visit had passed infinitely more slowly than the hours before his arrival, and try as she might to convince herself that this was because she was becoming bored with hospital life, she knew in her heart of hearts that it was distinctly more complex than that. It wasn't as if he had made her feel a part of the family. On the contrary, she had had the definite impression that, as a family, they were anything but close. But, if he had come back to see her, perhaps she had been wrong. How could she make any assessment when she had no previous experience to go on?

But the person who followed the nurse into the room was most definitely not her father's cousin. It was a woman; a small, dainty pearl of a woman, with a curly aureole of silvery blonde hair framing features tinted with the delicate bloom of a rose. She was dressed in white, a soft chamois leather suit, that clung to her gentle curves with the tenacity of a second skin. High heels—heels that Jessica doubted she could ever walk in—added inches to her diminutive size, but no one could doubt her presence, or the disturbing air of calculation that came into the room with her.

Jessica hesitated, and then got nervously to her feet. 'I—should I know you?' she ventured, when the woman didn't immediately say anything. 'I'm sorry. I'm afraid I don't remember.'

The woman gazed at her consideringly. 'I'm Laura Bentley,' she declared after a moment. 'Surely Jamie mentioned me.'

'Jamie? Oh, you mean you're related to James Bentley.' Unaccountably, Jessica's heart lurched. He had mentioned someone called Laura, but foolishly she had thought she would be older.

Laura Bentley's brows arched. 'So he didn't tell you,' she remarked, with biting certainty. 'I should have known he wouldn't. My dear, I am—I was—your father's wife. Adam Bentley was my husband. That's the only way Jamie and I are related.'

The young nurse apparently decided she wasn't needed, and beat a hasty retreat. Jessica wished she could do the same. What did this woman mean? *She* had been Jessica's father's wife? They had told her her mother was dead. Besides which, this woman was scarcely old enough for that.

'His—wife?' Jessica struggled to comprehend the fact that her father must have married twice. 'I see. You're my—stepmother. I'm sorry. I must seem addled. I just don't seem to——'

'I'm not your stepmother,' said Laura Bentley shortly, withdrawing the matching leather gloves she was wearing from her hands, and using them to flex her fingers. 'Look,' she seemed to notice Jessica had gone rather pale, 'why don't you sit down? What I have to say might come as something of a shock.'

Jessica did sit down again, rather quickly, her brain trying uselessly to come to terms with what Laura Bentley was saying. What did she mean, she wasn't her stepmother? She must be her stepmother, unless—unless her parents had never been married.

The look of dawning comprehension on her face seemed to please her visitor. 'I see you understand me,' Laura Bentley remarked, snapping the fine skin gloves against her palm. 'To put it plainly, you are illegitimate, Miss Devlin. You have absolutely no right to Adam Bentley's estate!'

Jessica's head was aching now with the effort of controlling the awful terror she was feeling. She didn't need to recover her memory to know that this woman had no liking for her, and the accusations she had levelled she had no way of defending.

'Well? Don't you have anything to say for yourself?'

Laura Bentley had come to stand over her, and Jessica felt a rising sense of claustrophobia. If only she'd move away, she thought faintly; if only she'd give her a chance to get some air. But the room was suddenly devoid of oxygen, and like a puppet whose strings have broken, Jessica crumpled bonelessly on to the floor...

She came to to find Dr Patel leaning over her bed, patting her cheeks with gentle persistence.

'So,' he said, when she opened her eyes, 'you come back to us, Miss Devlin. It was very naughty of you to overdo things. If you were feeling tired, you should have got back into bed.'

Jessica blinked as coherence returned, and her mouth dried a little as her eyes darted swiftly about the room. But the woman had gone. Only Dr Patel, and a rather anxious-looking young nurse, were in the room. Whatever Laura Bentley had wanted, she had evidently gone away empty-handed. Did that mean she would be back? From the very bottom of her consciousness, Jessica hoped not.

If she had expected Dr Patel to mention her visitor, she was disappointed, however, and, meeting the young nurse's troubled gaze, she guessed she had not told him. Perhaps it hadn't happened; perhaps it had all been a dream, reflected Jessica idly. But Dr Patel's departure stirred a distinctive trace of perfume in the air, and, even without the nurse's look of gratitude, she knew it had been no dream.

'Thanks,' murmured the young nurse as she straightened Jessica's sheets. 'I shouldn't have let her in without asking Staff, but she seemed to know her way around, and I didn't know what to do.'

'It's all right.' Jessica managed a faint smile, even though her heart was heavy as lead. 'I had to meet her sooner or later.' *I suppose,* she added silently. The only positive thing about it was that *she*—Laura Bentley, that was—wasn't James Bentley's wife. But why had he been so unwilling to explain just who he was?

It was the evening of the following day when Staff Nurse Jennings came to find her in the recreation room. Unable to stand the labyrinth of her chaotic thoughts any longer, Jessica had asked if she might watch television during the hour when most patients received their visitors. She had no desire to get involved in conversation with other patients, but she judged it reasonable that at this time the recreation room would be unoccupied.

It was—apart from an elderly man, whose expression at her appearance seemed to indicate a like-minded wish for seclusion, and Jessica seated herself in a chair near the door, ready to make her escape if the room became busy.

'So there you are!'

The staff nurse halted beside her with a smile, but Jessica's reaction was scarcely complimentary. *What now?* she was asking herself anxiously, and a little of her consternation must have shown in her face.

'Is something the matter?'

The nurse was perceptive, and Jessica moistened her lips. 'I—I was about to ask you that,' she confessed nervously. 'Did you want me?'

'Yes.' Staff Nurse Jennings nodded. 'There's someone waiting to see you.'

Jessica stiffened. 'Who?'

'That nice Mr Bentley,' replied the staff nurse smoothly. 'Come along. You don't want to keep him waiting, do you?'

Jessica wasn't sure. Her enthusiasm to see members of her family had waned considerably since Laura Bentley's visit. And as this man was related, however distantly, to Laura Bentley, he must know about that visit, too. And obviously he knew about her parentage. Her father had been his cousin, after all. Just because he hadn't told her the circumstances of her birth was no reason to suppose he felt any differently about it than his cousin's wife. Was that why he had come back? To reinforce the accusation Laura Bentley had made?

Walking at Staff Nurse Jennings' side, back to the small private ward which had become the only familiar place she knew, Jessica's knees were shaking. Since Laura Bentley's visit, she had tried not to think of what she was going to do when the time came for her to leave here. Until that brutal revelation about her parentage, she had naturally assumed that once she was well enough to leave hospital, she would go home to wherever it was she had lived before she went to London. But learning that she was illegitimate had changed all that, and, if she allowed herself to wonder how she was going to cope on her own, the panic that was never far away returned to overwhelm her. Why had James Bentley come back? she wondered, to the rhythm of her palpitating pulse. Was he to deliver the family's ultimatum? The final *coup de grâce*?

He was waiting, as the nurse had said, in her room, standing by the window, staring out at the squares and quadrangles created by the hospital buildings. But he heard her slippered feet as she came into the room, and turned to face her with the same guarded expression she remembered.

'Hello.'

'Hello.' Jessica's response was clipped, but she couldn't help it. What was he doing here? What did he want?

'You'll be all right, won't you?'

Staff Nurse Jennings had noticed the lack of warmth between them, and Jessica, unwilling to conduct any kind of conversation with this man in the nurse's presence, nodded quickly.

'Thank you,' she said, forcing a smile to her tight lips, and Staff Nurse Jennings shrugged.

'Well, if you want me, just call,' she commented, giving James Bentley a thoughtful glance. 'I'll just be along the corridor.'

She pulled the door to behind her, but she didn't close it, and Jessica froze in alarm when James Bentley came impatiently towards her. But he didn't touch her; only passed her to secure the door with a definite click, saying as he did so, 'I think we could use a little more privacy, don't you?'

Jessica shrugged, half turning to look at him. It was a warm evening, and the sleeves of his shirt were rolled back over muscular forearms. He wasn't wearing a tie, and the scent of warm male skin drifted from his opened collar. His appearance certainly bore no comparison to Laura Bentley's elegance, but in his way he was just as sophisticated and probably more dangerous.

'Don't you want to sit down?'

He was regarding her coolly with those strange light eyes, but, although Jessica would have liked to do just that, she stood her ground.

'I'm all right,' she managed, drawing the lapels of the silk wrapper closer about her. 'What do you want? Why have you come here?'

His narrow lips twisted in either resignation or derision. 'You're obviously feeling better,' he remarked, sliding his hands into the pockets of black denim trousers. 'Have you remembered anything yet?'

'No.' Jessica drew a steadying breath. 'Didn't your—cousin-in-law tell you? I can't believe you don't know about her visit.'

'Laura's coming here had nothing to do with me,' he retorted harshly. 'And I didn't know about it. Not until it was over, that is. I'm sorry if she upset you. Laura's like that. She's inclined to act on impulse.'

Jessica trembled. 'Is that what you call it?'

'It serves the purpose.' He sighed. 'Look, Laura's not knowingly malicious. She just—well, she's just had something of a shock. We all have.'

Jessica stared disbelievingly at him. 'Are you trying to tell me that—that Laura Bentley cared whether I lived or died?' she demanded.

He frowned then. 'I'm afraid I don't know what you mean.'

'The accident,' she prompted tremulously. 'That is what you were talking about, wasn't it?'

'Oh.' James Bentley's mouth compressed. 'No. No, it wasn't. I meant the fact that—well, that none of us knew of your existence until my cousin died.'

## CHAPTER FOUR

'YOU'VE done what?' Laura Bentley's face was a contortion of itself as she stared disbelievingly at her late husband's cousin.

James shrugged. 'Do you really want me to repeat myself?' he enquired evenly. 'All right. I've invited Adam's daughter to stay at Aspen until she's well enough to look after herself again. It was the least I could do after your little outburst.'

'I don't believe it!' Laura was incensed. 'James, the girl is a usurper! I thought we'd agreed to do everything we could to overturn Adam's will before it's too late.'

'You agreed; I never did,' James retorted, riffling through the papers on his desk without really seeing them. 'Laura, you shouldn't have gone to the hospital. For heaven's sake, that was why I agreed to go in the first place—so that you wouldn't go rushing in and causing all kinds of complications.'

Laura faced him across the heavy desk in his office. 'What kind of complications?' she demanded. 'You said the girl had lost her memory. All I did was tell her the truth——'

'And arouse her suspicions about my motives in seeing her,' James interrupted grimly. 'Christ, Laura, she's just recovering from a serious accident! Couldn't you at least have some compassion? It's not her fault that Adam chose to impregnate her mother!'

Laura held up her head. 'It's not mine, either.'

'No.' James conceded the point. 'I admit, you couldn't have been around when Adam was having this affair with Maggie Devlin. But the fact remains, when Adam died, you were hardly a grieving widow! Until you learned of Jessica Devlin's existence, that is.'

'Oh, James!' Laura's lower lip pouted. 'That's a cruel thing to say.'

'But true,' said her cousin-in-law drily. 'I'm sorry, Laura, but facts have to be faced. And do you think you're going to get anywhere in this matter if you persist in making an enemy of the girl?'

Laura met his level gaze. 'You can't honestly expect me to make a friend of her!'

'Why not?'

'Why not?' Laura gasped. 'James, you saw the letter her solicitors sent to me. She was only coming here to identify her assets with a view to selling. She didn't give a damn about the traditions her father and her grandfather created. She simply wanted to realise their—their cash potential!'

James nodded. 'I know.'

'You know?' Laura's small hands gripped the rim of scarred wood. 'So why are you telling me to be civil to her? Why should I be civil to someone who intends to throw me out into the street?'

'Hardly that,' James murmured quietly.

'Don't split hairs. You know what I mean. I'm left without a penny——'

'I think we've been through this before.' James sighed. 'Laura, listen to me——'

'Why should I listen to you, when you've taken her side?'

James's lips thinned. 'I haven't taken her side.'

'You've invited her to stay here. You've never invited me to stay here.'

'And you know why,' said James flatly. 'In any case, Laura, if you'd listen to what I have to say, you might—you just might—start thinking with your head, instead of with those greedy little hands of yours.'

*'James!'*

'Well, I mean it.' He hesitated for a moment, before coming round the desk to where she was standing, and smoothing gentle fingers over her shoulders. Laura immediately moved closer to wind her arms around his neck, but when she would have caressed his lips with her tongue James held her away from him.

'Listen,' he said, thwarting her efforts to rub herself against his lean, taut body, 'hasn't it occurred to you that the girl's losing her memory could work to your advantage?'

'To my advantage?' Laura looked sceptical. 'How?'

James considered his words for a moment before speaking. Then he said carefully, 'She doesn't remember anything. Not anything. Not Adam's death; nor inheriting his estate; nor her intentions to sell. Now do you understand me?'

Laura's arched brows drew together. 'I understand you, but——'

'Doesn't it occur to you that you—that we—have been given a breathing space?'

Laura blinked. 'A breathing space,' she echoed, as what he was saying began to make sense. 'To get her to change her mind.'

'Well, to get her to think about it, anyway,' James amended. 'Look, so far as Jessica Devlin is concerned, the most important thing at the moment is that she's illegitimate. Your informing her of that actuality may have been unfortunate, but it could have favourable repercussions.'

'How?'

'Well——' James paused. 'Right now, she's vulnerable. And I don't just mean because she's lost her memory. Thankfully, you didn't get the chance to remind her that her sole reason for coming here was to arrange for the sale of the property, and if—before she regains her memory—we can convince her that it wouldn't be in her best interests to do so, all may not yet be lost.'

'Oh, James!' Laura gazed up at him excitedly. 'I never thought of that.'

'No. Well, as I say, you don't think, you act, and face the consequences afterwards.'

Laura's lips curved. 'Then it's just as well I have you to keep me in order, isn't it, darling?' She ran stroking fingers along the roughening curve of his jawline. 'Aren't you clever? And I thought you felt sorry for her.'

James abruptly drew away from her caress. 'I *do* feel sorry for her, Laura,' he declared, taking her hands in his and pressing them down to her sides. 'And you would, too, if you had any natural feelings. Can't you imagine how terrifying it must be to have no recollection of who you are or where you came from? It must be like a living death!'

'Well, of course I can, darling,' she protested. 'But you have to consider my position, too. This hasn't been easy for me either.'

'That's why I'm prepared to forgive you,' said James wryly. 'So—do you approve of the arrangements now?'

Laura pulled a face. 'Well, I don't exactly approve of them. In fact,' she paused, 'it occurs to me, perhaps I should invite her to Bickersley.'

James's lips twisted. 'And do you think she'd come, after the way you behaved?'

Laura looked a little sulky now. 'She might. If I could convince her I didn't mean to be unkind.'

'I doubt it.' James shook his head. 'She may be vulnerable, but she's not a fool.' In truth, he was strangely loath to expose the girl to Laura's mercurial moods. She had had enough to cope with recently; and besides, she was *his* flesh and blood, not Laura's. 'I don't think Bickersley would be big enough for the two of you,' he added. 'Here at the farm, we have lots of space.'

Laura pulled away from him. 'And what does dear little Leonie have to say about that?' she demanded sarcastically. 'Or haven't you told her yet?'

'I've told her,' said James shortly, unwilling to get into yet another discussion about his daughter. 'And now, I'm afraid, I'm going to have to ask you to excuse me. This is a commercial enterprise, Laura, and I've got work to do.'

It was later that same evening when James had time to consider the wider implications of what he had agreed to. The night before, he had been too angry with Laura to give any serious thought to his impulsive gesture, and that morning, when he had mentioned the matter to Leonie before she left for school, he had not had the time to worry about her reactions. Oh, she had not been enthusiastic, of course, but they had had no time then to discuss what was involved, and James had managed to avoid thinking about his daughter's feelings for most of the day. But Leonie's expression at supper was eloquent of what she was thinking, and after Mrs Hayes had served the steak and vegetables, James decided something had to be said.

'So—what do you think about our cousin's coming to stay at the farm?' he ventured, watching his daughter merely picking at her food. 'I thought she could have the room next to yours. What do you think?'

Leonie regarded him through her lashes. 'There's not much point in asking me now, is there?' she replied stiffly. 'Whatever I say, you'll just go ahead and do what you want. You always do.'

James expelled his breath heavily. 'That's not true.'

'It is true. You know how I feel about Laura, but you still persist in bringing her here.'

'We're not talking about Laura,' said her father levelly, doing his best not to lose patience with her. 'I want to know how you feel about Jessica. The girl's been through a lot, and I don't want to bring her here if you're going to spend your time sniping at her.'

Leonie shrugged. 'It's nothing to do with me.'

'It *is* to do with you. As I say—she's your cousin.'

'Is she?' Leonie looked sceptical. 'How do we know Adam really was her father?'

James was taken aback. 'How do we know?' He shook his head. 'Well—because as I've said before, the facts are there.'

'Mmm.' Leonie hunched her shoulders. 'Well, I think he'd have done *anything* to get back at Laura. Even pretending he had an illegitimate child, when everyone knows he couldn't have any children.'

James stared at her. 'Who is everyone?' he enquired tersely.

Leonie's pale face took on a deepening colour. 'Oh—it's just gossip, I suppose.'

James's lips thinned. 'Gossip, from whom?'

'Daddy!'

'From whom?'

Leonie bent her head. 'I can't tell you.'

'It wouldn't be Mrs Hayes, would it?'

Leonie's startled glance was enough.

'It was Mrs Hayes, wasn't it?' her father demanded grimly. 'Well, I shall have a few words with her before she makes that kind of accusation in front of Jessica.'

'Oh, Daddy.' Leonie sighed. 'You know she and Mrs Oakes are as thick as thieves. If Mrs Hayes thinks that, she's probably got it from Mrs Oakes.'

'What Laura's housekeeper says or doesn't say is no concern of mine. But when my staff start gossiping to my daughter about things that are no concern of theirs...'

'She didn't,' said Leonie suddenly, and James frowned.

'Didn't what?'

'Didn't gossip to me,' admitted Leonie unwillingly. 'Oh—if you must know, I overheard her and Ted Paisley talking.' She sighed again as her father's expression darkened. 'Well, it's natural that they would talk, isn't it? They've both known you and Cousin Adam for years and years. And—and this Jessica is bound to cause gossip. Even if she is who she says she is.'

James regarded the juicy steak on his plate without appetite. For all his anger that his staff should find Jessica Devlin's advent into their lives such a choice source for speculation, he couldn't deny that Leonie's words had given him food for thought. Throughout the past weeks, since Adam's death, he had never once considered that Jessica Devlin might not be his cousin's daughter. It had never occurred to him to suspect that Adam had had the time and the opportunity to make changes to his will, and his frequent visits to the heart specialist in London could have enabled him to thwart his wife's expectations. He had been ill for a long time. The congestive heart disease, which his doctors had thought might have emanated from a childhood attack of rheumatic fever, had deteriorated rapidly in a matter of months, but even so, Adam had had time enough to trace this girl who was supposed to be his daughter and make her his sole beneficiary. What if there had been no daughter? What if, as Leonie had suggested, Adam had been sterile? Certainly, he and Laura had been married long enough to produce half a dozen offspring. And Adam had liked children. He had been very fond of Leonie.

'What's she like?' his daughter asked suddenly, and James had to force himself to abandon such negative thinking.

'Who? Jessica?' he asked, knowing full well who she meant, but needing the time to reassemble his thoughts. 'Hmm—well, she's very nice, I suppose.'

'She's twenty-one, isn't she? And blonde.' Her mouth turned down. 'Is she like Laura?'

James was glad he could reply truthfully. 'Not at all,' he said, seeing the relief in Leonie's face. 'She's taller, for one thing, and darker. Oh, not dark like you and I are dark, but less fair than Laura. I suppose you'd call her hair light brown, rather than blonde. It's sort of streaky, and she wears it in a braid.'

Leonie frowned. 'Is she pretty?'

'Pretty?'

James knew a momentary feeling of distaste. Jessica wasn't pretty. She didn't have the stunning good looks and even features that people regarded as *pretty*. The first time he had seen her, he hadn't even thought she was attractive, with her lids swollen from the tears she had shed in his presence, and her wide, generous mouth tight with fear.

But the second occasion had been different. Then he had glimpsed a delicate symmetry in the bones of her face, and even real beauty in the depths of eyes as haunting as violets in springtime. Indeed, he had been made aware that a man might find her quite startlingly attractive, and he had known the same sense of distaste at this awareness that he was feeling now.

'Yes, pretty,' Leonie prompted, impatient at the delay, and James moved his shoulders in a dismissive gesture.

'Not pretty, no,' he replied, pushing his steak aside and reaching purposefully for the bottle of wine he had opened to accompany the meal. 'I should say she's fairly ordinary. I think you might like her.'

'Because I'm ordinary, too?' asked Leonie bitterly, and James stifled an inward groan.

'I won't dignify that remark with an answer,' he said, refilling his wineglass and getting to his feet. 'I'm going to do some work in the study. I suggest you do the same. You've got your exams next year, remember.'

Leonie's jaw dropped. 'But, Daddy, I promised Ted I'd help him bring the mares into the paddock!'

'I dare say he and Cliff can manage without you,' retorted James unforgivingly, and Leonie groaned.

'Oh, please, Daddy,' she begged. 'Don't make me spend all evening doing homework. You know I want to leave school next year and help you with the horses. What's the point of doing maths and history when all I want to do is animal husbandry?'

James regarded her dourly. 'And you know my intention is for you to go to university,' he said. 'Working with horses is not for a girl. Not a girl with your opportunities, anyway.'

Leonie's jaw quivered. 'Don't be chauvinistic!'

James was about to remonstrate with her again, but her woeful expression suddenly reminded him of Jessica. 'All right,' he said, after a moment, 'I'll make a bargain with you. You be nice to Jessica when she comes here, and I'll promise to consider you leaving school in three years. How about that?'

Leonie hesitated. '*Three* years?'

'Yes, three years,' said James firmly. 'And if you still want to work here, I may be persuaded to change my mind about university.'

Leonie sighed, but it was obvious she realised it was the best offer she was likely to get. 'All right,' she mumbled. 'I'll try and be nice to her. But if she treats me like Laura does——'

'She won't,' said James flatly, heading towards the door. 'And don't spend too long outside. You've still got school tomorrow.'

* * *

James collected Jessica from the hospital on Friday morning.

He went alone—Leonie was at school, naturally, and he had managed to persuade Laura that it would not be a good idea for her to accompany him. 'Let her get settled in at Aspen first,' he said, when she had demurred. 'That's going to be quite enough for her to cope with in one day. Besides, it's far more natural if you come to visit Leonie and me after our guest has got used to her new surroundings. What's she going to think if you come with me to bring her home? Hell's teeth, the last time you saw her, you scared her half to death!'

Laura hadn't liked it, he knew, but she hadn't put up much of an argument. He hoped she'd decided he had a point. After all, if she wanted to change Jessica's opinion of her, the longer she waited, the easier it might be.

Jessica was waiting for him in her room, dressed now in a beige silk dress that looked at least a size too big for her. 'I must have lost some weight,' she said at once, aware of his eyes upon her, and James felt a heel for noticing and causing her embarrassment.

'You'll have to get some new clothes,' he commented, observing the way she picked up the sable coat from the foot of the bed and hugged it to her. Familiarity, or avarice? he wondered, remembering Toby had said she had been found clinging to the coat. Despite Laura's allegations, he would have guessed the former; there was something almost pitiful about her as she prepared to leave.

Dr Patel and two of the nurses came to say goodbye, the doctor drawing James aside for a moment to issue last-minute instructions. 'She'll be easily tired,' he said, fixing James with a warning gaze. 'And easily upset, too. She needs patience and understanding; and no mental stimulus until her natural resilience returns.'

'I understand, Doctor.'

'I hope you do.' Dr Patel bit his lip. 'Your solicitor told me the circumstances that brought Miss Devlin north, but I can only impress upon you, as I did upon him, that any damaging discussions must wait until she's stronger.'

'Of course.' James nodded, and then added softly, 'When do you think her memory will return? When she's stronger?'

'Perhaps.' Dr Patel frowned. 'Amnesia is one of those conditions that no one can really speculate upon. She could recover her memory tomorrow, or alternatively it could be weeks, months, even. The brain still guards its secrets jealously. We are only just beginning to understand its complexities.'

James sighed. 'Oh, well...' He shrugged. 'Until next week, then.'

'Until then,' agreed Dr Patel, who had suggested that Jessica ought to be examined at least once a week for the immediate future. 'Take good care of her, Mr Bentley. I'm sure it's what your cousin would have wished you to do.'

'Yes,' said James politely, wondering exactly what Adam's reaction would have been in similar circumstances. One thing was for certain: Laura would not have welcomed another woman into her home, particularly not a younger woman, especially if she was her husband's daughter.

They didn't speak much as James negotiated the hazards of driving in the city, but once the dual carriageway out of Leeds was left behind, and the road was enfolded by fields and hedges and copses of trees, Jessica relaxed visibly.

'It's so pretty,' she said, gazing out of the window of the estate car with fascinated eyes. 'I never expected it would be like this. I thought it would be all dark and industrial, and scarred with pit shafts.'

James glanced quickly at her. 'You remember that?'

'What? Oh, yes.' Jessica gazed at him appealingly. 'Yes, I do remember some things.' She frowned. 'For instance, I'm almost sure I didn't want to come here.'

'Where?'

'To the north, to Leeds.' Jessica pulled her lower lip between her teeth. 'Oh, not now. I don't mean that. I'm looking forward to staying on a farm. I can't be certain, of course, but I don't think I've ever stayed on a farm before.'

James concentrated his attention on the road. 'Tell me what you do remember. Perhaps it would help if we talked about it.'

'Perhaps.' But she didn't sound enthusiastic, and James wondered if he was going too fast. But something was warning him that perhaps inviting her to Aspen had not been the most sensible thing he had done in his life, and the sooner she recovered her memory and took up her own life again, the better it would be.

Still, he was loath to upset her on her first day out of hospital, and, changing the subject, he said, 'Do you like horses?'

She smiled then. 'I don't think I've met any,' she said ruefully. 'At least, not on a one-to-one basis, I'm sure. They don't frighten me. That is, I don't think they do. Do you have many? Are they easy to look after?'

'We have quite a number of animals,' admitted James, nodding. 'As I told you, I breed them. As for whether they're easy to look after—well, that rather depends on the horse.'

'Illness, you mean?'

'That, of course.' James nodded again. 'But horses are a lot like humans. They come in all moods and temperaments.'

'Oh, I see.' Jessica was evidently interested. 'You mean they can be mean or temperamental. What do you do with a bad-tempered horse? You can't just use a whip to get it to behave, can you?'

'No.' James agreed. 'But in many cases there's a reason for an animal's unsociable behaviour. Often it's boredom, particularly with nervous, highly strung horses; they need constant supervision to ensure they don't acquire bad habits.'

'What sort of bad habits?'

Jessica was half turned towards him in her seat, and he couldn't help noticing the downy hairs at the nape of her neck, exposed by the plait of hair that fell over her left shoulder. There was something disturbingly vulnerable about her at that moment, and although he knew she was only trying to show some interest in his work, there was an edge to his voice as he responded tautly,

'You'll find out soon enough. Ask Leonie to tell you. She's got a lot more time than me.'

Jessica's enthusiasm was extinguished in a moment. 'I'm sorry,' she said stiffly. 'I didn't mean to be inquisitive.' She moistened her lips. 'How—how much further do we have to go?'

James wanted to kick himself for his insensitivity, but something about this girl unsettled him. It wasn't the fact that she couldn't remember anything. He could live with that. Indeed, he had the greatest sympathy for anyone in her situation, and he would do everything he could to help her to recover her memory. But, none the less, she troubled him, and he could only assume that it was because she was so *unlike* Adam that he found her presence disturbing.

'We turn here, and it's about another three miles,' he said now, using the vehicle's indicators to signify his intentions to turn left. 'Bickersley, where your father used to live, is over there, to our right. Maybe when you're feeling stronger, you'd like to go and see the house.'

Jessica didn't look at him. 'Is that where Mrs Bentley lives?' she asked in a cold little voice, and James cast her a considering glance.

'Yes. Why?'

'Then I don't think I'd like to go there,' declared Jessica firmly. 'Mrs Bentley doesn't like me. She thinks I'm an intruder. I can understand that, I suppose, if she didn't know of my existence until after my father was dead, but I don't have to associate with her, do I?'

James's fingers tightened on the wheel. 'Perhaps you'll change your mind.'

'Why should I?'

'Well——' James sought for words. 'She was your father's wife.'

'And my mother was just his mistress, I know.' Jessica bent her head. 'But would your wife react like she did, to someone she didn't even know? I've thought a lot about what you told me, and I've come to the conclusion that it's not my fault that my father behaved as he did. I didn't ask to be born. And for the past twenty years, I didn't even know I had a father. He never tried to recognise me while he was alive. Why should I feel guilty because he finally decided to acknowledge his obligations?'

Even as James conceded the strength of her argument, something else she had said struck him. 'You mentioned my wife,' he said. 'I told you, didn't I, that she died when Leonie was born?'

'No.' Jessica turned her head to look at him now, and the wide, pansy-soft eyes were strangely anxious. 'Leonie—I thought Leonie *was* your wife.'

'No, Leonie's my daughter,' said James, knowing a quite uncharacteristic urge to swear at her. 'For Christ's sake, that doesn't bother you, does it? My not having a wife—it's not going to be a problem?'

Jessica swallowed. 'Why should it?' she asked, although he had the distinct impression that her words were more bravado than conviction. 'You—you're my father's cousin, aren't you? Just because we hardly know each other is no reason to doubt our relationship.'

## CHAPTER FIVE

JESSICA'S room was situated at the back of the house. Although she couldn't remember where she had lived before she made that fateful journey, she was sure she had never had such a lovely room before, and she said as much to Mrs Hayes, James Bentley's housekeeper, when that lady showed her into it.

'It's beautiful!' she exclaimed, an unexpected lump manifesting itself in her throat as she admired the candy-striped quilt and matching curtains, whose billowing folds brushed the velvety-soft pile of a shaggy cream carpet.

'Yes, it is a nice room, isn't it?' agreed the housekeeper, flicking the curled edge of the quilt into place, her keen eyes ensuring there was no speck of dust on the dark wood chest and vanity unit, or hiding in the buttoned seat of the ottoman that rested at the foot of the bed. 'Now, would you like me to unpack for you? Mr Bentley says you haven't to overdo things, not on your first day.'

'Thank you, I can manage,' Jessica assured her a little stiffly, distinctly aware of a certain coolness in the woman's manner. Mrs Hayes was not hostile exactly—certainly nowhere near as hostile as Laura Bentley had been—but she was not exactly friendly either, and Jessica was beginning to wonder if it had been such a good idea to accept James Bentley's invitation, after all. Whatever reason she had had for boarding that train, it was becoming increasingly obvious it had not been at the invitation of her father's family. She was the usurper here. So why had she come? What had been her purpose? Had it something to do with the inheritance that Laura Bentley had said she didn't deserve? But what inheritance? As yet, no one had told her.

'Very well, then, I'll leave you to it.' Mrs Hayes walked towards the door. 'Why don't you take a rest before lunch? Mr Bentley eats at one, so when you're ready, just come downstairs.'

'Thank you.'

The door closed behind the housekeeper, and Jessica's strength suddenly deserted her. Sinking down on to the ottoman, she buried her face in her hands for a moment, trying to still the sudden shaking of her shoulders. What was she doing here? *Who was she?* she wondered desperately. Dear God, if only she could remember. If only there was not this awful void where her memories of the past were supposed to be.

When the worst of the emotional spasm was over, she straightened and surveyed the soft leather suitcase lying on the seat beside her. Even the suitcase bore no resemblance to any suitcase she could remember, and the clothes inside were just as unfamiliar. In any event, they were hers, and she would have to wear them. Although there was some money in her purse, there was not nearly enough to replace her whole wardrobe, and until her financial situation was explained to her she would have to conserve what little she had.

She had asked Dr Patel if she had had a job before the accident, and he had explained she had given that up before she left London. Why would she do that, she wondered, if she had not expected to be welcome here? In time, she would have to go back there and find out, but for the present Dr Patel didn't want her exerting herself. In any case, she was in no state to make such a journey now. But maybe someone, some friend from those days, would contact her. She apparently had no relatives, other than her father's family. But someone might care enough to find out how she was, and surely she would remember them, better than these virtual strangers.

Leaving the ottoman, she walked to the window, enjoying the breeze that drifted in through the open casement. Outside the windows, the view was quite breathtaking: acres and acres of lush green fields, interspersed with hedges of hawthorne and shady copses of oak and ash and willow. Closer at hand, beyond a paved terrace, where tubs of fuchsias and geraniums spilled their beauty, were lawns and flowerbeds that dropped away to white-fenced paddocks where a group of mares and their foals grazed contentedly. It was all unbelievably peaceful and soothing, and Jessica's spirits rose a little in concert with the day. She *would* get well here, she told herself firmly. In time, and with so much beauty about her, her bruised brain cells were bound to assert themselves again, and once she regained her strength she wouldn't tire so easily. Dr Patel had said that the headaches she got now were nature's way of guarding her against stress. But they couldn't last for ever. Sooner or later, she would remember.

The bathroom adjoining her room was just as attractive. After hanging her clothes away in the capacious closets in the bedroom, she took a wash in the green porcelain basin, admiring the circular tub and shower stall as she dried her face on the fluffy olive green towel.

She took another of the tablets Dr Patel had given her before going down for lunch. She hadn't rested and her head had begun to ache, but she was determined not to give in to it, not until lunch was over.

The house was large, but not difficult to find her way about in. They had entered by way of a cool panelled hall, with a shallow staircase running at a right angle up two walls. Although she had been shown almost directly to her room, she had observed the various rooms opening off the hall below as she climbed the stairs, and the gallery at the top ran from one side of the house to the other.

Mrs Hayes must have been expecting her to come downstairs, for she was waiting in the hall as Jessica made her descent. 'Lunch is ready,' she said, her eyes assessing the quality of the ill-fitting silk dress which Jessica had not thought to change, and finding it wanting. 'I've laid the table in the breakfast-room. If you'll come with me.'

She led the way beneath an arched lintel, which formed a natural break between the oak panelled hall and a kind of sitting-room beyond. Here, cream and gold velvet sofas faced one another across an exquisitely patterned Chinese rug, an octagonal table in the centre providing a frame for a sprawling spider fern.

But Mrs Hayes gave Jessica little chance to admire the room, or take much note of the pictures of thoroughbred horses that were hung between long casement windows. Instead, she opened a door to their right and urged the girl into a sunlit parlour, where french doors opened on to the terrace, and a deliciously mouth-watering aroma of food scented the warm air.

The table, a circular one this time, was only laid for one, however, and Jessica turned doubtfully to the housekeeper.

'Oh—Mr Bentley has had to go out, miss,' declared Mrs Hayes, bustling forward to take the lid off a tureen and adjust a fork more to her liking. 'Now—there's a chilled consommé, and some smoked salmon; quiche, and salad; and a nice dish of summer pudding, with a jug of cream to go with it. Are you able to serve yourself?'

'Um—well, of course, but——' Jessica sighed. 'I mean—there was no need to go to so much trouble for me.'

'It's no trouble, miss. It's my job,' replied Mrs Hayes, with just a trace more warmth in her voice. She hesitated. 'You look as if you could do with a good meal, if you don't mind my saying so. That dress is fairly hanging on you.'

'Oh, this.' Jessica plucked unhappily at the beige silk. 'Yes, it does look a mess, doesn't it? I can't think how I came to choose it. It doesn't seem to suit me at all.'

'I wouldn't say that, miss,' declared the housekeeper consideringly. 'But it does want something doing to it, that I would agree. I've got a friend who's a bit of a hand with a needle. Would you like me to ask her if she could take it in for you?'

'Oh, would you?' Jessica was eager, but then the realisation that alterations cost money made her bite her lip. 'That is—it's very kind of you, of course, but—um, I don't know if I can afford it.'

Mrs Hayes's expression, which had definitely been softening, changed abruptly. 'Really, miss?' she said, in a tone that made Jessica want to cringe. 'You know, you'd only to say no. I'm not one to push myself where I'm not wanted.'

'It's not that.' Jessica was horrified that the woman should think she was just making excuses. 'Honestly, I——'

'That's all right, miss. I quite understand.' The ice was definitely back in the housekeeper's voice again now. 'If you'll excuse me, I have got other jobs to do.'

Jessica expelled her breath on a heavy sigh as the door closed behind the woman. What a mess she had made of that! she thought miserably. And just when Mrs Hayes had appeared to be thawing, too. The housekeeper had evidently thought she could just ask James Bentley for anything she wanted, and Jessica was reluctant to explain why this simply wasn't the case. How could she ask him for anything? He might be her father's cousin, but that didn't mean much in the circumstances. Indeed, she found it difficult to regard him as a relative at all. She would have felt far more comfortable addressing him as *Mr* Bentley. James sounded too familiar, and totally unreal.

She drank a little of the consommé, and ate a few mouthfuls of the quiche, but she didn't touch the summer pudding. The nerves in her stomach were not conducive to her enjoying the delicious meal, and she half wished James Bentley had been there, to take her mind off other things.

A girl, a couple of years younger than herself, brought her coffee afterwards, and Jessica managed to smile an apology as the young woman cleared the table. 'I'm afraid I wasn't very hungry,' she said, hoping that the maid would be more sociable, and the girl gave her a friendly grin as she loaded the plates and the tureen on to a tray.

'I dare say you need some fresh air, after spending all that time in the hospital,' she declared. 'That's one thing you'll get here. Plenty of fresh air.'

'I hope so.' Jessica paused. 'You work here, do you?'

'Part-time in the house, and part-time in the stables,' agreed the girl unhesitatingly. 'I'm mad about horses, see, and Mr Bentley lets me help out in the stables when Mrs Hayes doesn't need me in the house.'

'I see.' Jessica nodded. 'Do you ride?'

'As often as I can.' The girl's face took on a dreamy expression. 'Sometimes Mr Bentley lets me help exercise the horses, and I love that! I don't know if you ride, but I think there's nothing more exciting than galloping across the moors in the early morning, with the scent of the gorse all around you, and the horse's breath turning to mist in the air.'

Jessica smiled. 'It sounds wonderful.'

'It is.' The girl grimaced. 'But mostly I get to do the unglamorous jobs. You know, like grooming the mares, or mucking out the stalls. There's a scent, if you like. Healthy, mind you, but pretty strong all the same.'

Jessica shook her head. 'Perhaps I could help you some time.'

'You? Help me?' The girl stared at her aghast. 'Oh, I don't think Mr Bentley would approve of that. You're here to rest and recuperate, aren't you? Not to get your hands dirty——'

Before she could finish, however, the door opened, and Mrs Hayes's irate face appeared. 'Vicky!' she exclaimed. 'Vicky, are you standing there wasting time?' Her gaze flicked to Jessica. 'I'm sorry, Miss Devlin, but Vicky has work to do in the kitchen. Come along now, girl, and mind you don't spill that soup as you go.'

Vicky spared Jessica a sympathetic look before allowing the housekeeper to hustle her out of the room.

'Hope you're soon feeling better,' she whispered, making Jessica feel she had at least one ally in the house.

'See you later,' she said, before the door closed behind them. Then she helped herself to more coffee with a stirring feeling of growing optimism.

Although she would have liked to step outside into the bright sunlight, and explore her surroundings, Jessica did as the doctor had told her and went upstairs to rest after lunch. With all the new things that were happening to her, she had thought she wouldn't be able to relax, but in actual fact she fell asleep as soon as her head hit the pillow. It was so peaceful in her bedroom, with the curtains drawn, but billowing in the breeze, and only the distant sound of a tractor to disturb her. After the busy hum of the hospital, she found it totally appealing, and she didn't stir until voices on the terrace aroused her.

It was a girl's voice she heard first, shrill and indignant, and then James Bentley's voice in reply, with a clipped edge she hadn't heard before.

'—and I said *after* you've done your homework,' were the first words Jessica could identify. 'I'm well aware of why you want to keep out of the way, but I will not allow you to be insolent!'

The mumbled response was inaudible, but Jessica had heard enough to know that this must be James Bentley's daughter, Leonie. Another cousin, she reflected unbelievingly, forcing herself up, and swinging her legs over the side of the bed. If only any of this seemed familiar to her, she would not feel so helpless. As it was, in spite of all she knew, she had an underlying sense of incredulity, and, like an actor, she felt as if she was playing a part, without any real conviction or commitment.

The argument was going on, although Leonie was making most of the running; not wanting to hear any more, Jessica hurriedly got to her feet, and went to close the window.

'Well, how long is she going to sleep, for God's sake?' she heard as she brushed aside the curtains, but James Bentley's angry remonstrance was cut off by the squeak of the dry abrasion of the window-frame.

Jessica's headache had gone, but her palms were sweating as she crossed the bedroom to rinse her face again in the bathroom. And she also saw, to her dismay, that the silk dress had not responded well to being slept in. Her reflection in the mirrored walls above the bath was scarcely prepossessing. She would have to change. But into what? Although she had hung the clothes from the suitcase away in the closet, she couldn't remember seeing anything particularly suitable for such an occasion. She wasn't sure, of course, but she thought perhaps jeans, and maybe a T-shirt, would have suited her best. But there were no jeans in her wardrobe. Just suede trousers and designer shirts that didn't appeal to her at all.

Was it possible that a head injury could alter one's personality? If it had wiped away her memories of the past, could it also have changed her taste in clothes? It was possible, she supposed, that experience was what gave one a particular liking for certain styles in fashion. Someone who never had to worry about the cost of things, for example, was obviously more likely to choose expensive items. But, unless she was very much mistaken, she had not fallen into that category. On the contrary, she didn't even appear to possess a cheque-book, and she could only assume she had gone on a shopping spree on the strength of making this trip.

But why had she made this trip? she wondered suddenly. It wasn't as if she was here for her father's funeral. According to Dr Patel, Adam Bentley had been dead for over a month. If only she could remember. If only the accident had never happened.

She eventually changed the despised silk dress for the least formal outfit she could find. The amber silk shirt and long, fringed suede skirt actually looked much better on than she had expected, particularly after she had cinched in the waistband with a tan leather belt. At least they looked as if they fitted her, and on impulse she unthreaded her hair from its braid and brushed it thoroughly, before using the elasticated ring it had been fastened with to secure its loose waves at her nape.

'Better,' she told her reflection determinedly, steeling herself to go downstairs and join her host on the terrace. 'Just take one step at a time, and you'll be fine,' she added. 'You've got nothing to be afraid of. No one's going to eat you, *are they*?'

It was easy enough to find her way out on to the terrace. Jessica just followed the route that Mrs Hayes had shown her at lunch time, this time not stopping in the morning-room, but stepping through the french windows into the sunlight.

James Bentley, and the girl she assumed must be his daughter, were seated in the shade of a striped umbrella. A white, wrought-iron table was set about with curly wrought-iron chairs, whose loose padded cushions matched the parasol above. There was a jug of iced fruit juice on the table, as well as several glasses and a dish of strawberries. As Jessica emerged from the house, Leonie Bentley was picking desultorily from the dish of strawberries, a look of bored resentment on her face. Her father meanwhile was studying a file of correspondence, a frown of concentration between his brows.

Although she tried to be discreet, Jessica's heels rang against the paved tiles of the terrace, drawing their eyes to her. Immediately, James Bentley put his papers aside and rose politely to his feet, while Leonie stopped picking at the strawberries, and regarded her with brooding calculation.

'You look better,' said the man who was related to her father, and Jessica took a deep breath.

'I feel better,' she admitted, wishing she could confess that her physical well-being was the least of her worries. 'Um—is this your daughter? You said her name was—Leonie?' She moistened her lips and forced a smile. 'Hello, Leonie. I'm sorry I wasn't up when you got home from school. Er—I'm Jessica.'

'Hi!'

Leonie's greeting was hardly enthusiastic, and earned a warning look from her father, but at least it wasn't overtly hostile either. But she made no move to welcome their guest, either by making room for her at the table, or asking if she would like some juice; she just remained where she was, slumped in her chair, the sleeves of her school blouse rolled back above her elbows, and her wine-coloured skirt hiked up above her knees.

She wasn't an attractive girl, thought Jessica, finding some solace in the knowledge. She had been half expecting a minor replica of Laura Bentley, although of course Laura Bentley was no blood relation. Nevertheless, she had thought that a girl of Leonie's impressionable age would try to model herself on someone like Laura, and the realisation that she hadn't brought an added sense of reassurance.

'Sit up, Leonie,' said James abruptly, and his daughter grimaced, but did as she was told. I would, too, if he spoke to me like that, thought Jessica drily. Whatever else James Bentley might be, he was not an indifferent father.

'This is lovely,' she murmured, hoping to relieve the tension in the air, and gesturing vaguely towards the view. 'You're very lucky living in the heart of the country like this. I envy you.'

'Cousin Adam didn't own this house as well, if that's what you're thinking,' exclaimed Leonie suddenly, and Jessica's face suffused with colour.

'I—I never thought he did,' she began, not quite knowing what the girl was getting at, but before she could say any more James intervened.

'You'll apologise for that remark, Leonie,' he snapped, glaring angrily at his daughter, and the girl's mumbled submission was an embarrassment to them all.

'I'm sorry,' James added, transferring his attention to Jessica with little more warmth in his expression. 'Look, sit down, why don't you? I'll ask Mrs Hayes to fetch us some tea. And Leonie, if you make any more remarks like that, you can consider yourself grounded until the holidays, do I make myself clear?'

The girl swallowed. 'Yes, Daddy.'

'Good.' A wintry smile appeared for Jessica's benefit. 'I'll leave you then to entertain our guest. Perhaps she'd like some fruit juice. You are capable of pouring a glass of juice without spilling it, aren't you?'

The sarcasm was perhaps a little unkind, but Jessica was still too shocked by the girl's unexpected aggression to feel any sympathy for her. Was James Bentley the only member of the family prepared to be civil to her?

she wondered. And if so, why? What had she done to deserve so much animosity?

James disappeared into the house to make his wishes known to the housekeeper, and for a few moments after his departure the silence was almost oppressive. But then, as if realising she had only a limited amount of time to redeem herself, Leonie leant forward and indicated that Jessica should join her at the table, pushing the dish of strawberries towards her, and taking charge of the jug of juice.

'Do you want some?' she asked offhandedly, glancing at Jessica briefly and then quickly looking away. 'It's freshly squeezed,' she added. 'Daddy bought Mrs Hayes a juicer.'

Jessica hesitated momentarily before taking the seat she was offered, but she shook her head at the offer of a drink. 'I'd prefer tea,' she said, not altogether truthfully, but she felt as if anything Leonie had had something to do with was bound to be sour. 'Thank you,' she appended, so that no one could accuse her of impoliteness, and shifting in her chair she returned her gaze to the view.

One of the foals in the paddock took it into its head to perform a curious little leap at that moment, and seeing its long, spindly legs splaying quite alarmingly Jessica couldn't suppress the gasp that escaped her. She was unutterably relieved when the animal landed safely, and went to nuzzle its mother's neck. As if it was seeking her approbation, she thought, with some amusement. How nice it must be to be so sure of yourself and your role in life. Had she ever known that kind of security? She supposed she must have, if only she could remember.

'Do you know anything about horses?'

Leonie's question was as unexpected as her aggression had been earlier, and Jessica was tempted not to answer her. But then, realising it would be childish to ignore what she was saying, she made a careless gesture. 'No,' she responded tolerantly. 'Nothing worth mentioning, anyway.'

'You've never ridden?'

Jessica turned then and, resting her elbows on the edge of the table, she cupped her chin in her hands. 'Not that I know of, no.'

Leonie's eyes darted in her direction. 'You've really forgotten everything?'

'Everything,' agreed Jessica, with just a twinge of weary resignation. 'You, I suppose, know all there is to know about horses, and everything else. You really are very lucky. Or is that a provocative statement, too?'

Leonie coloured hotly. 'I've said I'm sorry,' she muttered, looking down at her hands.

'Yes.' Jessica nodded. 'But I'd like to know what you meant by it? Why should I even imagine my father might have owned this place?'

'You wouldn't. You didn't. Oh——' Leonie looked uncomfortable now. 'It was just a stupid thing to say, that's all. Look—won't you have a strawberry? Mr Hayes grows them in his greenhouse. That's why we get them early, before there are any local ones around.'

Jessica sighed. 'No, thanks.' She studied the younger girl thoughtfully. 'I guess you didn't want me to come here, hmm?'

'Yes! No! I mean—it's not up to me who my father invites to stay here.' Leonie groaned. 'Oh—does it matter what I think?'

'I think so.' Jessica paused. 'If you have some reason for disliking me, I'd like to know what it is.'

'I don't. I haven't. That is—well, I don't know you, do I?' Leonie's eyes darted nervously about the terrace. 'Oh, look—can't we just forget what I said before? Daddy's going to be back any minute, and if he thinks I've been upsetting you again, I'll be in deep trouble!'

Jessica frowned. 'This hasn't anything to do with my father's wife, has it? She hasn't—well, she hasn't been trying to poison your mind against me?'

'Your father's wife? You mean Laura!' Leonie stared at her disbelievingly. 'When did you see Laura?'

'In the hospital.' Jessica bent her head. 'She came a couple of days after your father first came to see me.'

'Did she?' Leonie's eyes were avid now. 'And?'

'And what?'

'Well, she must have said something pretty nasty for you to think she might have poisoned my mind against you!' declared Leonie reasonably.

'Oh, yes.' Observing the girl's obvious animation, Jessica half wished she had never started this. 'Well...'

'Oh, hurry up.' Leonie was impatient now. 'Daddy'll be back soon. What did she say?'

Jessica still hesitated. 'I——' She knew she had to say something, but she was choosing her words with care. 'She—told me about my father, that's all.'

*All!* Inwardly, Jessica cringed. The recollection of the other woman's malice was still able to drain all the blood from her cheeks, and she shivered. She had avoided thinking about that encounter too deeply until now, but Leonie's questions had forced her to remember, and she didn't like the memory.

'You mean—she told you about the will?' urged Leonie eagerly, but Jessica wasn't listening to her. A sudden pain was tearing her temples apart, and with a muffled sob of pain she groped for the table's rim and got unsteadily to her feet.

She was vaguely aware of Leonie's horrified awareness that something had happened, but then James Bentley came striding along the terrace towards them and she swayed back against the table.

'What the hell have you been saying to her?' she heard James swear angrily, and then his arms were around her, and he was sweeping her off her feet and carrying her towards the french doors into the house.

'Nothing! I didn't say anything, honestly,' protested Leonie, following them, practically running to keep up with her father. 'We were getting along fine, really. Then, she just sort of went pale and started staggering about——'

'I'll speak to you later, Leonie,' James retorted harshly, ignoring her excuses. 'Right now, you can find Mrs Hayes, and ask her to place a call to Dr Patel at the hospital——'

'Oh, no, really...' The pain was receding again, and Jessica didn't want to cause any more trouble. 'Um—Leonie's right. We were just talking, that's all.' She ran her tongue over her dry lips, intensely conscious of the hard strength of James's arms across her back and beneath the curve of her legs. 'Please—don't bother calling Dr Patel. If—if you'll just put me down, I can walk up to my room.'

'Forget the call, then, Leonie,' said James, over his shoulder to the frightened girl, but he made no attempt to release his burden. 'Just ask Mrs Hayes to bring a tray of tea up to Jessica's room. And then you make yourself scarce. You've got some homework to do before supper.'

'Yes, Daddy.'

Leonie sounded relieved, and Jessica couldn't blame her. In his present mood, James was not a man to be argued with, and she said nothing more when he started to mount the stairs with her still in his arms.

'It's my fault,' he said, as he reached her room, and kicked open the door with his booted foot. 'I should have left instructions for you to stay put for today. It's obviously been too much for you. I should have had more sense.'

'I'm not a child, you know,' murmured Jessica unevenly as he set her down upon the bed, and for a moment those light silver eyes bored into hers. He was close too; too close, she reflected unsteadily, realising as she did so that since he had taken charge of her the pain in her head had disappeared entirely. Perhaps that was because the blood was now pounding through her veins, she thought uneasily, acknowledging with some dismay that her reactions to this man were disturbing to say the least. She had to keep reminding herself he was her father's cousin, and in this instance her present memory seemed distinctly unreliable.

'You're all right, then,' he said, straightening, and in the cream and gold beauty of her bedroom his dark masculinity was very marked.

'Um—I think so,' she murmured, avoiding his eyes, and then had to clear her throat as the final word choked on the dryness. 'Thank you.'

'And Leonie wasn't annoying you?'

'No.' Jessica looked up then, but he was already turning away, the heated scent of his body a tangible presence in the warm air.

'Good.' He halted by the open doorway. 'Then I suggest you rest for the remainder of the day. Mrs Hayes will bring you supper when Leonie has hers at eight o'clock, but I probably won't see you until tomorrow. Anyway, if there's anything you need, don't hesitate to let us know.'

He left, and Jessica expelled the breath she hadn't realised she was holding until then. Then, pressing a hand that trembled a little to her chest, she got to her feet and made her way into the bathroom to splash her face with cold water. She was so hot, she thought shakily, using a face cloth to dampen the moist hollow between her breasts. And, as she pressed its coolness to her forehead, she realised it wasn't just a physical condition.

## CHAPTER SIX

James Bentley parked the Range Rover on the paved forecourt in front of the house, and sat for several seconds just gazing at its ivy-clad façade. Called, at various times, Bickersley House, Bickersley Grange, and Bickersley Park, it had been home to James until his cousin's marriage twenty years before. It was where he had been born, his own father never properly recovering from injuries he had sustained during the Second World War, so that his widow had been glad to accept her father-in-law's offer of a home only weeks after she'd discovered she was pregnant. James's grandfather, a widower, had always been like a father to him, and when his mother married again when he was eight, to a marine biologist whose work entailed a great deal of travelling about the world, he had been quite content to stay at Bickersley and continue with his education.

Adam had been like an elder brother to him at that time, although the fifteen years or so between them had precluded any real companionship. Like James, Adam had been brought up at Bickersley, too, the rambling old house being plenty big enough to accommodate both his grandfather and his sons' families.

It was ironic, James thought now, that it was through him that Adam had met his future wife. They had all thought that Adam was a confirmed bachelor. At thirty-three, he had shown little interest in women, but that was before his parents were killed in a freak storm in South America. At that time he had gone a little wild—not unnaturally, James had felt, but his attitude had changed when he introduced Laura to his cousin. She had soon discovered that not only was he heir to the Bentley fortunes, but also that he was quite dazzled by her own individual beauty, and James, still at university, was simply no competition.

James's mouth compressed. It was strange to think the house no longer belonged to his family—or at least, to no legitimate member of it. Even with the knowledge that Jessica Devlin was staying in his house at the moment, it was hard to accept that all this belonged to her now. Of course, she didn't know it, and Laura's attitude had made it all the more difficult to broach the subject with her, but nevertheless, as Adam's heir, she was a comparatively wealthy young woman.

It was strange, too, that she should have turned out so differently from what he had expected. The solicitor who had handled Adam's affairs in London had described her as tough and aggressive, with a definite chip on her shoulder regarding her sudden windfall. Although James was prepared to admit that Laura's opinion of the girl was bound to be a negative one, he couldn't deny that Adam's lawyer had reinforced her point of view.

So, was it possible that that blow on her head that had robbed her of her memory had also mellowed her character? Stranger things had happened, he supposed, but somehow it was difficult to see the Jessica Devlin he knew in the role of a tough operator. Oh, he realised that once she recovered her memory she would not appear as vulnerable as she did at present. Right now, she was defenceless, groping desperately for her identity, in a world that seemed totally alien to her. But when her memory came back, when the clouds of anonymity had been swept away, and she knew exactly where she was going, she was bound to feel and act differently. Nevertheless, he could not see the girl he knew in the role Laura and Adam's solicitor had laid out for her. She simply didn't seem that kind of girl. Or was he being absurdly credulous? Could those pansy-soft eyes and quivering lips be hiding a rapacious greed? Was her appearance of innocence only spurious? When her memory returned, would she still be as determined to dispose of her father's assets? And if so, wasn't he being incredibly naïve in supporting her at this time?

He sighed. It was an impossible question. Until something positive happened, there was no way of knowing whose opinion of her would prove to be the right one. The fact remained, he had felt sorry for her, and because of that—and Laura's involvement—he had felt obliged to help her. Would he live to regret it? Who could tell? One thing was for certain: it had given them all a breathing space.

He was locking the estate car when Laura herself appeared. She came out on to the porch of the house, and stood waiting for him to join her. 'You're late,' she greeted him, as he climbed the steps to bring him level with her. 'But I'll forgive you.' She reached up to touch his cheek with her lips. 'I've missed you.'

James accepted the salutation without comment, but he allowed her to lead him into the entrance hall, aware of her fingers caressing his wrist where it escaped from his cuff. Laura was evidently full of curiosity but she was controlling it well, and he had no wish to precipitate an outburst until they were positively alone. So he accompanied her into the library, which served equally well as a drawing-room, and accepted the Scotch and water she offered him from the tray of drinks set on the desk that had been his grandfather's.

'So,' she exclaimed at last, as he leaned back against the closed door, 'did you collect her?'

James didn't pretend not to understand what she meant. 'Yes,' he said, taking the glass she handed to him, and swallowing a generous mouthful before continuing. 'Yes, she's safely installed at Aspen. No problem. She's really quite a pleasant girl.'

'Pleasant?' Laura was impatient. 'You can't be serious.'

'Why not?' James regarded her over the rim of his glass. 'What did you expect me to say?'

Laura snorted. 'Well...' She lifted her slim shoulders, one of which was bared by the cut of her dress of rose-coloured tissue. 'You might at least have some sympathy for my feelings. How do you think I feel, when I hear you describing the girl who is threatening to destroy my life as *pleasant*?'

James sighed. 'Don't over-dramatise the situation, Laura. You know as well as I do that Adam made that qualification in his will so that you could continue to live at Bickersley——'

'But if I marry again, I have to leave,' Laura burst in hotly, and James shrugged.

'Is that unreasonable? One would assume the man you were going to marry would expect to support you himself. And he wouldn't want to live in another man's house, either.'

Laura pouted. 'You know *you're* the only man I want to marry!'

'Do I?'

'Of course you do.' Laura abandoned her independent stance, and crossed the room to slide possessive arms about his waist. 'Darling, how can you doubt it?'

James made no attempt to return her embrace. Instead, he said quietly, 'You didn't feel that way twenty years ago, as I recall.'

'Oh, can't we forget about that?' Laura groaned. 'James, you know perfectly well I was too young and foolish to know what I wanted when I was eighteen years of age. I was attracted to Adam, I admit it, but you were the one I loved.'

'Was I?' James didn't sound totally convinced. 'What you mean is, I was just the poor relation, with few prospects beyond a university education and an apparently unprofitable interest in horseflesh. I wasn't my grandfather's golden boy, his natural successor, with a burning desire to take over the family business when he returned. Adam was. He joined the firm straight from school, just as my grandfather wanted, and I dare say it was his intention to hand it on to *his* son when he retired. Only you didn't give him a son, did you, Laura? You didn't even have a daughter.'

Laura drew back. 'You bastard!' she exclaimed tremulously. 'How can you say such things to me? You know it wasn't my fault we didn't have any children. Adam just wasn't a sexual man. My God, you know that!'

James looked down at her with mildly cynical eyes. 'And what about Jessica Devlin?'

'What about her?' Laura was sulky.

'How do you explain her existence?'

Laura pulled a face. 'I don't have to.'

'You do if you persist in this argument that Adam couldn't have children.'

Laura sighed. 'All right, all right. But that was before I married him. Who knows who this woman was? She might have said the child was his, and it wasn't.'

'Yes.' James had to acknowledge that was a possibility. But how to prove it was something else. 'Actually—Leonie said something like that too.'

'Did she?' Laura sounded surprised. 'Well, well. Perhaps there's hope for me yet. I must have a word with Leonie. Perhaps we can join forces. That would be a novelty.'

'I'd rather you didn't say anything to Leonie,' replied James flatly. 'I've had a hard enough time getting her to accept the situation as it is. I don't want you coming over and confusing her again. Let's let it ride for the time being, shall we? There may be other ways of resolving the situation. You're not being threatened at the moment.'

Laura hesitated. 'You do understand how I feel though, don't you? I mean—Bickersley was your home, too. It could be your home again——'

'No, Laura.'

'What do you mean, no?' She stared at him.

'I mean—if we ever—get together, for want of a better description—it's got to be on my terms this time, not yours. You say you love me——'

'I do!'

'Well—OK. So be it. But if you do, you'll live with me at Aspen, not Bickersley. Whatever happens to this house, I want you to understand that.'

'All right, all right.'

But Laura pressed herself against him as she spoke, so he couldn't see the expression in her eyes, and James wondered if she was really as willing to sacrifice her role as lady of the manor as she protested. He loved her—he had loved her since he was eighteen, in fact—but he was not blind to her failings. The daughter of one of his grandfather's managers, Laura had had her sights set on becoming the next Lady Bentley, from the day she first visited the house. And if Adam's premature demise had prevented her from one day acquiring the title which had been granted to his grandfather in his lifetime, that could not be helped. She was still the châtelaine of one of the most prestigious houses in the district, and as Adam Bentley's widow she should have enjoyed that status for many years to come.

His lips twisted. And all because *he* had brought her to Bickersley to meet his family. On his first vacation from Durham University, he had encountered Laura during a visit to his grandfather's office in Wakefield, and learned that she was working there as an office junior. The attraction between them had been mutual, and for the whole of the Christmas holidays he had spent all his free time with her. Looking back, he was fairly sure that Laura had had no particular ambitions at that time, but a few days before he returned to Durham he had made the mistake that had cost him her affections.

He had known, as soon as Laura saw the house, that she was dazzled by its size and elegance. Until then, her world had been bounded by the road of comfortably middle-class detached homes in which she lived. The idea of owning a house like Bickersley had never even occurred to her, but he, in his ignorance, had made such a prospect not only commendable, but possible. And when Adam had shown his infatuation for her blonde beauty, James had known his own days as her escort were numbered.

Oh, he had been bitter, and angry, but it had all been to no avail. He had had to return to university a few days later, and in his absence Laura had wasted no time. He supposed, to be fair to her, that without Adam's co-operation she could not have achieved her ends, but he, poor fool, was as besotted with her as she was with Bickersley and all it meant. James had tried to tell his cousin what was going on, but he had been accused of sour grapes for his pains, and after that he had kept his own counsel. But he had drawn the line at being best man at their wedding, and from the minor role of usher he had watched the woman he still loved marry the cousin he was fairly sure she didn't.

In the years that followed he had kept away from Bickersley as much as he could, and when his grandfather had seen that he had no interest in the family business he had helped him to buy the Aspen property, when it was just a few acres of run-down pastureland, and a rather dilapidated farmhouse. His grandfather had had reservations, James knew, but he had managed to convince the old man he knew what he was doing, and his boyish dreams of running a stud farm had eventually become a reality. It had taken a great deal of hard work, and there had been times when he had been tempted to give it all up and accept an alternative role in life. But determination, and a need to prove himself in his own eyes, had driven him on, and the inspired purchase of a troublesome colt who, with his own and Ted Paisley's care, had proved a world-beater, had given him the necessary capital to grow and expand.

During this time, he had met and married Leonie's mother, and, although he had not loved her as he had once loved Laura, he had been devastated when she died. For a while, he hadn't even been able to look at his baby daughter without seeing Irene's pale face as it had looked on the hospital pillow, and that was when Laura had taken advantage of his weakness to insinuate herself into his life again. Perhaps that was why Leonie had always resented her, he reflected. Even as a little girl, she had objected to the other woman's presence, and the attention her father gave to her.

Not that James exactly welcomed Laura's intervention in his affairs. To begin with he, like Leonie, resented her assumption that she would be welcome in his home. Just because things were not flowing smoothly at Bickersley, it was no reason for her to use Aspen as a kind of bolt-hole, and they had many arguments when she persisted in invading his domain. His grandfather had died, leaving Adam in sole control of the family business, so that aside from any personal problems they might be having Adam spent long hours in his office, and Laura was bored. But James had little sympathy for her. She had chosen her fate and she had to deal with it.

All the same, she was useful in obtaining a nanny for Leonie, and it was at her suggestion that he hired a firm of interior decorators and had the house stripped and redesigned. 'James, the kind of people you're hoping to be dealing with will not expect you to be living in a hovel!' she had declared, when he had offered a token resistance. 'You want this to become one of the most prestigious horse-breeding establishments in the country, don't you? Take my word for it, surroundings are important.' And she should know, James had thought bitterly, still at that time able to feel the pain of her earlier betrayal.

But no one could deny that the renovations had proved an enormous advantage. In the hands of experts, the sprawling farmhouse had been transformed into a luxurious family home, with plenty of space for guest-rooms to accommodate the buyers who came to visit the farm. In addition to which, it enabled James to entertain more freely in his own home, and the Aspen stud began to appear in books and magazines with a frequency previously only enjoyed by the larger establishments.

And, over the years, his animosity towards his cousin's wife had gradually dissipated. He had succeeded in relegating that youthful indiscretion to the back of his mind and, if he hadn't actually forgotten it, he had, at least, found it in his heart to forgive her. He also learned, from what she told him, and from things he heard independently from other people, that her relationship with Adam was anything but blissful. Even without Laura's fairly doubtful reasons for choosing him as a husband and the demands of the business, Adam himself had been a bachelor too long to find his wife's needs of paramount importance. Besides which, she was too young for him, her tastes did not ally with his; and if his friends bored her, her friends felt uncomfortable at the house.

They had soon found they had nothing in common—beyond their mutual aspirations for Bickersley—but neither of them had been prepared to take the step that might result in losing it.

Maybe that was why, in spite of the fact that he still loved Laura, and felt a not-unnatural satisfaction that her life with his cousin had proved to be such a disappointment for both of them, James had never taken advantage of the frequent invitations she had offered him. He might not have felt a great deal of loyalty towards the cousin who had taken his own happiness at the expense of James's, but for his own sake, and for Leonie's, he had listened to the warnings of his conscience. In the years since Irene's death, he had found there were plenty of other women more than willing to satisfy any physical cravings he might have, and there had been some compensation in knowing Laura knew what he was doing, and could do nothing about it.

However, since Adam's death, the situation had changed. Laura was free now, and she had wasted no opportunity in reminding him of that fact. But James had no intention of moving back to Bickersley, whatever the outcome of this affair with Jessica Devlin. Aspen was his home and it was Leonie's home; and if Laura thought she could persuade him to leave, she was going to be disappointed.

As a result of a late night, James slept in the next day. He was annoyed, because he had intended being present when their newest young stallion was put on a lunging rein that morning, and when he went down for breakfast he was not in the most equitable of moods. Planning only to stop for coffee, he was not best pleased to find his guest already at the table in the morning-room, and her tentative greeting met only a muttered response.

'It's another lovely morning,' Jessica persisted, clearly not understanding his reticence, and James was forced to hook out a chair from the table and sit down to pour his coffee.

'So it is,' he remarked, reluctantly aware of how much more rested she looked this morning than she had done the previous afternoon. She had replaited her hair again, which made her look younger, and a creamy yellow cashmere sweater complimented her slender frame. The contrast between her and Laura had never been more marked, he reflected broodingly, resenting the intrusive thought. Where Laura was small and curvaceous, and excessively feminine, Jessica was tall and slim, and infinitely more controlled. In spite of the clothes she wore—the sable coat, which had been—what? An aberration brought on by learning she had inherited her father's company? A gesture of independence?—he got the feeling that this girl was unlikely to be impressed by affectation. As to what she wore, he would have guessed she would look best in tailored skirts and trouser suits, or softly draped dresses in primary colours. Clothes that would flatter her height and natural elegance, he thought unwillingly, and then knew a growing incredulity that he should actually be considering her appearance. How she looked, how she moved, what she wore, should be of supreme indifference to him. Yet he knew that this was not so, and the knowledge did not improve his temper.

'I feel much better today,' she volunteered, as if reminding him that he had been remiss in not asking after her health, and James's anger flared.

'I'm so glad to hear it,' he responded cuttingly. 'Perhaps, then, you can refrain from either bursting into tears or suffering another relapse if I tell you that Laura—that is, Mrs Bentley—is likely to show up here today, to apologise for her rudeness.'

Jessica's cheeks briefly flamed with colour but, before he had the opportunity to either consolidate his offensive or feel remorse at its cruelty, she sprang to her feet and shocked him into silence.

'I wondered—I wondered how long it would be before you showed your true colours!' she exclaimed, controlling the tremor in her voice with admirable fortitude. 'I thought it was unlikely that as every other member of the Bentley family evidently hates my guts, you could be the exception! Well—perhaps you'd be good enough to give me the telephone number of a taxi firm, so that I can arrange to have myself and my belongings removed from here immediately. I knew you couldn't really want me here, and I'm glad you won't have the chance to accuse me of taking advantage of your hospitality for any longer than is absolutely necessary!'

James listened to this outburst with a growing sense of self-disgust. For Christ's sake, he had been the one who had supposedly taken pity on her, and now, because of his own mood of irritation, he had virtually destroyed the tenuous communication there had been between them.

'Look—I'm sorry,' he muttered gruffly, thrusting back his own chair and getting to his feet too, but she flinched away from the placating hand he stretched towards her and backed away towards the door.

'Don't bother to apologise,' she choked, waving agitated arms out in front of her. 'It's my fault. It's all my fault. I should never have come here. It was a stupid thing to do.'

'It wasn't stupid at all. It was necessary,' contradicted James grimly, going after her and resisting her efforts to evade him. With a sudden lunge, he grasped her forearm and halted her uneven retreat with determined fingers, narrowing the space between them, and drawing her irrevocably towards him. 'For God's sake, Jess, stop fighting me! I've said that I'm sorry, and you've got to believe I am.'

'Why should I?' She faced him bravely, and James felt an unwilling awareness of her vulnerability. He was also unhappily aware of his own careless brutality, and that the insistent need to reassure her was only a part of the complicated emotions she continually aroused.

'Because—because I'm a brute and a bully,' he declared heavily, conscious of the brittle bones of her arm, easily tangible through their narrow coating of flesh. It would take so little to break it—and her, he reflected bitterly. And he was going the right way about it, just to pacify his own mood of impatience. 'Hell, I didn't mean what I said. I was just taking out my own frustrations on you!'

'Frustrations I created!'

'No.'

He lifted the arm he was holding and, sensing her weakening strength, worked his thumb over the pale skin.

It was amazingly soft and smooth, a potent contrast to the callused hardness of his own palm, and almost without his knowing it his touch became a caress.

'I've got a lot on my mind at the moment,' he continued, his voice harsh, but not aggressive. 'You'll have to get used to me flying off the handle. I growl a lot, but I don't often bite, as Leonie would say.'

Jessica was trembling. He could feel it, and the urge to reassure her took on a physical shape. He wanted to comfort her; he wanted to take her in his arms and prove to her that his earlier words had been the product of a deliberately induced self-indulgence; he wanted to wipe that look of anxiety off her face, and recapture the confidence she had shown before he smacked her down. He didn't deserve that she should forgive him, but he badly wanted to try.

But he didn't do any of those things. Something, some inner safety mechanism, warned him that giving in to such impulses was not only unwise, but reckless. The situation was becoming far too intense, and, meeting her tremulous gaze, he knew he had to defuse it right away. She was his cousin's *daughter*, for God's sake! His role in her life ought to be that of an uncle, or a *father*! Not the emotionally charged relationship that was presently being created by his curiously compulsive caress. He could just imagine Laura's reactions if she were to walk in on them now.

With an abrupt gesture he released her, but when she would once again have turned away he put out a hand across the doorway, successfully barring her chance of retreat.

'Look,' he said, 'can't we forget what just happened, hmm? Haven't you ever got out of bed on the wrong side? Or don't you remember that old adage?'

'I remember it.' Jessica's tongue appeared to moisten her lips, and James squashed a most un-uncle-like urge to follow its path with his thumb. 'I—all right. I'll try and do as you suggest. So long as you're serious. So long as you really don't mind my—being here.'

'I invited you, didn't I?'

'People make impulsive gestures they later regret.'

James's lips twisted. 'Like your accepting my invitation, perhaps?'

'Perhaps.' She was not about to let him off the hook so easily. 'And now—if you'll excuse me...'

'Where are you going?'

Jessica sighed. 'Does it matter?'

'As a matter of fact, yes.' James cast a thoughtful glance over his shoulder. 'If you'll give me a few minutes to finish my coffee——'

'Why?' She was showing more spirit than he would have imagined before this altercation, and he wondered if his words had sparked some latent energy inside her. One thing was certain, given time and confidence, she might even be a match for Laura, he mused, although that particular contest would need a little more stamina.

James dropped his arm and straightened. 'I thought you might be interested in looking round the place. If I promise not to tire you.'

Jessica hesitated, but he could tell by the sudden alertness in her gaze that she was intrigued by the prospect. 'Um—do you have the time?' she ventured, and one of James's dark brows ascended.

'I'll make time.'

Jessica stiffened her spine. 'And—Mrs Bentley?'

'What about her?' James's tone was clipped, but he didn't want to think about Laura right now.

'What if she comes when we—when we're not here?'

'She'll wait,' replied James, with sudden impatience. 'Look, do you want to come, or don't you? You'd better make up your mind.'

## CHAPTER SEVEN

LAURA BENTLEY came to meet them as they walked back to the house.

It was almost midday, and Jessica wondered if the woman had timed her arrival deliberately so that Mr Bentley—*James*, as he had told her to call him—would invite her to stay for lunch.

Just seeing the woman again brought on a wave of nausea that Jessica had to fight to overcome. She was tired, it was true, and although the morning had not been strenuous it had sapped her strength, so that any prospect of conflict left her feeling quite exposed. Laura's appearance was associated with pain and accusation, and the awful feeling of helplessness she had hardly ever escaped in the hospital. She couldn't prevent the tight knot of fear and apprehension that contracted in her stomach, and she wished with all her heart she could avoid this confrontation.

It was all the more distressing after the morning she had spent. Visiting the stables; feeding the mares in the paddock; even bumping along in a dusty Land Rover, to check on the boundary fencing, had enabled her to put herself and her own problems to the back of her mind, and Laura Bentley's intervention was an unwanted intrusion.

She sensed that James Bentley was not entirely pleased to see his cousin's wife, either. He didn't say anything, but somehow she could feel hostile vibrations emanating from him. It was strange how easily she could detect his mood, and its derivation. There had been times during the morning when she had sensed he didn't altogether relish the task he had set himself in appointing himself her protector; times when she had caught him looking at her with a strangely hostile expression, that she couldn't quite explain. She had wondered why, if he didn't really want her here, he had argued so convincingly to keep her. It didn't altogether make sense, but then, so much of what was happening to her didn't.

All the same, until she saw Laura Bentley walking across the paved forecourt in front of the stable block, it had been a reasonably successful morning. James had shown her the barns and tack-rooms; the foaling boxes and indoor exercise arena, where untrained horses were schooled, and expensively bred stallions were put through their paces. He had even told her a little about how the stud was run, and she had discovered a wholly unexpected attraction for horses, which seemed to point to some latent family trait at least.

She had also been introduced to James's manager, Ted Paisley, a somewhat dour Yorkshireman, who evidently had a great respect for his employer, but distinctly less enthusiasm for his latest acquisition. If she could call herself an acquisition, she reflected. In some respects she was, and in others she most definitely wasn't!

The two youths who assisted Ted Paisley had been infinitely more friendly. One of them had been grooming a mare when they walked across the stable yard, and he had been only too willing to take time out from his task to meet the boss's cousin.

'If you'd like me to give Miss Devlin a few riding lessons, sure you've only to say the word, sir,' he exclaimed, when Jessica confessed she couldn't remember ever being on a horse before. But James was not impressed.

'Thank you, Pat,' he said, with a cool politeness Jessica found just as off-putting as his anger earlier. 'But that won't be necessary. If Miss Devlin does wish to learn to ride, I'm sure either myself or Ted will share that responsibility.'

Pat acknowledged the set-down with a wry smile that did nothing for his popularity with his employer. Jessica couldn't help wishing James had not been so adamant. She might have liked talking to the young groom. At least he had no reason to dislike her, she reflected. He might even have been able to tell her what it was her father had put in his will which had created such a conflict within his family.

But now the minor irritations of the morning faded into insignificance. Laura Bentley's appearance put every nerve in her body on edge, and it was with the utmost difficulty that she continued to put one foot in front of the other. Even Laura's cream silk dress, with its delicate tracery of gold thread, was not unreminiscent of the white leather suit she had worn to visit the hospital, and Jessica wondered fancifully if she wore light colours deliberately to disguise the darkness of her character.

This morning, however, there was no reference to that unpleasant encounter in her manner. On the contrary, the smile she turned on the girl had all the warmth Jessica could have wished for at their first meeting, and her face held a look of entreaty, as if begging her forgiveness. If Jessica had been less wary, this unexpected display of almost maternal goodwill might have made her doubt the veracity of that earlier confrontation. But Laura's eyes were not half as remorseful as her words would have the girl believe, and Jessica would have done almost anything to avoid having to speak to her.

However, to her surprise, Laura's first words were to James. Jessica watched in some amazement as the woman placed scarlet-tipped fingers on James's wrists, before reaching up to bestow a most uncousinly kiss on his unsmiling mouth. 'Darling,' she chided, as Jessica's astonishment turned to embarrassment, 'I've been waiting *ages*!'

'Have you?' To Jessica's relief, James was not seduced into a passionate response. 'Well, I've been giving Jessica a guided tour of the place. I think it's important that she gets to know her immediate surroundings, don't you?'

If there was a challenge in that statement, Laura chose not to respond to it, but Jessica wondered why he had called her Jessica just now, when earlier on he had abbreviated it to 'Jess'. She had liked the abbreviation much better than *Jessica*, but she could hardly tell him that, and particularly not now.

'Of course, darling, of course,' the older woman responded instead, in an unmistakably conciliatory tone, giving a little *moue* of protest when James released himself from her seemingly unwilling fingers. 'We all want to do what we can to make sure—Jessica—feels at home with us. I mean that, my dear,' she added, turning to the girl. 'Whatever I said earlier, you have to believe I didn't mean to upset you.'

Jessica's fingers clenched. Laura was lying, of course. She was almost sure of it. But she had no way of proving it; no real way of convincing anyone, even herself, how she sensed that this was so. It was an instinctive thing, a sureness born of that first unforgettable encounter, when she was sure Laura had at least been honest with her. During the past few days, she had had to come to terms with what Laura had told her, but she had still to face the consequences of what her father had done.

'Um——' She looked rather helplessly in James's direction, before making any response at all. 'It's all right.'

'I knew you'd understand.' Abandoning her efforts to influence James in some way Jessica had yet to fathom, Laura slipped her arm through Jessica's as they walked back to the house. 'Now, could we try to be friends, do you think? I know it's expecting a lot, but we do have something in common: your father deceived us both.'

Jessica wanted to pull her arm out of Laura's grasp as James had done a few moments before, but she didn't have the strength. Whatever Laura had said, she was not convinced the woman was sincere, but the idea of instigating another argument filled her with alarm. Even though James was there, and surely himself providing the reason for Laura's sudden volte-face, she did not have the courage to make any protest. After all, she didn't really know James Bentley well enough to be confident of his support, and, although he had suppressed Laura's greeting, that kiss had been exchanged, and there was obviously a reason for it.

'So—are you feeling better?' Laura continued as they mounted the shallow steps that divided the gardens from the paddocks, and the narrow paved track that led down to the private road that circled the property. 'At least you're not stuck in the hospital. Wasn't it sweet of Jamie to offer you an alternative? But really, you ought to be at Bickersley. That was your father's home, and I'm sure that's what he would have wanted.'

Before Jessica could find words to respond to this invitation, however, James intervened. Much to her relief, he did not allow her the opportunity to make some stumbling objection that Laura could easily subvert. Instead, he moved ahead of them, so that his words could not possibly be misunderstood, and meeting Laura's gaze with a somewhat challenging stare of his own he said smoothly, 'I think, in the circumstances, it wouldn't help to change Jessica's surroundings once again. She's just becoming used to this place. We don't want to confuse her, do we?'

Laura's mouth compressed. 'Surely she's more likely to remain confused here?' she countered.

'Why?' James arched a dark brow. 'She doesn't know Bickersley. It's as foreign to her as Aspen. And besides, Dr Patel made her my responsibility, and I can't discharge my duties if she's not here.'

Jessica didn't like the way they were talking about her as if she wasn't there, but she liked the idea of moving to Laura Bentley's home even less, so she kept quiet. All the same, it was impossible not to wonder why she had chosen to come here at all, and Laura's game of cat and mouse didn't help her puzzled thoughts.

'Let's have a drink, shall we?' said James at last, terminating the discussion. 'Oh, I see Mrs Hayes has already provided you with some coffee, Laura. Would you like the same, Jessica, or would you prefer a soft drink?'

'Coffee's fine,' said Jessica, not wanting to cause any further disagreement, and the appearance of the housekeeper simplified the situation.

'Could we have some more coffee? And I'll have a beer,' said James, thereby confounding Jessica's intention of making do with the pot that was already there. 'How about you, Laura? Can Mrs Hayes get you anything else?'

'A martini,' declared Laura ungraciously, releasing Jessica's arm, which she had been squeezing unpleasantly tightly and flinging herself into one of the cushioned wrought-iron chairs. 'With lots of ice.'

'You got that, did you, Mrs Hayes?' James appended, adding a tight smile to soften his guest's words, and the housekeeper nodded.

'Of course, Mr Bentley,' she responded, giving Jessica a faintly speculative look. 'Will you have it out here, or shall I bring it to the library?'

'Oh, I think it's warm enough to sit out here, don't you?' said James, addressing his remarks to no one in particular. 'We'll have lunch in half an hour, if that's OK. It's got to be fairly prompt. I've got a meeting with a customer at half-past two.'

Mrs Hayes departed, and James pointedly held a chair for Jessica to sit in. It was nearer to Laura than she would have liked, but she felt obliged to take it. Sooner or later, she was going to have to come to terms with this woman who had been her father's wife, and this matter of a legacy was not going to go away.

James seated himself across the table from them, resting the ankle of one leg across the knee of the other and allowing one hand to lie negligently across both. His other arm he looped over the back of his chair, but although his pose was casual Jessica sensed his mood was anything but.

For her part, she felt an uneasy compunction to say something—anything—to make a voluntary contribution to the conversation. But it was incredibly difficult to think of any spontaneous topic that would not involve her in areas which were still so nebulous to her, and she was still struggling desperately for words when once again Laura raised an offensive.

'Don't you remember anything?' she asked, assuming a more elegant position, and fixing Jessica with a penetrating stare. 'I mean—exactly what kind of amnesia have you got? How long is it likely to last? Don't any of our names mean anything to you?'

'I believe it's called hysterical amnesia,' ventured Jessica reluctantly, recalling something the doctor had told James in her presence, and Laura snorted.

'*Hysterical* amnesia!'

'It's just a term,' put in James quietly. 'It can mean anything from a subconscious suppression of a memory, to a full-scale blanking out of the past, brought on by pain or stress—or conceivably a blow to the head.'

'So there's really nothing physically wrong with her memory?'

James sighed, his expression hardening. 'Not if you mean some physical pressure on the brain, no. At least, Dr Patel doesn't think so.'

'Then how do we know she really has lost her memory——'

'Oh, really——' began James impatiently, but Jessica had had enough of being made to feel like some dumb creature, incapable of speaking for herself.

'You don't imagine I'm enjoying this, do you?' she exclaimed, putting a hand to her temple as the unaccustomed surge of blood to her brain caused a distinct throbbing to manifest itself. 'For goodness' sake, I want to remember who I am as much as anyone else. More, probably. I know finding out your husband had an illegitimate daughter must have been a shock for you; but it's not my fault, and I wish you wouldn't blame me for it.'

'Do you?'

Laura would have said more, but once again James intervened. 'That's enough,' he said grimly, a muscle at his jawline jerking spasmodically as he looked at each of them in turn. 'For Christ's sake, can't we even have a drink together without it degenerating into an argument? The facts are plain. We have to live with them. Now, can we talk about something else? What's happening at the mills?'

Laura cast Jessica another brooding glance, but then she evidently decided that now was not the time to pursue this. Instead, she began to talk about some problem over recruitment at the plant in Bradford, and the uncertainty of tenure in the present situation. As Jessica didn't know what situation they were talking about, it was a simple matter for her to switch off and transfer her attention to the less demanding task created by Mrs Hayes's reappearance. While Laura sipped her martini, and James ripped open his can of beer, she busied herself with the tray of coffee the housekeeper had set before her, and only when the name Ripley was mentioned did she feel an unfamiliar spasm of concern. That name meant something to her. She could almost swear it. But whether it was in this connection, or simply the name of someone she had known in London, was difficult to decide.

But still, it was worth a try, and summoning up her courage, she said quietly, 'You mentioned someone called Ripley.' She flushed. 'Um—would I know him?'

'It's not a him, it's a firm,' said James patiently, ignoring Laura's sceptical expression. 'A firm of textile designers, if that means anything to you. Your father has used some of their designs for his worsted.'

Jessica blinked. Textile designers, she echoed silently. Yes, she had known that, too. But how had she known it? And what did it mean to her?

'Are you all right?'

James was looking at her rather concernedly now, and Jessica guessed her face had lost what little colour it had possessed. But the idea that something, even a little thing, like the name of some firm of textile designers, might mean something to her, was altogether shocking and unnerving.

'I'm—fine,' she managed now, shaking her head a little dazedly. 'It's just the name—Ripley—means something to me. I'm almost sure of it. I recognise that name, and the fact that they're textile designers.'

'Do you?' James's response was guarded. 'And do you know why? I mean, is it just a name? Or is there more?'

Jessica tried to think, but it was no good. The throbbing in her head she had suffered earlier returned as soon as she tried to concentrate. Swallowing back her disappointment, she slumped weakly in her chair, aware that Laura was watching her without much sympathy.

'No,' she admitted dully, after a moment. 'No, there's nothing more. Just the name, like you said. Do you think I could have heard it in London? Is that why you don't think it's important?'

James sighed, and exchanged a look with Laura. 'I didn't say it wasn't important.' He lifted his shoulders. 'Of course it is. Any memory, however small, is important. I'm—just sorry it isn't a more personal memory. You see,' he hesitated, 'Ripley's was the firm the girl who was killed was going to work for. The police told us. She was on her way to Leeds for an interview. You must have talked to her. You were apparently sharing the same table.'

Much to Jessica's relief, Laura left when James went to attend his meeting. She had been prepared to say she had to rest every afternoon, whether she needed to or not, but in the event it wasn't necessary. Instead, she was able to spend the afternoon familiarising herself with the downstairs layout of the house, braving Mrs Hayes's disapproval by not asking her to be her guide.

In all honesty, she was glad of the activity, to keep her mind from dwelling on what James had told her. Until then, she hadn't realised how close she had come to death in the aftermath of the crash, but hearing that the girl who had been sitting with her had died put everything into painful perspective. It made her injuries, however distressing, seem so paltry, somehow. Here she was, brooding about the fact that she couldn't remember anything, when this other girl, probably someone of about her own age, was already dead and buried, a real victim of that terrible accident.

Mrs Hayes came upon her at last as she was studying the pictures of blood stallions that hung on the walls of the cream and gold sitting-room, and asked if she would like afternoon tea.

'Leonie will be back soon,' she added, her tone less abrasive than it had been the previous day. 'Perhaps you'd like to have it with her. She's usually ready for something when she gets home.'

'All right.' Jessica did not bear grudges. Then, 'Er—are these horses Mr Bentley has bred?'

'Those?' Mrs Hayes's lips actually twitched. 'Bless you, no, miss. Don't you recognise any of the names? Oh, no, perhaps you wouldn't,' she added hastily, remembering Jessica's condition. 'Well, now, that's Eclipse. He was bred in the eighteenth century, and became one of the most famous horses ever. And that's his uncle, or great-uncle or something, Flying Childers. He was born in 1715, isn't that what it says?' She moved closer to read the inscription at the bottom of the painting. 'He was the first great British racehorse, and you can bet Mr Bentley would like to think he could breed a horse like that.'

'I see.' Jessica gave a rueful smile. 'Now that you mention it, I do seem to have heard of Eclipse, but I might be wrong. They're beautiful animals.'

'Beautiful paintings, too,' added Mrs Hayes, smoothing her thumb along the dark wood of the frame. 'The man who painted them, Stubbs, he was a famous artist, too. Mr Bentley says he was a genius. But me, I don't know much about such things.'

'Nor me,' murmured Jessica automatically, although as she looked at the paintings, she did feel an odd sense of affinity with them. It was as if she understood the effort that had gone into them. As if the classical lines of brush and canvas held more than a casual interest for her.

'Well, never mind,' Mrs Hayes remarked now, with evident sympathy. 'I suppose you didn't have much time for artistic things, working in a supermarket.'

'No.' Jessica forced her thoughts into more realistic channels. 'I wonder if I was any good at it; working in the supermarket, I mean. I believe Dr Patel told me I used to sit behind one of the tills. It must have been fairly easy. I was never any good at maths.'

'How do you know?' exclaimed Mrs Hayes at once, and Jessica's brow furrowed.

'You know—I don't know,' she admitted bewilderedly, feeling the familiar sense of panic that always gripped her when she tried to co-ordinate what she remembered. 'It's just an—instinct, a *feeling*. I don't have anything to base it on. I don't even remember where I went to school.'

'Well, don't worry about it,' said Mrs Hayes hurriedly, noticing how pale the girl had gone. 'As I say, sooner or later something will click and you'll remember everything. Now, you sit yourself down and I'll fetch the tea. By the time the kettle's boiled, young Leonie will be home.'

The housekeeper was a little out with her estimate, but Jessica heard Leonie's entry into the house as she was pouring herself a second cup of tea. A door slammed, and footsteps sounded in the hall, and then the girl appeared in the doorway, flushed and perspiring, and evidently less than overjoyed to see her new cousin.

Obviously the school she attended insisted on a uniform, but Leonie's interpretation of it left something to be desired. The shirt she was wearing was at least two sizes too big for her, so that her tie sagged about the loose collar like a sloppy scarf. Her skirt was too long, and although it was the compulsory burgundy in colour, it was so narrow-fitting that she needed the slit at the back to enable her to move. Jessica guessed her intention was to hide the fact that she was both tall and thin, but anyone could see she was going completely the wrong way about it.

'Hello,' Jessica greeted her, hoping what had happened the previous afternoon was not going to sabotage any chance of their becoming friends. 'Have you had a good day?'

Leonie looked as if she wasn't going to respond, and then evidently changed her mind. Perhaps she was remembering what her father had said, reflected Jessica ruefully. She hoped their relationship was not going to be based on coercion. She wasn't used to having to persuade people to like her. Once again, it was only a feeling, but she thought that she used to make friends fairly easily.

'It's hot,' Leonie said, by way of a reply. 'Blood—blooming hot!'

'Are you thirsty?' Jessica glanced at the tray. 'Would you like some tea?'

'I'd prefer Coke,' said Leonie, just as Mrs Hayes appeared behind her. 'But I'll get changed first,' she added, including the housekeeper in her comments. 'I want to take Becca out before Dad gets home.'

'I think your father would prefer you to keep Miss Devlin company, instead of disappearing until supper time,' remarked Mrs Hayes smoothly, bringing a scowl of irritation to her employer's daughter's brow. 'At least, that's what he said to me. Tell Leonie to get to know her new cousin, I think that was how he put it. In any event, you're not to go out until he gets back.'

'Oh, knickers!'

'Leonie!'

'Well——'

'There's really no need for Leonie to keep me company,' Jessica inserted quietly. The last thing she wanted was to become an encumbrance to the girl. 'Honestly, I was thinking of taking a shower myself. And by the time I've dried my hair it will be almost supper time.'

'Do you mean it?'

Leonie was unflatteringly eager to convince herself that Jessica meant what she said, and the older girl swallowed her pride. 'Of course,' she said, ignoring Mrs Hayes's disapproving shake of her head. 'I spoilt your afternoon yesterday, and I don't want you to think I need a nursemaid.'

'All the same——' began the housekeeper, only to be overridden by Leonie's burst of relief.

'Gosh, yes,' she exclaimed. 'I forgot to ask if you were feeling better. You obviously are,' she continued, without giving the other girl time to answer. 'You don't look half so pale as you did yesterday. Anyway, I'll just go and get changed, if that's OK. I'll get that can of Coke when I come down, Mrs Hayes. And I'll see you at supper, Miss Devlin. I really do appreciate this. Thanks.'

## CHAPTER EIGHT

IT WAS lunch time the following day before Jessica saw James Bentley again. Much to Leonie's relief, she knew, he had not appeared at supper time the previous evening, and Mrs Hayes had informed them that he had rung to say he was dining elsewhere.

'Bickersley, probably,' Leonie had muttered, but Mrs Hayes had swiftly disabused her of that notion.

'No, he's not come back from Harrogate,' she retorted, saving her smile of satisfaction for Jessica. 'And you can thank your lucky stars he hasn't. Coming to the table in that state! If Mrs Bentley could see you, she'd be horrified.'

Leonie had the grace to look a little shamefaced that she had come into supper in the same shirt and jodhpurs she had worn for riding. But Jessica guessed the girl had delayed her return to the stables to avoid a confrontation with her father, and when she discovered he was not home she had taken advantage of the situation. Not that Jessica minded. She didn't find the smell of horse that lingered on Leonie's hair and clothes particularly unpleasant. On the contrary, she remembered smelling the same earthy scent when James had taken her around the property in the Land Rover, and in her mind it was associated with worn leather and male skin.

She shivered suddenly. Now why had she thought of that? she wondered. The scent of James Bentley's skin was far too personal an image for her to nurture, and it brought to mind again that kiss between him and Laura Bentley which she had been trying so hard to forget. And it was not the only thing she would have liked to erase from her mind, she reflected ruefully. It seemed that everything that had to do with Laura Bentley had an unpleasant connection in her mind, and whenever she tried to remember the past, that woman's image constantly got in the way.

Leonie's muffled, 'Do you think I care what *she* thinks about me?' was almost a reflection of her own feelings towards her father's wife, but she couldn't say so. Not then; not ever.

Even so, Laura was like an unspoken presence at the table, and in consequence Jessica's conversation with Leonie was stilted, to say the least. Apart from a brief explanation from the girl that the horse she had been riding was not a mare called Becca, as Jessica had assumed, but a bay gelding called Bekahra, their exchange was mostly confined to Leonie's schoolwork and the food. And as Leonie had little time for one, and little interest in the other, they spent most of the meal in silence, each occupied with their own thoughts.

The next morning Jessica felt much stronger, and after breakfasting alone, as on the previous day, she decided to spend the morning going through the contents of her handbag. She had thought there just might be something she had missed when she first glanced at its contents in the hospital, and almost immediately she was struck by the presence of the heavy gold cigarette lighter.

So far as she knew, she didn't smoke, or at least it was not something that held any attraction for her. But maybe she used to, she reflected, examining her hands for any traces of nicotine staining. But there was none. Not that that meant a lot either, she decided, weighing the lighter in her hand. It was weeks since the accident, and she hadn't touched a cigarette in all that time. Stains could have disappeared, or she might never have had any in the first place. It was odd that there were no cigarettes in the bag, but that wasn't important. Nevertheless, she thought she ought to try one just to see if she found it enjoyable. She had no recollection of what it was like to smoke, and certainly she had suffered no craving for the drug. The lighter could have been a gift, and she had never actually needed it. But it had been used. The fuel in the reservoir proved that. Or perhaps it didn't actually belong to her, which seemed distinctly more believable.

But it was obviously valuable, and she didn't like the idea that she might have kept something that wasn't hers. That smacked of dishonesty, and although she couldn't be sure, of course, she could have sworn she had never stolen anything in her life. Yet how could she be really sure? she asked herself anxiously. She could be a notorious shop lifter. How would she ever know?

Consequently, she was in a distinctly depressed frame of mind when she went down to lunch and found James Bentley already seated at the table in the morning-room. He was evidently studying some correspondence when she appeared, but he thrust his papers away and rose to his feet politely when she came into the room.

'Good morning,' he said with a tight smile, drawing out a chair for her and waiting until she was seated before resuming his own. 'I was beginning to wonder if you were all right. Mrs Hayes tells me you've spent the morning in your room.'

'Yes.' Jessica was non-committal, regarding the meat casserole, steaming on the table in front of them, without enthusiasm. She certainly did not feel hungry, and the idea of making polite conversation with this man, who might or might not be sympathetic to her plight, was not appealing.

James hesitated a moment, and then pushed the casserole dish towards her. 'Please,' he said, 'won't you have some?'

'Thank you.'

Jessica suppressed a sigh and, lifting the serving spoon, ladled a small portion of the meat and vegetables on to her plate. Then, picking up her fork, she made an effort to appear interested in the food as James served himself.

'Is something wrong?' he asked at last, and Jessica schooled her features before looking up at him.

'No.' She paused. 'Should there be?'

'You seem—troubled,' said James evenly. 'Did something happen that I should know about? Leonie hasn't been upsetting you again, has she?'

'No,' Jessica answered at once, eager to allay any thoughts of that kind. The last thing she needed was for Leonie to think she had been telling tales to her father. Their relationship was precarious enough as it was. 'I—er—I've been trying to piece things together, that's all, and I don't seem to be making much of a job of it.'

'Piecing what things together?'

'Oh—I was looking through my handbag. I found a lighter—a cigarette lighter. I just don't remember smoking at all.'

James frowned. 'A lighter, you say?'

'Yes.'

'Well—perhaps it doesn't belong to you. Perhaps it belongs to someone else.'

'That's what I'm afraid of.'

James regarded her curiously. 'Why?'

'Well—because it's an expensive lighter, that's why. You don't suppose I could have stolen it, do you?'

'Stolen it?' James stared at her disbelievingly. 'That's not what you think, is it?'

Jessica caught her breath. 'I don't know, do I? I don't know anything. I—I could be a thief; you don't know.'

James lips curved into a reluctant smile. 'No, I don't know,' he agreed humorously. 'But you don't strike me as being a second Bonnie Parker!'

Jessica bit her lip. 'That's not funny.'

'I'm not suggesting it is.'

'But you're not taking me seriously.'

'Yes, I am. I just don't think you have to worry about being a thief, that's all.'

'How do you know?'

James ignored her question. 'Is it possible the lighter could have belonged to the girl who was sitting with you. The one—the one who——'

'Died?' suggested Jessica tensely. 'It's possible, I suppose. But why would I have put it in my handbag? It doesn't make sense. It has to be mine.'

'OK. Then, perhaps you gave up smoking and kept the lighter,' said James reasonably. 'Whatever the solution is, I don't believe you stole the lighter. And nor should you. You may have lost your memory, temporarily, but your character hasn't changed. Surely you can believe that?'

'Can I?' Jessica put down her fork and pushed her plate away. 'Sometimes I wonder if I'll ever remember anything. Surely something should have clicked by now? But nothing has, has it?'

James sighed. 'You recognised Ripley's name.'

'Yes. But as you pointed out, that wasn't really of any value. It was just something the other girl said to me.'

James drew a breath. 'Well, maybe I was too negative about it. It was something, after all.'

Jessica's jaw quivered. 'Don't humour me, please.'

'I'm not humouring you.'

'Yes, you are. Pretending it matters that I've remembered the name of some woollen mill or other. God, I don't even remember what the girl's name was.'

'It was Chambers. Cecily Chambers,' said James patiently. 'Jess——'

'Cecily Chambers?' Jessica said the name slowly, wondering if the fleeting feeling of familiarity when James had said the name held any encouragement. But no. There was no reassuring follow-on of meaning. Only the awful blankness of not feeling any identification with anything, and with a sudden surge of panic she thrust back her chair and made for the door, desperate to escape the sense of terror that suddenly enfolded her.

However, James Bentley reached the door before her, his instincts recognising her hysteria almost as quickly as she did. And because he was fitter, and had longer legs, he easily overtook her despairing flight. Consequently when she reached the door, his lean, powerful body blocked her way, and she gazed up at him defensively, silently begging him to move aside.

'Panicking isn't going to solve anything,' he said quietly, as she fought to hold back the tears she was desperate to shed. 'Don't lose hope so easily. You've only been here a couple of days. Give it time.'

Jessica struggled to speak. 'Th—that's easy for you to say,' she got out chokily, and then disgraced herself completely by bursting into tears.

Turning away, she scrubbed frantically at her eyes, trying to stem the tide of hopelessness that was sweeping over her. If only he would show some compassion for her and go away and leave her alone, she thought fiercely. Oh, God, yesterday she had actually felt some optimism about her condition, but today...

She was totally unprepared for what happened next. For the past few seconds there had been an ominous silence from the man behind her, so that she had been half inclined to believe that her wish that he would leave her had been granted. But when his hands closed on her shoulders she knew at once how mistaken she was, and when he stepped close behind her, and with a muffled exclamation pulled her back against him, she experienced a disturbing sense of guilt that he had not.

'You've got to stop feeling that there's some kind of time limit to regaining your memory,' he declared harshly, and she knew his lips were only inches from her neck as he spoke. The warmth of his breath fanned the nerves contained within the quivering skin of her throat, and in spite of her state of mind she knew a reckless desire to turn her head and close the gap.

'I—feel as if there should be,' she said tensely, unable to even think coherently with the taut strength of his arm about her waist, and James expelled a sigh.

'You can stay here as long as you like,' he said, lifting a hand to tuck the strand of silky fair hair that was brushing his face behind her ear. 'Just—stop putting pressure on yourself, hmm? Things are going to get easier, believe me. Relax; live each day as it comes. And if the memories refuse to come back, well—so be it.'

Jessica trembled, holding herself away from his hard body, even though the idea of letting herself rest against him was unbearably tempting. She wanted to give herself up to the warmth and the strength and the reassurance of his embrace, but she was afraid of her emotions, and where they might lead her. James was sympathetic because she was his dead cousin's child, not for any other reason. She, on the other hand, was aware of him as a man with every fibre of her being, and the fact that he was so much older than she was didn't come into it at all.

'I—that's easy for you to say,' she got out at last, and with an impatient expletive James swung her round to face him.

Now it was impossible to avoid an eye-to-eye confrontation, and Jessica shook her head helplessly as he grasped her chin with determined fingers and forced her to look up at him.

'What do you want me to say?' he demanded, his eyes raking her tremulous features with the sharp penetration of a blade. 'No one's harassing you here. No one's forcing you to do anything. You have total freedom to go where you like, when you like. All right, so in an ideal world you'd have recovered your memory by now, but you haven't. Be thankful it was only your memory you lost. Cecily Chambers lost her life!'

Jessica swallowed. 'I know that.'

'Do you? Do you?' James stared at her. 'Perhaps what you need is shaking up, not calming down. This is not a matter of life and death, Jess. It's just a temporary inconvenience!'

'I know.' Jessica would have moved out of his grasp then, but he still wasn't satisfied with her response.

'Are *you* humouring *me* now?'

Jessica knew a momentary sense of mirth. 'Are you admitting you *were* humouring me before?' she countered, and his expression relaxed somewhat.

'That's better,' he said, his hands on her shoulders relaxing slightly. 'For Christ's sake, Jess, things could have been a lot worse. At least you're with people who—who care about you.'

'Am I?' Now her eyes sought his. 'You can't pretend Mrs Bentley cares about me, and—and you're her—*friend*, too, aren't you?'

James held her for a few moments longer, his fingers digging painfully now into the thin covering of flesh on her shoulders. Then, with an abrupt movement, he let her go, and she knew a moment's bereavement at his consummate withdrawal from her.

'My—relationship with Laura is of no concern here,' he said harshly, and she had to force herself to sustain his gaze.

'Isn't it?' she ventured. 'Then you have no conflict of loyalties in befriending me as well as her? I may not understand all the nuances here, but I find that hard to believe somehow.'

James's brow darkened. 'Leonie has said something to you, hasn't she?' he demanded bewilderingly, and Jessica blinked.

'Leonie?'

'Yes, Leonie. My daughter. The other occupant of this house.'

Jessica held up her head. 'I know who Leonie is.'

'Well?'

'Well, what?'

'What has she been saying? I warned her——'

'Leonie hasn't said anything,' retorted Jessica tremulously. 'But I'm not stupid. I—I saw the way that woman greeted you yesterday.'

'Did you?' She could feel his antagonism reaching out towards her, but she had started this now and she had to finish it.

'Yes.' She moistened her lips. 'It's nothing to do with me, of course——'

'No, it's not.'

'—but it's obvious she resents me.'

'How do you know that? Laura wasn't unkind, was she?'

'Not yesterday. Not exactly, anyway.' Jessica hesitated. 'But when she came to the hospital——'

'She was upset. Overwrought. You have to remember, she didn't even know of your existence until your father died.'

'I know that.' Jessica groped for words. 'But why blame me——?'

'It was the shock,' said James curtly. 'She did apologise.'

'Did she?' Jessica could feel her own anxiety giving way to a surge of resentment. It wasn't *all* her fault, but she was being made to feel it was. 'As I remember it, her remorse was fairly short-lived!'

James looked positively grim now, his lean, dark features taut and controlled. Even the curious lightness of his eyes had absorbed a smouldering shadow, hiding their expression behind an opaque veil of darkness.

'I think this discussion has gone far enough,' he declared bleakly. 'You expect people to be tolerant of your condition, yet you apparently have little sympathy for other people's frailties.'

'Frailties?' Jessica had not realised how angry she could feel. 'You are asking me to believe that Laura Bentley's attitude to me is the result of some inner vulnerability?'

James's jaw tightened. 'You don't understand the whole situation. Until you do, I suggest you suspend your disbelief.'

'I'm simply trying to understand the situation,' retorted Jessica shortly. 'Just because you are apparently—enamoured of the woman...' She caught her breath. 'Just out of interest, did my father know about your affair, or is that something I should suspend interest in, too?'

As soon as the words were spoken, Jessica realised how utterly unforgivable they were. Whatever James's relationship with Laura Bentley might be, he had always treated *her* with kindness and consideration, and to accuse him of something so outrageous was to reject his hospitality in the most ungracious way.

But before she could formulate any words of apology, his temper exploded in her face. 'How dare you?' he exclaimed, grasping her upper arms in a painful grasp and half lifting, half hauling her off her feet, so that his face was a bare couple of inches from hers. 'I ought to throw you out of here for a remark like that. You know, the solicitor in London said you were a tough lady, but I wouldn't accept that, not after the act you put on for my benefit, that is. But Laura, whom you persist in speaking about in the most objectionable terms, saw through you, didn't she? That's what really galls you. It's nothing to do with the way Laura behaved. It's because even if you have lost your memory, you're still the same selfish little bitch inside, and Laura recognised that!'

'That's not true!' Jessica was horrified. 'I'm not selfish——'

'How do you know?' he demanded, and, realising he was hurting her, he let her go. 'If you *really* don't remember who you are——'

Jessica gulped. 'Don't you believe me?' she choked piteously, and as if her desperate cry at last struck some sympathetic chord inside him, he uttered a weary oath.

'Christ,' he muttered, gazing down at her with unconcealed self-loathing, 'do you have any idea of the trouble you have caused?'

'I'm sorry.'

'So you should be.'

'I wish there was something I could do.'

'So do I.'

For a moment she thought he was going to turn away, but then, as if their exchange had put other thoughts into his mind, he continued to gaze intently at her.

'You know,' he said at last, 'you're nothing like Adam. I can see no single resemblance to him. You must take after your mother's side of the family. Either that, or you're a changeling.'

'Are you implying I might not be who you say I am?' she asked, causing him to draw a sudden intake of air.

'No,' he muttered heavily. 'No, that's not what I'm saying. God, I don't know what I'm saying any more. Let's forget it, shall we? Before this discussion gets completely out of hand.'

Jessica swallowed. 'I'm sorry.'

'Yes. So am I,' he conceded, his temper dispersing as quickly as it had come. 'I guess we both need more time to come to terms with the situation. I'll forget what you said about Laura if you'll forgive my spurt of brutality, hmm? I am sorry if I upset you. It's what comes of having more brawn than brain, I suppose.'

Even Jessica managed a faint smile at this blatantly obvious untruth, and then, realising it was up to her to restore the situation completely, she took a deep breath. He was her father's cousin, after all, she told herself as she divined what to do. Almost an uncle really, even if she found it difficult to think of him that way. Summoning all her courage, she reached up to plant a kiss, as an olive branch, on his cheek.

But James, for some reason best known to himself, turned his head at the exact moment Jessica's lips sought his skin, and instead of feeling the faintly abrasive brush of his shaven flesh, her mouth encountered the parted heat of his. And immediately everything went wrong. Instead of drawing back, some unguarded instinct made her lips cling to his, and, although he made a muffled sound of protest, the illicit kiss went on.

Her own response to the unwilling pressure of his mouth was devastating. With or without the memory of any previous liaisons, Jessica was made insistently aware of her own unfamiliarity with the strong emotions that were sweeping about her, and, although it was scarcely a mutual attraction, she sensed James was initially as incapable as she was of breaking the contact.

His hands gripped her arms again, but not painfully this time, and she wondered if he was aware that his thumbs were moving convulsively against her quivering flesh. Her breasts, brushing against the taut cage of his ribs, felt tender and sensitised, and she knew without looking at them that the button-hard peaks were straining against the thin material of her shirt. Even her hips ached with the need to press herself against him, but something—some lingering thread of sanity, perhaps—kept her from destroying all pretence that this could be forgotten, by either of them.

And, predictably, it was James who came first to his senses. With a constrained laugh that was more destructive than any force of anger could have been, he dragged his lips away from hers and, stepping back, put a distinctive space between them. 'Hey,' he said, wiping the back of his hand across his mouth, 'I guess this makes us kissing cousins, doesn't it?' He smiled, and if there was a certain tenseness in the gesture, it was quickly hidden. Then, transferring his gaze to the thin gold watch on his wrist, he uttered a convincing groan. 'My God! Look at the time! I've got to go. I've got a buyer coming in fifteen minutes. We'll have to—talk again later. Who knows, maybe I'll be able to persuade you and Laura o kiss and make up, too.'

Jessica was frozen with embarrassment. Nothing he ·ould have said could have been more designed to put what had happened in its real perspective, or to inspire in her a feeling of complete ignominy. The storm of emotion she had experienced had been wholly self-induced, that was what he was saying, and although he was giving her a chance to laugh it off too, she was crushed and hurt and totally humiliated.

'You will excuse me, won't you?' he said, opening the door behind him, and happily Jessica had only to nod in reply. 'Great!' He forced another apologetic smile. 'See you this evening, then. 'Bye.'

## CHAPTER NINE

A WEEK after she had left the hospital, James drove Jessica into Leeds for her first check-up. Dr Patel had made the appointment for half-past two in the afternoon, and although James might have wished he could have transferred the responsibility for escorting her to Ted Paisley, the appointment he himself had with Toby Langley made such a proposition unviable.

Consequently, the drive into town was quite a tense affair. It had been a tense week, all things considered, and although James had found plenty of reasons to keep himself out of the house, and therefore out of Jessica's company, the awareness of her presence in his home seldom actually left him.

It was the aftermath of that disastrous scene in the morning-room that had left him in the state of anger and frustration that had soured his week. Ever since he had been reckless enough to imagine he had the ability to influence the situation by using his own ham-fisted methods of psychoanalysis. How catastrophic that idea had been! Not only had he reduced the girl to floods of tears, but he had compounded his felony by trying to comfort her, and thus provoked a far more devastating error.

He was still unsure how that unbelievable kiss had happened. Oh, he knew the mechanics of the situation: Jessica's attempt to restore an element of normality to the scene by depositing a cousinly kiss on his cheek was reasonable enough, and even the mistake he had made by turning his head could have easily been explained. But what was more difficult to assimilate was the unholy urge he had had to consummate the kiss, or why the innocent brush of her lips should have provoked such a surge of desire inside him. And it *had* provoked his desire, of that there was no doubt. For a moment he had forgotten everything—Leonie, Laura, Adam, *everything*—and all that had been real had been the all-consuming hunger his cousin's daughter had evoked.

Of course, he had had to shake it off. He was a man of almost forty, not a schoolboy. Whatever it was that had gripped him had had to be most stringently denied, and he had been left with anger and frustration that he should have so adolescently lost his cool. It wasn't like him. He wasn't some sexually starved youth, desperate for the excitement of an illicit relationship. Besides which, there was Laura—and Leonie. He could well imagine how his daughter would react if she ever discovered his behaviour.

Only it shouldn't have meant anything, he told himself fiercely. One kiss, however uncontrolled, was not in any way grounds for such a storm of self-remorse. For some reason, Jessica had caught him off guard—off balance, if you like—and in his blind confusion he must have mistaken her for Laura.

And yet, he had to admit that since the scene with Jessica he had had no stomach for any other emotion. It was some days since he had seen Laura alone, and this arranged meeting at the lawyers had been her way of showing her displeasure. She had phoned him the night before, telling him of the appointment, deliberately giving him no chance to announce a prior engagement. 'Be there!' she had said with ill-concealed resentment, and although in other circumstances James might have objected, his conscience told him that her feelings were justified.

As far as Jessica was concerned, he hoped his feelings had proved less easy to interpret. After all, he had had a busy week, commercially, and Leonie had shown no particular interest in the fact that he found a different reason for his absence at the supper table every evening.

On the contrary, to his relief, his daughter seemed to have resigned herself to his plans for her to stay at school for another three years. There had been no further outbursts on that score, and without his personal aberrations he should have been feeling fairly optimistic. But he didn't. He felt raw and sensitive, and overpoweringly resentful of the girl beside him, and her unwanted invasion into his previously sanguine existence.

'I could have taken the bus, you know,' she said now, as if sensing his animosity, and once again, James felt a bitter surge of impatience at his own apparent inability to hide his feelings.

'The bus?' he echoed, deliberately giving himself time to consider his reply. 'Why should you want to take the bus?'

'Well—to save you making this journey,' said Jessica reasonably. 'I'm quite capable, you know. I haven't had a real headache for days, and I really think I ought to be considering a change of scene.'

'A change of scene?' he repeated again, unable to prevent the automatic rejoinder. He shook his head impatiently. 'What the hell is that supposed to mean?'

Jessica looked a little discomfited now. 'Um—well, I don't want you to think I haven't appreciated your hospitality or anything like that, but it is some weeks now since the—accident, and—well, as I haven't recovered my memory, perhaps I should begin to take responsibility for myself——'

'Don't be ridiculous!' To his astonishment, James found himself repudiating her suggestion with some violence. In spite of his earlier irritation with her presence, the idea that she might be considering leaving of her own accord inspired an angry intolerance. 'You're not fit to attempt looking after yourself. Where would you live? Where would you go?'

Jessica's cheeks had paled a little at his onslaught, but her voice was steady as she answered. 'I—I imagine I do have a home, somewhere,' she ventured. 'I must have, mustn't I? I didn't live with my father, as we all know, and if I was on the train from—from London, I must have lived there.'

'No.'

'What do you mean, no?' She swallowed a little convulsively. 'I must have. There's probably a flat—or—or a bed-sitter.' She frowned. 'You know—yes. Yes, I do remember a room.' She caught her breath, but whether with pain or concentration, he could not be sure. 'A—a bed-sit. I'm almost sure of it.'

James's mouth compressed. 'How convenient!' he remarked, knowing he was being bloody-minded, but unable to prevent the sarcastic comment. 'And I suppose this sudden rush of memory is entirely spontaneous. So why do I get the feeling that it's totally without foundation?'

Jessica gasped. 'It's not without foundation.' She gazed at him indignantly. 'You don't imagine I'd make something like that up, do you? Just—just for a moment there, I did have the image of a room in my mind. It's not much, I agree, but *I* think it's worth investigating, even if you don't.'

James sighed, hiding his temper with some difficulty. 'And what do you propose to investigate?' he demanded.

'What do you think?' Jessica held up her head. 'Where I lived until the accident, of course.'

And, of course, he had known what was coming. It had only been a matter of time, after all, before she worked that solution out for herself. But how could he explain that from what they had learned she had severed all her ties with her old life before leaving London, without getting into areas that were, for the time being at least, best kept in abeyance?

The trouble was, he was being torn in three totally opposing directions. On the one hand there was Laura, to whom the precipitate restoration of Jessica's memory would prove so expensive; and there was Jessica, herself, obviously unaware of the anguish created by her father's will, to whom the truth might still prove destructive; and finally, there was his own unwanted, but undeniable, unwillingness to surrender his responsibility for her future—for, whatever way you looked at it, she wasn't going to find it easy to pick up the threads.

Now James drew a breath before saying tersely, 'I don't think you're ready for that kind of investigation yet. We've discussed this before, Jess. There's no need for you to go rushing into rash measures. Take your time. Be patient.'

Jessica stared at him. 'You know, if I didn't know better, I might suspect you were trying to balk my remembering,' she declared tensely, and James knew a moment's misgivings.

'But you do know better,' he improvised at length. 'Don't you?'

'Do I?' Jessica was evidently loath to abandon the subject, and James's hands tightened on the steering wheel.

'You should,' he countered, and heard her involuntary sigh. 'For Christ's sake, Jess, what do you think I have to gain from keeping you at Aspen?'

She bent her head. 'I don't know.'

'There you are, then.'

'Maybe I just haven't figured it out yet,' she added, and James had some difficulty containing his impatience.

'You can't imagine I don't want you to get well?' he protested harshly. 'Of course I do.'

'But does Mrs Bentley?' murmured Jessica, almost under her breath, though not low enough for James not to hear her.

'Mrs Bentley?' he exclaimed, and Jessica nodded, evidently deciding there was no point in pretending she had not said what she had.

'Well,' she said defensively, 'she is your—relation, isn't she? You must know how she feels.'

'I know she's concerned about you, just as I am.'

'Oh, don't play games!' Jessica's response was strained, but vehement. 'You know what I'm talking about. Who better?' Her hands clenched in her lap. 'You are involved with her. Don't bother to deny it. I may be slow-witted, but I'm not completely stupid.'

James's nostrils flared. 'I don't see what my relationship with Laura has to do with this,' he argued.

'Don't you?' Jessica's lips twisted. 'It's obvious Mrs Bentley resents the fact that my father left me something in his will.'

James managed to hide the full extent of his disconcertment. 'What do you know about that?' he demanded, briefly shocked into an unwary admission, but fortunately she was too absorbed with what she was saying to notice his error.

'Well, I suppose he must have left me some money,' she went on steadily. 'Mrs Bentley said something about his estate, so I suppose that's what she meant. But I didn't ask him to do it, did I? I just wish she didn't blame me for something I didn't even know about until he was dead!'

They were running down into Leeds now, the elegant homes on the outskirts of the city giving way to the narrower streets and light industry that lay just outside the centre, and James was obliged to abandon the conversation in favour of concentrating on his driving. Which was probably just as well, he reflected, in spite of a fleeting feeling of frustration. He needed time to gather his thoughts before continuing this discussion. Time to find satisfactory answers to her undeniably justifiable questions.

'Anyway,' she said now, jolting him into an awareness of her presence again, 'I'm going to ask Dr Patel what he thinks I should do. At least I can be sure his opinions aren't self-motivated.'

James breathed deeply. 'And you think mine are?' he asked roughly, and now she had the grace to look discomfited.

'I—didn't say that,' she murmured ruefully. 'I don't know what to think.' For a moment her eyes, darkly purple now and full of uncertainty, met his brooding gaze. 'You've been kind to me, I know, but—well, sometimes I have to ask myself why.'

James suppressed the wholly unwelcome urge then to stop the car and take her into his arms. Instead, he channelled his energies into watching the stream of traffic lights that punctuated this road like so many semi-colons. It was crazy that he should feel this way, when Laura's future depended on his—*their*—ability to persuade this girl that selling the mills that had been in her father's family for generations was not only callous but foolish. But it was so difficult to associate the Jessica he knew with the gold-digging female his cousin's London lawyer had described, and, while he was forced to accept that she might be a better actress than he knew, his instincts were all against it.

'Are you angry with me?' she ventured suddenly, and once more he was cast into the arena of his emotions.

'No,' he said shortly, letting her make what she liked of his brevity. 'No, of course not.' And thereafter there was silence between them.

James arrived at Toby Langley's office a little after the stipulated time of a quarter to three. Although Jessica had insisted she could find her way to Dr Patel's office unaided, he had insisted on accompanying her along the rubber-floored corridors of the hospital, and in consequence he had been obliged to exchange a few words with her physician before leaving. Patel had suggested James might like to speak to him after the examination, and it had been arranged that when he had completed his own business he would return to the hospital and talk to the doctor then. It was nothing more than he had expected, but it did retard his progress, and Laura was pacing the solicitor's office when Toby's secretary let James in.

'Where have you been?' she exclaimed, almost as though he was an hour and not simply ten minutes late, and James exchanged a faintly embarrassed look with Toby.

'Getting here,' he responded, ignoring her outrage. 'Hello, Toby. It's good to see you again.'

'And you, James,' said Toby, taking his cue from his client. 'Um——' He indicated the two chairs across the table from him. 'Won't you both sit down?'

James looked at Laura and, sensing the uncertainty of his mood, she subsided abruptly, reaching for his hand below the level of the desk. 'Sorry for the outburst,' she murmured, squeezing his fingers, and James allowed the intimacy in spite of his irritation.

'No sweat,' he assured her smoothly, and Toby looked relieved that a potentially explosive situation seemed to have been defused.

'So,' he said, steepling his fingers, 'shall we have some coffee?'

'I'd rather get down to business,' said James at once, causing Laura's expression to stiffen a little. 'I have to meet Patel at the hospital in a little under an hour. Jess is having her first post in-patient examination this afternoon, and he may be able to give me some idea of how her case is progressing.'

'Is that why you were late?' demanded Laura at once, and James wondered rather caustically what he had done to warrant being put in such an invidious position.

'Perhaps,' he replied, and then, addressing himself to Toby, he added, 'There's no change, you know. Jess still hasn't remembered anything.'

*'Jess!'* echoed Laura sarcastically. 'My, aren't we familiar?'

'She is my cousin's daughter,' countered James coldly, and then, restraining himself again, he continued, 'She was asking me today why you blame her for Adam's generosity. As she sees it, she's just the innocent beneficiary.'

Laura caught her breath. 'You mean she—*knows* about the will?' Her cheeks had paled. 'Did you tell her?'

James drew a breath. 'No, of course not,' he retorted, and then, taking pity on her, he added, 'You have only yourself to blame that she knows anything about the will.'

Laura breathed more freely. 'You're talking about what I said before I knew she had no memory of what had happened.'

'Yes.' James's lips twisted. 'Nevertheless, you put the thought in her mind. You can't blame her if she's curious about your attitude.'

'Which brings us to the point of this meeting,' interjected Toby, evidently deciding their argument was becoming too personal again. 'Look, it's like this: Adam's will states quite categorically that—that Miss Devlin is his chief beneficiary. And while I appreciate the difficulties engendered by Miss Devlin's continued—absence of mind, shall we say, there are certain obligations to fulfil.'

Laura gave him her full attention then. 'What obligations?'

'Well...' Toby was obviously uncomfortable in the role he was obliged to play. 'Notwithstanding Miss Devlin's condition, she is still her father's heir, and sooner or later she is going to have to be informed of that fact.'

'Why?' Laura was resentful. 'What good will that do?'

'I imagine Toby means that the terms of Adam's will stand, whatever Jess's state of mind might be,' put in James flatly, and the solicitor nodded.

'Exactly,' he affirmed, giving James a grateful look. 'Quite frankly, Higgs—that's the London solicitor, who dealt with your late husband's affairs,' he explained swiftly, 'is agitating for some action, and unless I can assure him that I have matters in hand, I'm afraid he'll come charging up here and see her himself.'

Laura caught her breath. 'But—can't you stop him?'

Toby sighed. 'On what grounds? As he sees it, the terms of the will are quite straightforward. Miss Devlin inherits everything, apart from a small annuity, which you already know about, and your right to stay at Bickersley as long as you remain a widow.'

Laura's lips twitched. 'Yes, Toby,' she said harshly, fumbling in her handbag for a handkerchief, and rapidly blowing her nose. 'Thank you for informing me of Adam's cruelty all over again. But it really wasn't necessary. The terms of the will are written on my *soul*!'

James sighed now. 'Laura,' he exclaimed, guiltily aware of his own growing ambivalence in all this, 'Toby is only trying to explain how difficult his position has become. He's not trying to hurt you——'

'Indeed not.'

'He's only giving you the facts as they stand, and I can quite believe this Higgs—is that his name?—considers someone's dragging their feet over this.'

'Exactly.' Toby nodded urgently. 'Do try to understand my position, Laura. If you could give me some idea of when the situation is likely to be resolved...'

'How can we?' protested Laura bitterly. 'What happens if she never gets her memory back? Am I to hand over everything to someone who doesn't even remember what her own name is? My God, it's barbaric! Bickersley should be *mine*!'

James exchanged a long look with the solicitor. Then he said quietly, 'As I see it, if you could give us another couple of weeks, Toby, we would be grateful. By then—well, by then, there may be some change in Jess's condition. You never know, Patel may have some news for us this afternoon. Whatever, if you could pacify this fellow in London for another fourteen days, physically Jess herself will be stronger; better able, I guess, to withstand the shock she has to come.'

'The shock *she* has to come?' Laura was incensed. 'Jamie, what are you trying to do to me?'

James deliberately cleared his face of all expression. 'I'm trying to be objective,' he said, although he wasn't absolutely sure that this was true. He turned back to the solicitor. 'Well, Toby, what do you think? Can you persuade Higgs to hold off for a few more days?'

It was after five when James drove back into the grounds of the hospital. The interview with Toby had been extended by his insistence on providing them with coffee after all, and once outside the solicitor's office Laura had been inclined to be tearful.

'You don't feel like giving me a lift back to Bickersley, do you?' she had sniffed, after James had taken her into a nearby café and plied her with cups of tea. 'I really don't feel up to driving home alone, and I can easily get someone to come and pick up the BMW later.'

In consequence, Laura was at his side when he was eventually admitted to Patel's office, and the doctor's brows arched interrogatively at the unexpected intrusion.

'Mr Bentley,' he said politely, in answer to James's rather rueful greeting, his lips parting thinly as the other man made his apologies.

'The—er—the discussions we had with the solicitor took somewhat longer than we had anticipated,' James explained, with some discomfort at the lie. 'Um—have you met Mrs Bentley? My late cousin's wife? Laura, this is Dr Patel. Jess—Jessica was in his care, when she was an in-patient at the hospital.'

'How do you do, Mrs Bentley?' Patel shook hands with his other visitor, but James could tell he was not altogether pleased by their assumption that she would be welcome here. And, in all honesty, James would have preferred their conversation to be private, but short of asking Laura to remain outside there was nothing he could do.

It was Laura who opened the conversation. 'So, Dr Patel,' she invited smoothly, 'do you have some good news for us?'

Patel's mouth compressed for a moment before he replied, 'That rather depends on what you mean by good news, Mrs Bentley,' and James took the opportunity to voice his own query.

'Where is Jess, anyway?' he asked, half alarmed that whatever Patel had found, he had decided to re-admit her, but the doctor was able to reassure him on that score at least.

'She's helping out in the children's ward,' he said, showing the first trace of warmth since they were admitted. 'As you were—delayed, she asked if she might be allowed to talk to the little ones, and in no time at all she was drawing them pictures and telling them stories.' He smiled. 'Your—niece?'

'Cousin.'

'Ah, yes. Your—cousin has a natural aptitude for drawing, Mr Bentley. I don't know if that's of any help to us, but her artistic skills are obviously considerable.'

'Really?' James was surprised. What little he had learned of Jessica Devlin's past had not led him to believe she had any particular artistic talent. But any enlightenment, however small, was welcome, and he exchanged a look with Laura to give himself time to think.

'Yes, really,' Patel continued, his eyes shifting to each of them in turn, as if making some calculation of his own. 'I gather this doesn't help us in any way? There's no history of creativity we might draw on?'

'Not to my knowledge,' admitted James wryly, remembering Adam's uninterest in all things academic. Adam had been a doer, not a thinker, and it was certainly not from his side of the family that she had acquired any imaginative leanings.

'Don't you think we're getting off the point?' Laura demanded abruptly, her own innate frustration with the whole situation bursting to the surface. 'For heaven's sake, whether or not she can draw pictures pretty enough to entertain a handful of children is not in question here, surely? What I want to know, and—and what I'm sure Mr Bentley wants to know—is whether there's any likelihood of her regaining her memory in the foreseeable future! Not how apt she is at playing games!'

'I would hardly call it "playing games", Mrs Bentley,' Patel retorted, before James could placate him. 'Anything your stepdaughter does, or can do, is of immense importance to her recovery. If we can reach behind the veil her mind has drawn over her past by this method, then we must do what we can to facilitate her progress.'

'She's not my step—that is,' Laura coloured, 'I'd never met her before—before the accident.'

'No.'

Patel inclined his head, and James wondered if he had actually known that or just guessed. He didn't remember telling the doctor anything about Laura's relationship with his patient, but then, he didn't know what Toby might have divulged.

'Well, anyway,' said Laura, refusing to be put down, 'is there any progress? Physical progress, I mean? Is she going to remember? Surely you must know something.'

'Not much more than you, I am afraid,' responded Patel after a moment, evidently deciding there was no point in prevaricating any further. 'As far as I can see, there is no reason at all to suppose she will not make a full recovery. Her health is good; she has recovered from the concussion; and apart from a very natural sense of disorientation, there are no other after-effects of her ordeal.'

'You don't think she's bluffing, do you?'

Laura's question came out of the blue, and James, as much as the doctor, was astounded by it. She couldn't be serious, he thought disbelievingly. What was she trying to do here? Make an enemy of the doctor?

And once again Patel answered before he could make any mitigating comment. 'Bluffing?' he echoed, his dark brows descending ominously. 'You are asking me if I think your stepdaughter is bluffing?'

'She's not my—oh, well—yes. Yes, that's what I'm asking.' Laura's fingers closed convulsively over the strap of her handbag. 'It's not such a crazy proposition,' she added defensively. 'People have been known to make mistakes.'

Patel snorted. 'But not in a situation like this, I think,' he declared bleakly. 'As I understand it, your step-daughter has no earthly reason to affect amnesia. She's your late husband's heir, is she not? And therefore she has everything to gain by recovering her memory.' He got to his feet. 'If you'll excuse me, I will tell Miss Devlin you are here.'

Left to themselves, while Patel went to send a nurse to inform Jessica of their arrival, James lost no time in making his feelings clear. 'Are you completely out of your mind?' he demanded. 'What did you hope to achieve by implying that she might be lying? As Patel says, she has everything to gain by telling the truth.'

'Has she?' Laura got to her feet to pace around the room. 'Well, I'm not so sure.' Then, stopping behind the chair she had been sitting in earlier, she smoothed long white fingers over its hide back. 'Consider,' she said, persisting in spite of his impatient expression, 'she's in a pretty comfortable position at the moment, isn't she? Living at Aspen. Enjoying the freedom. No responsibilities——'

'Oh, Laura——'

'Being with *you*,' she went on determinedly. 'An attractive proposition in itself. You do realise the girl's attracted to you, don't you? Her father's cousin, her benefactor, her hero! What a pity you don't ride a white charger, darling. I'm sure she sees you as her knight in shining armour!'

James felt an overwhelming urge to silence her, but he restrained himself. None the less, her words were uncomfortably close to his own perception of the situation, and, although Jessica herself might be unaware of it, James sensed his loyalties were being stretched to the limit.

# CHAPTER TEN

As Jessica had hoped, James was still at the breakfast table when she entered the morning-room. Lately, the occasions on which she could count on seeing him were getting less and less, and since her visit to the hospital last week he definitely seemed to be avoiding her.

Oh, she could understand why. Mrs Bentley had been with him when he came to pick her up after her consultation with Dr Patel, and it was obvious from *her* attitude that they had spent the afternoon together. Laura lost no opportunity to illustrate to the younger woman just how close her relationship with James was, and if James himself balked a little at her deliberately open affection, it was obviously just embarrassment in front of an audience. Jessica was quite sure that when they were alone he was not half so reticent, and she herself had evidence that he was not a cold-blooded man.

Indeed, it was the memory of what had happened between them that had made her put off any approaches to him. The last thing she wanted was for him to think she had any ulterior motives for seeking his company, and yet he was the only person she could talk to; the only person she could share her anxieties with.

And no doubt Laura's involvement made the situation that much more difficult. It was obvious, whatever he said, that there was a conflict of interests, and although blood might be thicker than water, a sexual relationship was closer than either. In addition to which, in spite of her denials to the contrary, Jessica knew Laura didn't like her. In fact, it might even be more than that, and how could Jessica hold her own against someone who hated her?

It was a worrying situation, made the more so by Dr Patel's unsatisfactory diagnosis. He still had no further prognosis of when she might begin to recover her memory, and although he spoke of other drugs and other tests, it was obvious they were all of them groping in the dark.

Therefore, the only sensible course seemed to be to return to the places she had known before the accident. She appreciated that until recently she had not been fit enough to attempt such an undertaking, but she was stronger now, and marginally more confident, and until she made the effort she wouldn't know how she'd take it.

She had had to accept the fact that no one from her past had been sufficiently concerned about her future to come and see her. She had been told she had no other relatives and she accepted that, but she would have thought there might be someone, her landlady even, who might have been concerned enough to write and find out how she was. After all, she must owe someone some rent, mustn't she? Or were they confident enough of this inheritance she was supposed to be getting to allow her an indefinite leave of absence? And what about her job? In a supermarket, they had told her. Had she got leave of absence from there too, or had she given up her job on the strength of her father's money?

In the past, thoughts like these had caused her so much pain and distress that she had been happy enough to delay thinking about them. But gradually, as her strength returned, she could feel a growing sense of urgency inside her. An urgency to know who she was, and what she had intended to do with her life; an urgency to regain her independence and put some purpose into her existence. But most of all there was an urgency to put her relationship with James Bentley into perspective, for, as long as she remained dependent on him, she could not escape her growing attraction to him.

If she had had any doubts that James did not share her feelings, they were quickly dispersed by the look of intense irritation that crossed his face when he looked up from his breakfast and found her standing in the doorway. No one could misinterpret his annoyance that she should have invaded his early-morning privacy, and for a moment she was daunted enough to consider turning round and leaving the room. But then tenacity, and a certain amount of indignation, stiffened her resolve, and taking a few steps forward she clutched the back of one of the chairs pushed in to the table.

'Um——' She cleared her throat. 'Do you mind if I join you?'

There was a moment's pause, while James pushed aside the half-eaten slice of toast he had been holding, and then he rose adroitly to his feet. 'Please,' he said, gesturing towards the chair she was holding, and watching as she clumsily drew it out and subsided into it. 'But, as a matter of fact, I was just about to leave. Ted and I have to go to Cumbria this morning, and I want to make an early start.'

'Oh, but——' Jessica got to her feet again when he would have moved past her, and put herself between him and the door. She was briefly reminded of that other occasion when their positions were reversed, but now was not the time to indulge in stupid reminiscences. 'That is—I mean—please, don't go. Not yet.'

James's mouth drew down at the corners. 'Jessica, I've just told you——'

'—that you have to go to Cumbria this morning, I know, and I also know that it's a long journey.' Jessica took a deep breath. 'But I have to talk to you, and lately there never seems to be an opportunity.'

James sighed. 'Jessica——'

'No. Listen to me. It's true. You've always had breakfast and gone out by the time I come down in the mornings, and if you're not lunching with clients, you have a sandwich with Ted down at the stables. Then at supper time—well, you usually dine elsewhere.'

James made an evident effort to control his impatience, before saying tersely, 'I can't help it if you don't get up before I go out in the mornings.'

'Can't you?' Jessica hardly let him finish before plunging in. She glanced at the clock, ticking away on the sideboard, and arched one silky brow. 'It's a quarter to seven, James. What time am I supposed to get up? Half-past six? Six o'clock, maybe? I'd have to if I wanted to eat breakfast with you, so that's hardly a reasonable complaint.'

James cast an impatient look at his watch. 'I'm not complaining, am I?' he retorted. 'I'm merely pointing out that this is a working enterprise, and I consider myself as much a part of the team as either Ted or Pat Grady.'

'All right.' Jessica's voice quivered a little, but she forced herself to go on. 'Nevertheless, I do want to talk to you, and I've made a special effort to get up this morning, just so I could do that thing.'

James shrugged. 'Well, I'm sorry.'

'You're not going to give me a few minutes, then?'

He seemed to hesitate for a moment, but then he spread his hands. 'Jessica, I can't.'

'Very well.' Jessica lifted her shoulders in a defiant gesture and stepped aside. 'But don't be surprised if I'm not here when you get back,' she added provokingly. 'I have things to do, too, and if——'

But she didn't finish what she had been about to say. James, who had automatically stepped past her when she moved, turned in mid-sentence, and swung around to face her. 'What did you say?' he demanded, and she had to steel herself not to succumb to his aggression as his eyes bored into her.

'I said——'

'Yes, damn you, I know what you *said*!' he snapped angrily. 'All right, let me phrase it differently—where the hell do you think you're going?'

'How about London?' she got out breathily. 'I know what you said, but don't you see? I've *got* to do something.'

'Why?'

'Why?' she echoed, playing for time. 'You know why.'

'Do I?' he essayed grimly. 'For Christ's sake, I thought we had all this out last week, on our way to the hospital. I thought we agreed——'

'We didn't agree anything,' said Jessica wearily. 'We just talked round the subject like we did before. And—and Dr Patel thinks I'm strong enough to start taking responsibility for myself.'

'That's not what he said to me.'

'What did he say to you?'

James breathed heavily. 'Not a lot, actually,' he admitted. 'But I'm damn sure he didn't give you permission to go charging off to London on your own. Be sensible, Jess. Give yourself a little more time.'

The 'Jess' almost persuaded her, but not quite. He probably knew how susceptible she was to his persuasion and used the diminutive form of her name deliberately.

'I don't think time is the answer,' she replied determinedly, bringing another scowl to his lean features. 'I need to do something positive. I can't just sit around waiting for inspiration to come any longer.'

James uttered an oath. 'All right,' he said at last. 'All right, I accept that you're beginning to feel—restless. But——' he glanced once more at his watch and she saw his lips tighten '—at least give me the chance to go with you. London is a hell of a long way to go on your own, particularly as you don't have the first idea where to go when you get there.'

Jessica hesitated. 'I might.'

'You might what?'

'I might know where to go when I get there.'

'Jess!'

His temper was daunting, and she reluctantly gave in. 'Well—all right. I won't take off for London while you're in Cumbria,' she conceded.

'That's a promise?'

She sighed. 'Yes.'

'OK.' His relief was palpable, and she wondered why. It wouldn't have been unreasonable if he had appeared eager to encourage her. But he had never made her feel as if she was unwelcome, even if, for the most part, he did avoid her company. She wondered, rather guiltily, if there was something else in her father's will, something she still didn't know about, that provided James with a motive for keeping her here as long as possible, but that seemed unlikely. Unless it had something to do with Laura Bentley. That was infinitely more conceivable.

But, before she could even formulate a way to voice her suspicions in any acceptable form, James excused himself and was gone, leaving Jessica to face a day made even longer by her early rising. It didn't help either that a faint drizzle was beginning to dampen the windows of the morning-room, or that the sky looked dull and overcast, promising more of the same. With a depressing deterioration of her spirits, she flopped down into the chair at the table again, cupping her chin on one hand and gazing into space.

Mrs Hayes had cleared James's dishes away and provided Jessica with the orange juice, coffee and toast she had lack-lustredly requested, when James's daughter appeared. Leonie came into the room where Jessica was still sitting, wearing corded trousers and a chunky sweater, and pulled out a chair at the table before helping herself to juice from the jug.

'Good morning,' she said, viewing Jessica over the top of her glass with her usual attitude of forbearance. 'Miserable morning, isn't it? Did Dad get away at first light?'

Jessica lifted her shoulders. 'I suppose so,' she responded dully, and then, acknowledging that Leonie was making a more-than-usual attempt to be civil, she added, 'He left about half an hour ago. I'm surprised you didn't go with him.'

'Me!' exclaimed Leonie ungrammatically, and Jessica nodded.

'Why not? As you've obviously got a day off school...' She indicated Leonie's casual attire. 'You have got a day off school, haven't you?'

Leonie made an offhand gesture. 'I am off school today, yes.'

Jessica's brows narrowed. 'That's not exactly what I asked. Is this a holiday or what?'

Leonie sighed. 'That's right,' she said, keeping her head down as she buttered a slice of toast, which Jessica was sure must be cold by now. 'It's a holiday.'

Jessica hesitated. 'For the *whole* school?'

'Does it matter?' Leonie looked up now, her sallow expression taking on a defiant cast. 'What's it to you? You're not my keeper.'

'No.' Jessica conceded the point abruptly. She was no one's keeper, she thought bitterly. Not even her own.

Leonie licked a crumb from her lip, and then said reluctantly, 'All right. It's not a holiday. I'm skiving off. Why shouldn't I? It's my life.'

Jessica shrugged. 'That's right. It's your life. Do what you want. But don't be surprised if you feel differently in a few years' time.'

Leonie put down her knife. 'As you did?' she suggested sarcastically. 'I suppose you regretted leaving school at sixteen, too.'

Jessica blinked. 'But I didn't.'

'Didn't what?'

'Leave school at sixteen.'

'Yes, you did.' Leonie stared at her. 'According to what the solicitor told Daddy, you had a dozen jobs before you started at the supermarket.'

Jessica quivered. 'Nevertheless, I'm sure—*I know*—I didn't leave school at sixteen.' She moistened lips that were suddenly dry. 'I—I think I went to college.' She swallowed. 'Do you think that's possible?'

Leonie looked troubled now. 'To work in a supermarket?' she murmured sceptically. 'I don't think so. Um, perhaps you ought to ask Dad. He might know.'

Jessica was trembling quite perceptibly now, and Leonie obviously didn't know what to do. But she evidently decided she had to do something, and before Jessica could stop her she had slipped off her chair and hurried to the door.

'Mrs Hayes! Mrs Hayes!' she called, keeping a wary eye on the other girl as she did so. And then, when the housekeeper came in answer to her cry, she gestured at Jessica. 'She—she thinks she's remembered something,' she explained jerkily. 'Something about going to college. Oh, hell! If only Dad was here. I don't know what to do.'

'I suggest you go and ask Vicky to find some brandy and bring it here,' said the housekeeper, taking in the situation at a glance. And when Jessica started to object, she overrode her protest. 'You need something to put the colour back in your cheeks,' she insisted firmly. 'My goodness, child,' she squeezed Jessica's fingers with some dismay, 'you're as cold as ice.' She tutted anxiously. 'Oh, come along, Vicky, what are you doing? Ah—at last! And haven't you brought a glass? Oh, well, put some in Miss Devlin's cup and give it here. There you are, my girl, sip a little of that.'

With Leonie and Vicky, as well as Mrs Hayes, standing guard over her, Jessica had no choice but to do as the housekeeper said, and in truth she did feel a lot better with the warmth of the raw spirit warming inside her. Even so, the memories Leonie had so innocently evoked had left her feeling distinctly unsteady, and she was glad she didn't have to put any weight on her legs at that moment.

'Thank you,' she said at last, and there was a concerted sigh of relief from the two girls. 'I—I'm sorry I lost control like that. It—it was just something Leonie said. It seemed to spark off something I remembered. But I honestly can't be sure.'

'What have you been saying, Leonie?' demanded Mrs Hayes at once, and, realising how ambiguous her words had been, Jessica hastened to explain.

'It wasn't Leonie's fault,' she exclaimed. 'We—we were talking about school, about leaving school. I seemed to remember going to college——' She broke off as a spasm of pain stabbed her temple. 'But—but it's probably just something I heard. Maybe even from that girl on the train. She was a college graduate, wasn't she? I'm sure that's what Dr Patel told me.'

'Maybe.' Mrs Hayes sounded as doubtful as Leonie had done earlier, but after exchanging a look with the younger girl she was abruptly diverted. 'Leonie!' she exclaimed. 'Why aren't you wearing your uniform? It's almost time for you to leave!'

'Er—Leonie isn't going into school today,' said Jessica swiftly, realising she was to blame for drawing attention to the girl's appearance. 'She—I—we're going shopping together. Mr Bentley was unwilling to let me go alone.'

The fact that James had been unwilling for vastly different reasons was something she determinedly put aside, and Leonie's look of gratitude was worth the deception.

'Really?' Mrs Hayes said now, and Jessica could tell she wasn't altogether convinced. 'Well, Mr Bentley didn't say anything to me.'

'We only discussed it this morning,' said Jessica at once, uncomfortably conscious of the ever-increasing number of lies one had to tell to support one untruth.

'He would have told you, I'm sure, but he was in a hurry to get away. He probably forgot.'

'Hmm.' The housekeeper looked sceptical. 'Well, I don't know if you're fit enough to go—shopping!' The way she said the word was a condemnation. 'Leonie, is that what your father said?'

Leonie straightened her shoulders. 'Are you calling Miss Devlin a liar?'

'No, of course I'm not calling Miss Devlin a liar.'

Mrs Hayes was on the defensive now, and Jessica felt a reluctant sympathy for her. But it was too late to retract her words, and besides, perhaps with Leonie's help she might begin to take some control of her own life again.

'Thanks,' said James's daughter, when they were alone again. 'I appreciate what you did just now. Particularly when you don't approve.'

The pain in Jessica's temple had subsided at last, and she managed a faint smile. 'Perhaps I had an ulterior motive,' she remarked, and saw the wary look that crossed the girl's face at her words. 'I meant it, you know. I would like to go shopping.'

Leonie subsided into her chair again. 'Shopping!' she echoed in dismay. 'You meant it?'

'Why not?'

Leonie grimaced. 'I hate shopping.'

'Do you?'

'Yes.'

'Why?'

'Well!' Leonie's shoulders sagged. 'Looking at clothes, make-up, that sort of thing. That's for people like Laura. Not for me.'

'Why not?'

'Why not?' she echoed bleakly. 'Isn't it obvious?'

'Not to me.'

'I'm not interested in clothes—in any clothes, except these.' She indicated the shabby sweater and trousers. 'I don't have the shape for present-day fashions.'

Jessica's concern over her own problems receded a little. 'I disagree,' she said, studying the younger girl with critical eyes. 'You're tall; and slim. I'd have said you'd look good in the kind of gear young people are wearing today.'

'Well, I don't.' Leonie looked sulky now. 'I just look gawky. Laura thinks I'm a beanpole.'

Jessica was shocked. 'Did she tell you that?'

'Yes.' Leonie hunched her shoulders. 'A—spotty beanpole, I think, were her exact words. But I don't care. I'm only interested in horses, and they don't care what I look like.'

Jessica shook her head. 'I see.'

'You needn't feel sorry for me,' Leonie exclaimed irritably. 'That's just Laura's way. Sometimes she gets mad at Dad because he won't do what she wants, and then she takes it out on me. She blames me, you see, for being a source of contention between them. If I wasn't here, she could stay at Aspen whenever she liked, whereas now she has to wait until she can persuade Dad to stay at Bickersley.'

'You mean——'

'That's right. Dad won't sleep with her at Aspen,' said Leonie matter-of-factly, apparently unaware of the bombshell she had just exploded. 'Not until they're married, anyway,' she added flatly. 'If they ever do get married, that is. So long as Laura has control of Bickersley, she won't give it up.'

Jessica swallowed and, seizing the least provocative thing Leonie had said, she murmured faintly, 'Bickersley. That's my father's house, isn't it?'

'It was,' agreed the younger girl ruefully. 'But not any more.'

'No.' Jessica nodded, relieved that Leonie hadn't noticed her disconcertment. 'Not any more.'

Leonie grimaced. 'Still, when you get your memory back, you may decide you want to live there, too, and that could change a lot of things.'

Jessica blinked now. 'Why on earth should you imagine I might ever want to live in Laura Bentley's house?' she exclaimed.

'Because, it's not *her* house,' retorted Leonie at once, and then, her pale face turning a brilliant shade of crimson, she added awkwardly, 'That is—I mean——'

She cleared her throat in embarrassment. 'Um—when did you want to leave?'

'To leave?' Jessica looked confused now, and the girl hurried to explain herself.

'Er—for Leeds,' she appended hurriedly. 'Or—or Harrogate. Yes, Harrogate would be better. You've never been there, have you?'

'Leonie——'

'Oh, God!' The younger girl gave up all attempts to evade the inevitable, and groaned. 'Oh, please, you won't tell Dad what I've said, will you?' she begged distractedly. 'Why did I open my big mouth? He's going to *kill* me!'

'For telling me that Bickersley doesn't belong to Laura Bentley?' asked Jessica mildly. 'I can't believe that.'

'He will.' Leonie got up from her chair and paced wretchedly about the room. 'Oh, lord, I always do the wrong thing.'

'You haven't.' Jessica shrugged. 'At least, I don't think you have. Why should it matter to me if—*oh!*' Like a streak of lightning, the significance of what Leonie had so carelessly revealed suddenly struck her. If Laura didn't own Bickersley, *who did?*

'You see.' Leonie came to stand in front of her, going down on to one knee and putting her face on a level with Jessica's. 'You've *got* to promise me you won't tell Dad what I've said. I'll be in enough trouble as it is when Mrs Hayes tells him I've had a day off school. If you tell him I've been blabbing about Laura, he'll never forgive me.'

Jessica could feel a return of her earlier unsteadiness, but she managed to control it as she said gently, 'All right. All right, Leonie. I won't tell your father what you've said—on one condition.'

'Which is?' Leonie scowled.

'That you tell me everything you know about my father's will.'

Leonie gulped. 'No.'

Jessica managed to adopt a resigned expression. 'Oh, well, then——'

'You shouldn't ask me!' burst out Leonie desperately. 'You shouldn't. Why don't you ask Dad to tell you? He will, you know, if you persist. After all, you have a right to know.'

'Do I?' Jessica's eyes narrowed. 'Do I take it then that my—legacy from my father is not just a small annuity?'

Leonie bent her head. 'I can't say any more,' she insisted, but she didn't have to. Jessica already knew, or at least, she thought she did. So that was why James Bentley had agreed to bring her to Aspen, she thought bitterly. To save Laura the embarrassment of having to give up her home to her husband's illegitimate daughter!

'All right.' Jessica stood up now, and Leonie pushed herself unhappily to her feet, too. 'So—Harrogate it is,' Jessica declared huskily. 'I think we should get ready, don't you? Have you any idea how we're going to get there?'

'One of the boys will take us, or maybe Mr Hayes,' said Leonie indifferently. 'Jessica——'

'It's all right. I've told you. I won't say anything to your father.' Jessica pressed her lips together. 'Nothing that will implicate you, at least,' she added cryptically.

## CHAPTER ELEVEN

In spite of its inauspicious beginnings, the day out in Harrogate proved to be a success. Jessica used the money from the wallet in her handbag to buy them lunch in a rather attractive restaurant, overlooking the Valley Gardens, and afterwards she persuaded Leonie to enter a store selling teenage clothes. The girl was unenthusiastic about trying on any of the pretty garments, but with Jessica's encouragement—and a certain amount of minor blackmail—she agreed to take a couple of cotton suits and a short-skirted polyester dress into the changing-room.

The transformation was amazing. The suits, one with a skirt and bloused top, and the other an all-in-one jumpsuit, put inches on to Leonie's skinny frame, accentuating the slight curve of bosom that was just beginning to appear, and giving shape to the long legs that weren't half so angular in the softer garments. Even the dress, with its swirling pleats that ended just above her knee, gave her a look of confidence, the silky orange print giving colour to her face.

Leonie was evidently surprised and delighted, and Jessica wondered how long it had been since James had taken the trouble to take his daughter shopping. Who had chosen those awful corded trousers, and the school clothes that were too long for a girl as tall as Leonie? Mrs Hayes, perhaps? Or Laura? It was obvious that the two females in James's life didn't like each other, and, although it seemed inconceivable that anyone could be so petty, was it possible that Laura had used this method to undermine Leonie's self-confidence?

Whatever the truth of the matter, Leonie was clearly convinced now that not all shopping trips need be a bore. And when Jessica began checking the money in her purse to see exactly which of the outfits she could afford, the younger girl surprised her.

'I'll just put them on Dad's account,' she declared, reminding Jessica that, whatever she looked like, Leonie was still the daughter of a man of means. 'Honestly, he'll be delighted I've got something different to wear. He's always telling me to buy some clothes, but—well, I wasn't interested until now.'

Jessica frowned. 'Why?' she asked, unable to prevent the question, and Leonie grimaced.

'Oh—I guess I've always regarded myself as a misfit,' she said offhandedly, and although she didn't elaborate Jessica knew that the expression was unlikely to be her own.

'Anyway, you should buy something, too,' Leonie exclaimed, eager to share her excitement, and change the subject. 'How about a dress? Or a suit? Please—I'd like to buy something for you. Just as a kind of thank you. Isn't there anything you would like?'

Jessica shook her head. 'If I buy anything, I'll buy it myself,' she demurred firmly. Then, seeing the girl's suddenly downcast expression, she added quickly, 'I don't think your father should be expected to buy my clothes, as well as giving me a temporary home, do you? But thank you for the offer. I do appreciate it.'

Leonie hesitated before allowing her expression to relax again. 'All right,' she said. 'Perhaps you're right. Although I don't think Dad would notice, one way or the other.' She grimaced. 'So—there must be something you need. What sort of clothes do you prefer? Or don't you remember?'

'As a matter of fact, that's something that troubles me a little,' confessed Jessica, finding it suddenly easier to talk to Leonie about it than anyone else. Perhaps they were both misfits, she reflected unhappily, but then thrust that thought aside in an effort to explain what she meant. 'The clothes in the suitcase I had with me—even the sable coat, although I was apparently hanging on to it for dear life when they found me after—after the accident—well, they just don't seem the kind of things I would wear.' She coloured as the younger girl turned to stare at her. 'Does that sound crazy?'

Leonie frowned. 'Not crazy, no.'

'But—odd?'

Leonie shrugged. 'Maybe.'

Jessica sighed. 'You see...'

'It is possible that when—well, when you found out you'd—inherited some money, you had a spending spree,' murmured Leonie awkwardly.

'Yes.' But Jessica was not convinced. 'Oh, well, I expect all will be revealed in time.'

'So why don't you buy something you really like?' suggested Leonie again. 'And if you need to borrow——'

'Oh, no that's all right,' said Jessica hastily, mentally calculating what the contents of the wallet would run to. 'What I'd really like is some jeans. And perhaps a couple of cotton tops.' She pulled a face. 'I've got enough—formal clothes. What I need is something I can—*breathe* in!'

It was the evening of the following day before Jessica had an opportunity to speak to James Bentley. It had been late the previous evening when he'd arrived back from Cumbria, and although she had intended to intercept him at breakfast again she overslept, and James had departed, this time for a race meeting, before she had a chance to interrupt his schedule.

In consequence, they met quite by accident.

For the first time, Leonie had invited Jessica to join her after school, when she went down to the stables. The shopping trip to Harrogate, following as it had upon the conversation they had had at breakfast, had broken the ice between them, and Jessica, just as much as Leonie, appreciated having someone to confide in. They had talked a lot since that uneasy confrontation the previous morning, and Jessica thought that, if nothing else, the accident and its subsequent difficulties had brought them together. Whether they would have become friends in other circumstances was arguable. Leonie was a prickly creature, and she had obviously resented the intervention of an unknown cousin into her life. But now her defences were down, and Jessica was grateful for it.

Pat Grady came over as they leaned on the rails, watching the mares in the paddock. He rested his elbows familiarly beside Jessica and subjected her to a critical appraisal.

'Well, well,' he said, admiring her trim figure, that was shown to advantage in the slim-fitting jeans and cotton shirt she had bought the previous day, 'you're looking very well, Miss Devlin.'

'Thank you.' Jessica wasn't embarrassed. Somehow she knew she had been dealing with youths like Pat Grady all her life. 'I'm feeling much better.'

'We were just admiring Minstrel and her foal,' put in Leonie enthusiastically. 'Do you think he'll be a winner?'

'Mr Bentley seems to think so,' answered Pat, turning his gaze with some reluctance to the animals. 'He's got good strong withers, and you can see the way he moves is good. But he's got a long way to go. I wouldn't like to speculate.'

Leonie grimaced. 'Well, I think he's beautiful.' She turned to Jessica. 'I was there when Minstrel foaled. You should have seen the way he tottered to his feet just after the delivery. Strong foals are looking for milk about half an hour after they're born. And Troubadour was just like that.'

'Troubadour,' murmured Jessica, smiling. 'What a nice name. Who chose it?'

'Well, Dad chose that one, but I've chosen names, too,' replied Leonie defensively. 'But when we sell the foals, the people who buy them often change the names for racing purposes.' She grimaced as she turned back to the yard behind them. 'You should hear some of the ghastly names they choose! Things like Tinker's Damn, or Put it There—names like that. We once had a beautiful filly called Serendipity, and the man who bought her raced her as Wither's Nag!'

Jessica left the rail to walk back with her, and Pat Grady fell into step beside them. 'Have you thought any more about getting up on a horse yourself?' he asked, pushing his hands into the pockets of his trousers, so that his bare forearm brushed against hers. 'We've got just the mount for you, haven't we, Lee? Sure, Angel Face wouldn't scare you a bit.'

'Hey, that's right,' exclaimed Leonie at once, unaware of her father's reaction to Jessica's learning how to ride. 'If you could ride, Jessica, you could come out with me when I exercise Becca. Would you like to do that? It's such fun, honestly.'

Jessica hesitated. 'Well——' she began, but before she could express any preference Pat Grady intervened.

'Sure, Miss Devlin might not be strong enough,' he declared, and it wasn't until she had instinctively declared that she was 'perfectly strong enough' that Jessica realised that was exactly the reaction he had hoped to provoke.

'Well, then,' said Leonie, clearly sold on the idea of teaching Jessica to love horses as much as she did, 'shall we give it a try?'

'Oh—I don't know——'

Jessica gave Pat an appealing look, but as she had expected she got no support from that quarter. 'Sure, a little walk around the lunging ring, and you'll be as right as ninepence,' he declared, striding off towards the stables. 'I'll get the mare saddled for you. Then we'll see how it goes.'

Fifteen minutes later, Jessica wondered why she had ever been apprehensive of getting up on Angel Face's back. The sturdy brown mare was as good-natured and docile as a rocking-horse, trotting round the circle of neatly cropped grass with all the patience of a well-behaved pony. Pat Grady held her on the end of the lunging rein, and, although Jessica was pretty sure she had never ridden before, she found a natural rhythm with the horse that made it really enjoyable.

'Do you want to try it without the restraint?' Pat asked, reining in the animal and coming to rest his arms familiarly beside her thighs.

Jessica hesitated. 'Do you think I should?' she asked, not altogether certain of herself even after almost half an hour of circling the ring.

'I don't!' declared a strong, familiar, but definitely aggressive voice.

The surprise Jessica received at this sudden intervention almost caused her to lose her balance on the horse, but she managed to stay where she was, even if a flush of colour stained her cheeks.

'Oh, hello, Dad!' exclaimed Leonie, looking every as bit as guilty as Jessica felt. 'We didn't expect you back until much later,' she added, and then realising what she was saying, she subsided into an awkward silence.

'Obviously,' observed her father, regarding the little tableau with ill-concealed irritation. The strange, icily cool eyes flicked to Pat Grady. 'I thought I told you that if Miss Devlin required riding lessons, I would give them to her.'

Pat's normally confident expression faltered a little. 'Sure, and wasn't it Miss Leonie herself who had the idea of teaching Miss Devlin how to ride?' he replied, ignoring the girl's look of indignation. 'Would I make a suggestion like that, I ask you?'

Jessica was beginning to feel as if her presence was of supreme indifference to all of them. Except perhaps for Leonie, who was subjecting the young Irishman to a series of stony stares. And, guessing that some kind of misplaced loyalty was preventing her from contradicting, Jessica chose to intervene. 'As a matter of fact it was my idea,' she stated, wishing she was as adept at getting down off the horse as her riding would have led her to believe. Unwilling to make a fool of herself in

James's presence, she remained where she was, meeting his disbelieving gaze with concentrated determination. 'I—oh—I thought it would be rather nice if Leonie and I could go riding together. I mean, everybody rides around here, don't they? And I felt rather out of it not being able to, so to speak.'

James's eyes did not waver. 'Really,' he remarked, coldly. 'And how long have you been feeling this deficiency?'

Jessica, who hadn't been feeling it at all, gave a determined shrug. 'Not long,' she replied defensively. She had seen James in many moods, and this sarcastic manner was the one she liked least.

'I can believe that,' said James drily. 'You certainly never professed such an interest to me.'

Leonie shifted uncomfortably from one foot to another. 'Oh, Daddy, does it really matter whose idea it was?' She forced a smile. 'Anyway, Jessica has been awfully good. I think you'll be really pleased. And Angel is such a gentle mount.'

'It's just as well for you,' said James, striding forward and taking all of them by surprise by lifting Jessica out of the saddle and down to the ground beside him. 'In future, I would be grateful if you would wait until I'm around before you run the risk of doing yourself some permanent injury. Have you any idea of what might have happened to you if you had fallen off the horse?'

'Oh, honestly, I'm not a child, you know!' exclaimed Jessica in some embarrassment. James really was making her feel like one, throwing his weight around, and hers too, if you considered the way he had hauled her down off the horse.

'Then stop behaving like one,' he retorted grimly. 'I can't leave you five minutes without you doing something you know I won't approve of. Like that trip to Harrogate yesterday, for example. Was it you who gave Leonie permission to take a day off school?'

'Yes—no, I—that is—perhaps!' finished Jessica lamely. The whole situation was becoming one of extreme embarrassment to her, and she was aware of Leonie and Pat Grady's eyes upon her, mirroring a mixture of apprehension and speculation. It wasn't as if anything disastrous had happened. As a matter of fact, riding around the small ring had given her a certain amount of confidence, a kind of reassurance that she was not completely incapable of caring for herself. But James was evidently in no mood to be conciliatory, and gazing up into his dark, almost vengeful, face she thought how odd it was that his usually controlled demeanour had given way to such uncharacteristic agitation.

He had evidently come immediately to look for them, for instead of the casual cords and sweaters he wore around the stud, he was quite elegantly attired in a well-cut pair of black trousers and a fine tweed hacking jacket, his tie indicative of the rather exclusive club of which he was obviously a member. His more formal attire made him seem more formidable somehow, but it was an awareness of his aggressive masculinity that made Jessica conscious of him in a totally unforgivable way. How could she be feeling like this? she wondered, with Leonie looking on in some confusion, and Pat Grady eyeing the pair of them with growing curiosity. It was shameful and ridiculous, and, realising the only way to end it was to give in to him, Jessica offered a tight smile.

'Thank you for your concern about my welfare,' she declared formally. 'But as you can see, no harm has been done, and now, if you'll excuse me, I'd like to take a shower.'

She had thought that would have been the end of the matter. Leonie evidently thought it was. With a rueful grimace in Jessica's direction, she sauntered off towards the stables, no doubt eager to take Bekahra out on his much delayed ride, leaving Pat Grady to unsaddle Angel Face, and dispose of the lunging rein and saddle. But although James allowed his daughter to escape his wrath, Jessica was not to be reprieved, for he fell into step beside her, apparently prepared to accompany her back to the house.

Deciding her only chance of keeping control of the situation was by taking the attack to him, for Jessica was fairly sure that James was not about to let the subject drop, she cast a defiant glance in his direction before saying flippantly, 'Did Mrs Bentley enjoy her day at the races?'

'Mrs Bentley?' James looked briefly perplexed. Then, evidently realising what she meant, he gave her a sardonic look. 'I'm sorry to disappoint you,' he said, 'but Mrs Bentley did not accompany me to the races. Laura is not overly fond of horses, as Leonie has probably told you. And as for spending a day in their company, well—I don't think that would be quite her scene.'

'Not even with you?' suggested Jessica rather provocatively, and James's expression darkened.

'Not even with me,' he essayed crisply, 'and I would be glad if you would refrain from discussing your late father's wife and myself with Leonie.'

'What do you mean?' Jessica was puzzled now.

James's mouth turned down at the corners. 'Oh, please, let's not get involved in needless argument. We both know how Leonie feels about Laura, don't we? And it's obvious you've been encouraging her to be indiscreet.'

'I have not.'

'Jessica——'

'Well, I haven't. Leonie's opinion of Laura is her own, just as mine is. And if it's not a favourable one, then Laura has only herself to blame.'

James sighed. 'All right. We'll say no more about it now. But I want you to know that stirring up trouble with Laura is not going to help your situation at all.'

They were nearing the house now, and whereas before Jessica had been eager to escape his brooding presence, now she took the opportunity he had unwittingly given her. 'My situation?' she enquired pointedly. 'Yes, I'd like to talk about my situation.'

Her steps had slowed as they neared the terrace, and now she turned, as if surveying the view, when in fact the slanting bars of sunlight sweeping across the fields had never been further from her thoughts. She guessed James would have rather put off this conversation till later but, short of walking out on her, and thus provoking suspicions he was probably more eager to subdue, he was obliged to turn and face her. But his eyes were definitely guarded now, in the early evening light.

'Am I supposed to glean something from that remark?' he enquired tightly, and although Jessica knew she had a right to ask, it didn't ease her nervousness at bringing the matter up.

'Well,' she said, giving herself time to choose her words, 'perhaps you should tell me what my situation is.'

James regarded her dourly. 'Let's stop playing games, shall we?' he said harshly. 'It's obvious you think you've learned something of some relevance, so perhaps you should tell me what you're talking about.'

Now it was Jessica's turn to sigh. She couldn't say what she knew without involving Leonie, and she had promised not to do that. Even so, the temptation to call his bluff was appealing, and she had to force herself to be as ambivalent as he was being. 'Look,' she said at last, 'I'm not a fool, whatever you believe. And—and, well, I've had time to do some thinking.'

'While you were riding, no doubt,' remarked James with some derision, and Jessica's cheeks flushed with colour.

'No, not while I was riding,' she replied tensely, resenting his easy ability to disconcert her. 'It was—it was earlier today, actually. I just—well—started to wonder why I should have been coming to Bickersley, when it's obvious I wouldn't be welcome. Perhaps—perhaps there was a more—serious reason for the trip. Hmm?'

She could tell by his darkening expression that Leonie's careless words had not been unjustified. But what motive could he have had for bringing her here? It had to be to do with Laura. And if Bickersley didn't belong to Laura, did it belong to *her*? The idea was breathtaking.

'You see,' she continued, finding it increasingly difficult to hide her increasing agitation, 'it seems fairly obvious to me that Laura would never have invited me here. So there has to be something else. Something that you know and I don't.'

'Go on,' said James flatly. 'So?'

'So—this legacy my father is supposed to have left me, what exactly does it entail?'

James shrugged his shoulders. 'I don't think it's my position to tell you.'

Jessica's lips tensed. 'So you haven't.'

James took a moment before saying quietly, 'You may remember, when you left the hospital Dr Patel said you shouldn't be upset in any way. He specifically warned me not to get involved in conversations of this kind. As you're evidently feeling better, perhaps you ought to make an appointment to see your father's solicitor in Leeds. I'm sure he'd be more than willing to give you all the details of your father's will.'

'But you won't?'

'No.'

James was adamant on that point, and Jessica realised that his whole intention was to protect Laura. And why not? she asked herself bitterly. If Leonie was to be believed, and it seemed she was, their relationship went far beyond the loyalty due to a hitherto unknown cousin.

Now Jessica took a deep breath. 'Then perhaps you'd be kind enough to make me an appointment,' she said, somewhat tremulously. Somehow she sensed it was not in her nature to make ultimatums of this kind, and it didn't help to have James staring at her as if she was some particularly obnoxious example of her sex. But living at Aspen, however pleasant, was not her only concern, and she knew that the longer she lived in James's house, the harder it was going to be to leave when that time came.

'Very well.'

James accepted her instructions without further comment, and would have turned away if some uncontrollable surge of desperation had not caused Jessica to lay delaying hands on his sleeve. 'James,' she began unhappily, 'you do understand how I feel, don't you?' She shook her head, the silken swirl of her hair, loosened by her ride, giving her face a look of haunting innocence. 'I have to do something. I can't just go on accepting your hospitality indefinitely. And—and if there is something I should know, perhaps it might help me to remember the rest.'

James had responded to her plea by remaining where he was, but his expression was no less forbidding as he met her candid gaze. 'I'm sorry,' he said, 'I didn't realise you were so unhappy here. But naturally, you are entitled to know the facts, and I'll get on to Toby Langley in the morning.'

'Toby Langley?' Jessica looked blank.

'Your late father's solicitor,' James explained without warmth. 'He may not be able to see you tomorrow, but I'll make the earliest possible appointment.'

'Well—there's no hurry.' Jessica was embarrassed now, half wishing she had never started this.

'Isn't there?' James's dark brows arched. 'Forgive me, but I got the impression that you were eager to proceed.'

The tensing muscle, tangible even through the fine wool of his sleeve, made Jessica aware that she was still holding on to his arm. And with a helpless little gesture she drew her hand away, but once again, when he would have entered the house, she demanded his attention. 'Did—er—did you have a nice day?' she asked, hoping against hope that she might redeem their relationship. But James was not responsive.

'It was a very pleasant day, until now,' he declared caustically, and without giving her another chance to try his patience he strode into the house.

## CHAPTER TWELVE

JAMES parked the Range Rover at the side of the house and, getting out, locked the door with not altogether steady fingers. He had been lucky to get home in one piece, he reflected grimly. Had he been stopped by the police, the amount of alcohol inside him would have certainly shown up on one of their breathalysers, but, after the evening he had had with Laura, the several Scotches he had sunk in the village pub had seemed a worthy compensation. He had known it wasn't going to be an easy evening before he left home. But he had had to tell her what Jessica had said. There was nothing else for it. And he had known she would be furious, and in the event he had not been disappointed.

Even so, her anger didn't altogether account for his own sense of irritation tonight. He had had little patience with Laura; little patience with himself. It was almost as if he sympathised with what Jessica had said. It was altogether ridiculous in the circumstances, but it was true. All right, she was his cousin's illegitimate child, and as such he should feel no earthly sense of responsibility towards her. And even the accident, which goodness knew had been unfortunate enough, couldn't entirely account for the feelings of frustration Laura's attitude had created. But the truth was, when Laura began blaming himself, Adam, Jessica Devlin, and the fates in general for ruining her life, he had felt only irritation, and he had been hard-pressed not to take Jessica's part. After all, as she had maintained, she was the innocent party in all this. Who knew, perhaps Adam had intended them all to suffer. Who knew what feelings of resentment he might have felt towards Jessica's mother. Had he blamed himself for abandoning her? Or had he never thought of her again, until this opportunity presented itself to make Laura pay?

James had known he should have felt sympathetic towards Laura. After all, he had known her a lot longer than he'd known Jessica Devlin. And in God's name, he had intended to marry her, as soon as they decently could.

But that was before Jessica Devlin had entered their lives. It was strange, but her advent had changed so many things. For years, Leonie had been trying to show him how selfish Laura was, but it wasn't until recently that he had begun to believe it was true. Oh, he had known Laura had faults. And he hadn't forgotten the mistakes of the past. But the Laura he was seeing now he didn't like at all, and it was this, as much as anything, that had contributed to his mood. He didn't like it. He didn't like the feeling that for the past twenty years he had lived with an imaginary image. But what was more galling was the fact that Jessica Devlin should have opened his eyes. He didn't want to feel grateful to her for anything. In many ways, he wished he had never laid eyes on her.

In consequence, after spending more than an hour listening to Laura, he had refused her offer of a bed for the night, and sought consolation elsewhere. He realised he had done a lot of that lately. Ever since Jessica came to stay at Aspen, he had found it increasingly difficult to put her out of his mind when he was with Laura, and as far as staying at Bickersley was concerned, he had found a variety of excuses for refusing her invitations. It hadn't been easy placating her, but on the other hand it hadn't been so hard either. The situation with Jessica provided ample reason for both of them to want to avoid the inevitable discussions about their future. But although he knew he ought to feel glad that Adam had left Bickersley to Jessica, thus obviating any possibility of Laura's having to choose between himself and the house, the idea of her moving into Aspen was no longer a desirable proposition. And why was that so? he asked himself now, trudging across the courtyard. He didn't know the answer, but he did know that that was another reason why he had chosen to soak his brain in alcohol.

To his surprise, there were still lights on in the house when he let himself into the hall. The Hayeses, he knew, were unlikely to be about, and Leonie, despite her assertions of maturity, was invariably in bed and asleep by ten o'clock. As most mornings she got up when he did to help with the morning stables, it was hardly surprising she was tired at night, and he hoped on this occasion the lights were just an oversight on Mrs Hayes's part, and not Leonie lying in wait with some new grudge to plague him with.

But to his astonishment it was Jessica who appeared in the arched entry to the sitting-room when she heard his key inserted in the lock. Tall and slim, and strangely vulnerable, still wearing the close-fitting jeans she had been wearing earlier in the day, with a chunky cardigan to supplement the T-shirt against the cooler air of evening, she looked very different from the rather wan female he had first encountered in the hospital. Her hair was clean now, shining, and healthily lustrous, her eyes bright and alert, if distinctly anxious.

James was tempted to walk straight past her. After the evening he had just spent, he was in no fit state to conduct a conversation with anyone, and, while she might have a better reason than most for delaying him, what he desperately wanted to do was to forget his thoughts in blessed oblivion. But he couldn't ignore her. Apart from anything else, he was curious to know why she had chosen to wait up for him. She couldn't possibly have been sure he would come home, not that night anyway, and it was inconceivable that there should be another reason for her being there, other than the obvious one of wanting to continue their discussion of her father's will.

The door closed behind him, and without really being aware of it he swayed revealingly back against it. His shoulders came up against the hard wood panels of the door, involuntarily steadying him, and he was eventually able to push himself away with a semblance of sobriety. 'Well, well,' he remarked, quite pleased that there didn't seem to be any slurring of his speech, 'it's been a long time since anyone waited up for me. To what do I owe this indulgence? Or is indulging me not quite what you had in mind? From your expression, I would say it probably wasn't.'

Jessica pushed her long, narrow fingers into the back hip pockets of her jeans. He couldn't remember ever seeing her in jeans before today. As he recalled it, all her clothes had seemed fairly big for her, with a predominance of long skirts and flowing dresses, none of which had shown her figure as the tight-fitting jeans tended to do. Indeed, he'd never noticed before what long legs she had, or how attractive she was becoming now that the gauntness had left her features. This latter thought caused him no small sense of irritation, and he was almost relieved when Jessica began to speak.

'I—er—I wanted to talk to you,' she ventured, not without some awkwardness. 'I realise it's late, and you probably don't want to talk to me, but I couldn't wait until tomorrow, not when the chances of my speaking to you then might be as remote as they've been recently.'

'Is that a criticism?' he countered, aware that his weight was shifting from his heels to his toes and back again with annoying regularity.

'No, I——' Jessica hesitated. 'Look, wouldn't you like to sit down? You're obviously tired. We both are. But I won't keep you long, and it is important.'

'I'm perfectly all right on my feet,' declared James, not altogether truthfully. 'And personally, I would rather speak to you in the morning, if that wouldn't inconvenience you too much. As you've noticed, I'm not altogether undistracted this evening, and I really would prefer to go straight to bed.'

'You've been drinking,' stated Jessica flatly, taking a deep breath and glancing behind her. 'I suggest you sit down and I'll get you some black coffee. I know where the kitchen is, and I'm pretty sure I could produce something fairly palatable.'

'I don't want any black coffee,' retorted James, loosening his tie and pulling it a couple of inches away from his collar. 'It's very kind of you to put on this little display of domesticity, but I'm really not in the mood for either your sympathy or your personal remarks.'

Jessica was indignant. 'Is it a crime to make a perfectly innocent observation?' she asked. 'You have been drinking. Anyone can see that. I can't imagine why, unless Mrs Bentley is angry because I've started asking questions.'

'Let's leave Laura out of this,' James retorted harshly. 'All right, I have visited the local hostelry, but that, also, is my business. I suggest you say what you have to say, and be done with it.'

It was easy to disconcert her. In spite of her spirited defence of her honesty, she was still not confident enough to counter his derision. Yet, for all that, he couldn't help feeling a certain amount of admiration for her tenacity, and that, combined with his unwelcome awareness of her, added to his own sense of irritation.

'Well——' she said, taking a couple of steps backward into the sitting-room behind her, so that he was forced to follow suit or risk awakening Leonie by raising his voice. 'I've been thinking.' She sighed. 'You must have known I would. About—about Mrs Bentley.'

'Oh, not again!' exclaimed James. 'I've told you——'

'I know what you've told me,' Jessica interrupted him. 'And what I'm about to say has nothing to do with Mrs Bentley's attitude towards me.' She lifted her slim shoulders. 'I just wanted to say, if—if my father has left me a share of his house, then she needn't worry. I shan't want to live there.'

James shook his head, and then wished he hadn't, as the room swam slightly before his gaze. But the idea that Jessica should have come to this decision by herself was totally amazing. He had spent the evening trying to persuade Laura to come to terms with the latest developments, and now Jessica was saying exactly what Laura had been agitating to achieve. Except that she still thought that Laura owned some part of Bickersley whereas, in fact, the house was completely hers. None the less, her innocent contention altered the situation considerably, although whether she'd feel exactly the same when she discovered that Laura shared no part in her inheritance was another matter entirely.

Feeling in need of a stiffener, James abandoned his stance in the doorway and walked, not altogether steadily, across to the tray of drinks residing on a polished wood cabinet. He was aware of Jessica watching him as he took the stopper out of the whisky decanter, and poured a generous measure into a glass of heavy lead crystal. Then, turning, using the side of the cabinet for support, he raised the glass to his lips, and met Jessica's disapproving stare with controlled deliberation. 'I know,' he said. 'This is most unwise. But you can blame yourself for causing me to need it. I assume this is why you were waiting up for me.'

Jessica bit her lip. 'So it's true, then,' she said. 'I do own part of—what did you say it was called? Bickersley?'

James hesitated, and then, deciding there was little point in prevaricating any longer, he said, 'Not part, *all*. Adam left everything to you. Now do you understand why Laura feels so bitter?'

Jessica was appalled. It was evident in every horrified line of her expressive face. 'You—can't be serious!' she faltered. 'But—that's unbelievable! No wonder Mrs Bentley hates me. What could—*he*—have been thinking of to do such a thing?'

Now it was James's turn to look non-committal. 'Who knows!' He expelled his breath on a heavy sigh. 'I dare say he had his reasons. After all, you are his daughter.'

Jessica shook her head. 'But why would he leave everything to me? He never even knew me. How could he be sure I would do what was best for his company?

I don't understand.' She lifted her slim shoulders helplessly, and then, as if illumination had suddenly dawned, she caught her breath. 'Unless... Unless...'

James frowned 'Unless what?'

A faint colour stained her cheeks. Evidently whatever it was that had occurred to her was not so easy to articulate. And, watching the changing expressions that sped across her face, James was pretty sure he could guess what she was thinking. She had already observed Laura's proprietary interest in himself, and as perplexity gave way to logic she was bound to come to the obvious conclusion.

Before he could speculate any further, however, Jessica chose to answer him. 'I think my father must have wanted to hurt Mrs Bentley for some reason,' she declared thoughtfully. 'Don't you?'

She was surprisingly calm, considering the shock he had just given her, and for a moment James didn't know how to answer her. He could agree. That would be the honest thing to do. But defending Laura had to be his first concern, and he balked at betraying her trust even now.

Jessica was staring at him intently, and as if she had decided he needed further provocation, she added, 'Do you suppose Mrs Bentley had hurt him?'

James strove for indifference. 'How would I know?'

Jessica allowed her breath to escape rather suddenly. 'It seems—logical,' she ventured carefully. 'And as you seem to know her better than most people, you should know.'

James finished his drink with a gulp and put the glass down on the tray behind him with heavy-handed precision. 'That's what you think, is it?' he remarked tautly. 'I wonder why?'

'Well——' Jessica looked visibly agitated now, but she stood her ground. 'We both know that your relationship with Laura must have been a source of bitterness to my father. I think you do know why he did what he did. You—you might even feel some responsibility for it.'

'Now, you listen to me,' James grated harshly, leaving the support of the cabinet to approach her, 'I've told you before, my relationship with Laura is not a topic for discussion, and as far as your father was concerned, he had nothing to reproach me for.'

Jessica was trembling now. He could see it. But she was still determined to have her say, and her hands, pulled out of the sheltering warmth of her pockets, clenched into fists at her sides. 'How can you say that?' she demanded. 'If you were having an affair with his wife——'

'We were not having an affair,' retorted James violently, half amazed that they should be having this conversation, that he should be defending himself to her.

'Do you expect me to believe that?' she persisted, controlling the tremor he could hear in her voice. 'I've seen the way she looks at you. I've seen the way she speaks to you, the way she touches you, whenever she gets the chance. *You* may not be having an affair, but she is, and my father must have known about it!'

James looked down at her without liking. His nerves were as taut as cat-gut and his pulse was racing. Despite the fact that everything she was saying had an element of truth in it, he could not allow her to go on thinking of him in that way. 'Listen to me, you stupid little bitch,' he said, using the coarse epithet to keep some sense of control here, and a spasm of pain crossed her face. 'If you want to know the truth, it was I who introduced Adam to Laura in the first place. It was I who brought her home. I lived at Bickersley in those days, too, and she was going out with me when Adam chose to cut me out. I was away at university. He wasn't. End of confession!'

Jessica looked up at him. 'My father must have fallen in love with her,' she said unsteadily.

'He was infatuated with her,' retorted James flatly.

'And—and you were jealous!' Jessica was determined to have the last word.

'Very probably.' James took a deep breath, controlling the impulse to shake her. 'But that didn't make what he did any the less despicable,' he replied. 'Adam was almost twenty years older than Laura. He should have known better.'

'So you decided to take your revenge,' said Jessica tremulously, and James knew an almost uncontrollable desire to choke her.

'No, I did not,' he declared instead. 'As I said before, while your father was alive, my relationship with Laura was entirely honourable.'

'And since he died?' Jessica seemed unaware of the dangerous path she was treading.

'Hasn't Leonie told you?' James's response was clipped. 'I can't believe she would have resisted the impulse to make Laura look bad. But as a matter of fact, whether you believe it or not, I did care about your father, and I do have some respect for his memory.'

Jessica seemed to be getting a crick in her neck from looking up at him, so she transferred her gaze to the knot of his tie, resting just below his collar-bone. Her breath fanned the underside of his chin as she struggled to compose a suitable response, and that barely tangible caress was unbearably sensual. It was obvious the amount of alcohol he had consumed that evening was responsible for the feeling of awareness she was arousing in him, but that didn't remove it or make it any the easier to dismiss. He found his eyes moving from the tip of her head, drifting across the wide expanse of her forehead to the downy curve of her cheek. There was colour in her cheeks now, and not all of it was the result of her present state of agitation. Her face was fuller too, without the angular hollows that had been there in the weeks following the accident. He had never noticed before what long lashes she had, or how their tips were bleached by the sun. Even the soft arch of her brows was unfamiliar to him from this angle, but the parted fullness of her mouth was an unconscious invitation. He remembered how that mouth had felt beneath his own, on that one unwary occasion when he had completely lost his head. There had been warmth there, and a hint of passion, and he knew a sudden reckless longing to experience that feeling again.

But why? he asked himself tensely. It wasn't as if he was starved of female companionship. Laura would have been only too willing to satisfy any desires he had, and if he had had any sense at all he would not have walked out of Bickersley in his present state of aggravation. He guessed it was the knowledge of this latent attraction that had sent him to the pub, and the amount of alcohol he had consumed should have suppressed any lingering desires he had. And it would have done, too, if Jessica had not been here, waiting for him when he got home. He would have gone straight to bed and lost himself in oblivion, safely anaesthetised against any mordant feelings of sexuality.

But it hadn't happened that way. Jessica had been here, balking his escape, and disrupting his reason. Not that she was aware of it. Not yet, at any rate. But unless he could get out of here pretty soon and seek the sanctuary of his own bedroom, he was very much afraid he might lose his head for the second time in his life.

Jessica took a deep breath. 'Well—at least I know now why you brought me to Aspen,' she said quietly. Small, even, white teeth appeared to draw her full lower lip between them. 'Was it her idea or yours? And how long were you prepared to let me stay?'

James closed his eyes against this new offensive. 'Jess—— '

'I'd like to know,' Jessica insisted tensely. 'It must have been quite a sacrifice. No wonder Leonie was dismayed.'

James groaned. 'Look, I know how this must appear to you, but it wasn't like that. My reasons for bringing you here were my own, and believe me, Laura was not in favour.'

'Why not?'

Jessica looked up at him then, and the look of wounded suspicion in those darkly violet eyes was James's undoing. Dear God, he thought, trying to fight the urge he had to comfort her and failing. When he had brought Jessica to Aspen he had had no idea of the trouble she could cause for him, but he was beginning to apprehend it now, even if it was too late to do anything about it.

Almost against his will, it seemed, his hands left his sides to grasp the yielding contours of her upper arms. He thought, momentarily, that perhaps she was as startled at his actions as he was himself, for to begin with she made no move to resist him. His mouth curved sensually as he felt the warm softness of her skin beneath the fine wool, and he paused. For a moment, it was enough to hold her like that, smoothing his thumbs over the veiled skin and feeling the sense of pleasure it gave him. But when her involuntary submission to his touch gave way to a concerted denial, his emotions got the better of him and he was no longer able to be gentle.

Her eyes were wide now, wide with anger and disbelief, and perhaps, unbelievably, fear. She had no reason to fear him, he thought uncomprehendingly, or had she? Did he even now know what he wanted of her?

'James, please——'

But her protesting cry was barely audible. Even then, he thought she was over-reacting. Although she must be aware of the heat of his body, and of the growing urgency in his touch, their relationship thus far had not led her to believe that he might ever act this way, but James hardly recognised himself in the emotive stranger who pulled her into his arms.

But it was good, so good to feel her slim, wriggling form against his. Even if it was against her will, the feminine warmth of her body was so satisfying. His hands left her arms to slide over her shoulders and down into the hollow of her back, urging her lower limbs against his and creating an intimacy between them that could not be denied.

'James, what are you doing?' she gasped, when one of his hands found the curve of her nape, and turned her face up to his. But he ignored the desperation of her protest.

'What do you think I'm doing?' he asked, though it was a purely rhetorical question. Before she could respond, his mouth had found the parted agitation of hers, and any reply she might have made was stifled by the possession of his kiss.

He had thought it would be the same, the same as the other time he had kissed her, when all hell had been let loose in his carefully ordered existence. But it wasn't. It was much more profound, much more disturbing, and although she continued to resist him it was infinitely more exciting. God, he wanted her, he thought with some amazement. He wanted to bury himself in her tender flesh, and spill his seed inside her. It was a totally primitive need, pagan almost, and neither Laura nor Irene had ever evoked such a hunger inside him.

Her resistance ceased abruptly when his tongue slipped between her lips and into her mouth. It was as if that intimate invasion broke down the barriers she had hitherto been sustaining against him. With a little groan deep in her throat, she succumbed to the searching pressure of his lips, and the frisson of excitement he felt at her sudden capitulation tore through his stomach with a devastating surge. Her slim, delectable thighs were no longer struggling to be free of him, and he parted his legs deliberately to deepen their embrace. His hand, still resting in the small of her back, slid down to cover her small buttocks and urge them even closer to his burgeoning masculinity, and he knew from the little jerks she gave that she was aware of the heat and size of his hard arousal.

His mouth left her lips to move down the slender column of her throat, pushing the thin T-shirt aside so that his lips could nuzzle her shoulder. She wasn't wearing a bra, and the firm swell of her small breasts was an unrestrained temptation. He wanted to kiss her neck and her shoulders. He wanted to kiss her slender arms, where the fine bones were almost translucent beneath her skin. He wanted to strip the offending garments from her, and caress her naked body, to feel her taut nipples hardening in his mouth, and touch her feminine sweetness with his tongue.

He kissed her again, more deeply this time, drugging her with his kisses as he ground his hips against her. He was beyond all thought of what was right and what was wrong, and he half believed he would have taken her then if Jessica herself had not innocently brought him to his senses. For it was when she whispered, 'Oh, Larry!' against his neck that he started back from her in blind disbelief, and the sudden sense of self-derision he felt was not simply anger at a mistaken case of identity.

Yet, for all that, and not withstanding his disgust at his behaviour, James couldn't deny the spasm of jealousy that gripped him at her words. *Larry,* he thought savagely. Who the hell was Larry? And for a minute the significance of what she had said completely escaped him.

But, if he was disconcerted, he was no more so than Jessica. When he stepped back from her, and put an arm's length between them, she gazed at him with horrified eyes. Whether she was aware of what she had said or not was not immediately apparent. But what was apparent was her complete abhorrence of what had happened between them, and conversely James's self-remorse abruptly lost direction. Why the hell was she looking at him like that? he asked himself silently, bitterness tearing his sense of decency to shreds. She had wanted him to kiss her, she couldn't deny it. And it was he who should be feeling disenchanted that she should have mistaken him for someone else.

*Someone else!* The sudden awareness of what she had actually said swept over him. Shaking his head to clear the after-effects of his reckless descent into madness, he forced himself to concentrate on the really important aspect of what had occurred. She had used a man's name—Larry—who was obviously someone she knew. He thrust his own recurring surge of anger aside. God, this was a clue, wasn't it? If she could remember who Larry was, she might remember the rest.

But while he had been suffering his own particular brand of soul searching, Jessica had withdrawn from him more fully than as if she had put the whole width of the room between them. Looking at her, he saw accusation, not excitement, in her eyes. And why not? he asked himself bitterly. He had only himself to blame. It was just as well she had spoken indiscreetly. Without her words of intervention, who knew where his whisky-soaked senses might have taken him?

All the same, he couldn't deny a feeling of indignation that she should be regarding him with such resentment. It was he who had been made to feel a fool, and it was through his teeth that he at last said icily, 'Larry?'

Jessica blinked. 'I beg your pardon?'

Her voice was slightly unsteady, but chilled, none the less. She almost had herself in control, and James wondered what it would take to rob her of that annoying air of innocence.

'Larry,' he said again. 'You called me Larry.' His mouth compressed. He suddenly felt sober as a judge. 'Forgive me, but I'm not used to being mistaken for someone else.'

Now Jessica's expression faltered. Her unsteady dignity gave way to utter bewilderment. 'I—I don't know what you're talking about,' she exclaimed tremulously. 'But if you're trying to confuse me, you're succeeding. However, if you're hoping this diversion will make me forget what you told me about my father's will, then you couldn't be more wrong!'

*'Jess!'* James took a grim breath. 'Stop talking such utter rubbish! You must know what you said as well as I do. You called me Larry. Do you think I'd lie about a thing like that?'

Jessica's small breasts rose and fell with the tumult of her breathing. 'I—I did what?'

'You called me Larry,' said James, not altogether coherently. 'For Christ's sake, Jess, don't tell me you didn't know!'

'I didn't.' Jessica was trembling quite visibly now.

James stared at her. 'Are you serious?'

'Yes! Yes!' Jessica returned his gaze, wild-eyed. 'Oh, God, what does it all mean? Who is Larry? Why did I use that name?'

James bit back his frustration. 'That's something we'd both like to know.' He lifted his shoulders in a bitter gesture. 'It was obviously someone you were pretty close to.'

Jessica flushed. 'Yes, I suppose so.' She cast a fleeting glance at his brooding face. 'Did I really call you Larry?'

Seeing the look in her eyes, James decided this conversation had gone far enough. He had the distinct suspicion that, if she suddenly chose to understand the reason for his withdrawal, he might not be able to resist the temptation to take up where they left off. Even if she had called him Larry, she had done it unthinkingly, and the idea of where their lovemaking could lead them could still arouse feelings he would rather subdue.

'I gather the name doesn't mean anything to you?' he said, endeavouring to speak formally. And at her obvious confusion, he added 'Then I suggest we abandon any further discussion until tomorrow.'

Jessica hesitated then, clearly torn between the desire to leave him, and an apparently equally strong desire to say something else. 'Um—there is one thing,' she ventured, and James steeled himself to remain immobile when her hand brushed his sleeve. 'About—about the will——'

'Oh, please!' James's teeth ground together. 'You'll get what is yours, don't worry.'

'I'm not worried.' Jessica swallowed with an obvious effort, and ignoring James's expression, she insisted on going on. 'About the house,' she said. 'I—I just wanted to explain about the house.' She licked her lips. 'You see—I don't want it. I don't know what I said before the accident—why I should have been coming here, when there doesn't seem any reason for me to do so. But you can tell Mrs Bentley, she can keep it. I—I'll see the solicitor and get the necessary papers drawn up. All I need, as far as I can see, is a little money to tide me over until I can get another job. I've always been independent—at least, I think I have. And I'd like to keep it that way, whatever you may think.'

## CHAPTER THIRTEEN

LATER on, it was almost impossible for Jessica to describe how she felt during the next couple of days. The accident, her loss of memory, even the sense of disorientation she felt whenever she tried to remember the past, paled into insignificance when compared to the tumult of emotion James's lovemaking had evoked.

It had all been so unexpected. It was the very last thing she'd ever expected of him. In spite of her own unwilling attraction to him, she had never in her wildest dreams imagined he might be aware of it. But he must have been aware of it. Why else had he behaved as he had? Oh, he had been drinking, it was true, but he would never have thought of laying a hand on her if he had not become aware of the uncontrollable vibrations emanating from her. She had done her best to disguise her feelings, and she had been angry with him. Not least because of his attempt to protect Laura. But underlying everything else was her uneasy awareness that, compared to how she felt about James, the ramifications of what he had told her had lost some of their significance. Even at this moment, when she should have been thinking of what she was going to do now that she had discovered the truth, her brain refused to concentrate on the relevant issues. Instead, all she could think about was the fact that her relationship with James would never be the same again. By compromising his position, she had made it impossible for her to stay here. But where was she to go? And who could she turn to for advice?

One thing was certain, his behaviour had successfully defused her anger. The feeling of betrayal she had felt when she'd discovered exactly why James had brought her to Aspen struggled painfully to the surface. It was obvious now that everything James had done had been to protect Laura, and she should have had her suspicions sooner. The truth was, she had wanted to believe his motives had been honourable, and she had stifled any doubts she had had because of how she felt. But not now. Not any longer. Her eyes were open to the full extent of his treachery. Even if she did feel a certain reluctant sympathy for Laura, nothing could alter the fact that they had both kept the truth from her, hoping no doubt that they could delay the revelation of what her father had done. And because she had lost her memory she had played into their hands.

But, although she knew all this, Jessica was still no nearer to deciding how she should proceed. In spite of the excitement she had evidently felt at learning that Adam Bentley had recognised her at last, she was now convinced she should not have come here. Had she indeed given up her job on the strength of this inheritance? Had she severed all ties with her life in London to make contact with a family who had never known of her existence until now, and obviously wished she did not exist? Surely she must have considered this before she left London? Or had she had some naïve idea that they might accept her as the innocent contender she was? Was that why she had brought that awful sable coat? Those terribly formal clothes? Had she hoped that by dressing as they did she could pretend she was one of them? All things were possible, as her grandmother used to say, she recalled ruefully, and then caught her breath at this amazing recollection. *Her grandmother!* she thought unsteadily. So she had had a grandmother! She sighed, pressing frustrated fingers to her temples. If only she could recover her memory. If only she could recall exactly what her intentions had been.

The day after her confrontation with James she spent in consternation, expecting every moment for him to send for her to ask her to leave. She couldn't believe he would want her to stay after what had happened, and she spent some time composing what she was going to say. But at lunch time Mrs Hayes informed her that Mr Bentley had had to go into Leeds to see Leonie's headmistress, and she really had no idea when he was likely to be back.

'There's not been any—well, trouble about Leonie taking a day off?' Jessica ventured uneasily, meeting the housekeeper's gaze with some confusion. 'I mean—I wouldn't like her to get into trouble because of me. And it was my idea that Leonie and I should go shopping.'

'But Mr Bentley knew about that,' said Mrs Hayes pointedly. 'You said so yourself. I believe it was you who asked him, wasn't it?'

'Well, yes.' Jessica crossed her fingers against the lie, and managed a thin smile. 'Even so, he might have forgotten, and I shouldn't like Leonie to take the blame.'

'Mr Bentley doesn't forget anything,' said Mrs Hayes, making for the door. 'Now, you enjoy your lunch. I'll be back later to clear the dishes.'

Jessica did her best to do justice to the meal, but although the slice of fresh salmon and crisp salad was delicious, she had little appetite for the food. She knew she ought to be grateful for James's absence, but she wasn't. Although she wasn't yet clear in her mind what she was going to do, nothing could be resolved so long as he was not here, and she owed him the courtesy at least of keeping him informed of her decision.

It was a glorious day. Beyond the windows, the garden was a blaze of colour. Mr Hayes, and the boy who came to help him, had tied back the late flowerings of tulips and daffodils, and in their place hyacinths and lilies rioted in colourful profusion. The almond trees that edged the path that led down to the stables had shed their blossom over the paving stones, giving them the appearance of a confetti-strewn pathway. The trees in the paddock too, cast luxuriant pools of shadow against the green turf, and even the mares were frisky as they grazed in the sun. If only she could ride, thought Jessica, with a rueful longing, remembering the previous day's fiasco. It was a crime to live in surroundings like these and not be able to make yourself a part of it, and the life she must have led in London seemed even more remote.

James came back in the late afternoon. Jessica heard the Range Rover as she sat on the patio, enjoying a glass of freshly squeezed orange juice that Mrs Hayes had provided for her. She expected him to join her, and steeled herself for the inevitable encounter, but although Leonie appeared on the terrace there was no sign of her father.

'Oh—hi!' she greeted the older girl a little lamely. 'That looks good.' She nodded towards the jug of iced juice resided on the tray beside Jessica's elbow. 'I'll go and get a glass.'

'Wait!' Jessica caught her lower lip between her teeth. 'There's—there's nothing wrong is there?'

Leonie looked puzzled. 'Should there be?'

'No.' Jessica sighed. 'I just wondered why your father had to go to the school.'

'Oh, that!' Leonie shrugged her shoulders carelessly. 'It was just the usual parents' afternoon. You know, it's when the teachers drop you in the proverbial—well!' She grimaced. 'What did you think it was? Did you think they were going to expel me for telling a few white lies?'

Jessica shook her head. 'I didn't know what to think.'

'Well, you can relax.' Leonie loosened her tie and pulled it off. 'Nothing untoward happened. I'm still a pupil at St Winifred's, worse luck!'

Jessica was relieved, but after Leonie went into the house to change she waited a little apprehensively for James to appear. However, once again he confounded her, and when Leonie reappeared it was with the news that her father had gone straight down to the stables.

'Do you want to come, too?' she asked, gulping down a glass of the orange juice before wiping her mouth on the back of her hand. 'You could ask Dad to let you ride Angel Face again. I'm not saying he'd let you, mind you. He's in a pretty foul mood.'

Jessica forced a smile. 'I think I'll stay here,' she said, even though the urge to see James again and gauge his reaction was tearing her to pieces. But another confrontation in front of Leonie, and possibly Pat Grady too, was not to be recommended. And if James was not in the best of tempers, anyway, it was hardly the time to choose to discuss her immediate future.

Leonie didn't argue. She was obviously too eager to get down to the stables and take her beloved Bekahra for a ride. But Jessica did notice that she was wearing the all-in-one jumpsuit that they had bought a couple of days ago in Harrogate, and with her pale face flushed with anticipation Leonie looked almost attractive.

'OK, see you later!' the girl said now, charging away towards the stables, and Jessica thought how ironic it was that just as Leonie was beginning to accept her, she was going to have to leave. Although she couldn't be sure, she really thought Leonie had begun to like her, and at least so long as she was there Laura was kept at bay.

Resisting the impulse to follow her, Jessica got to her feet and walked regretfully into the house. What was she going to do? she wondered as she slowly climbed the stairs to her room. As she saw it, she had only two alternatives. Firstly, she could try and put what had happened between her and James behind her, and wait until her memory returned before attempting to leave. In spite of everything, that was still the most attractive alternative, even if it was the least acceptable in the circumstances. Or secondly, she could do what she had suggested to James himself. And that was to go back to London and try and jolt her unconscious brain into action. It was still reasonable that familiar names and familiar places might achieve what unfamiliarity had not, and just because the idea was a little frightening, was no reason to dismiss it out of hand.

If only someone had shown some interest in what had happened to her. Had she had no friends? Or had she alienated them all when she so unexpectedly became an heiress? *An heiress!* She frowned. Every now and then, something she thought or something she said seemed to spark some latent nerve inside her. And they were becoming more frequent, she thought more optimistically. Somehow she knew she had heard those words before. Someone, somewhere, had used them to her, but when she tried to tax her brain to remember who had said them, she experienced the same feeling of blankness that she had felt before. But soon, she told herself grimly, soon she would remember. There was nothing to stop her. Dr Patel had said so. She just had to wait and be patient, and nature would do the rest.

She took a shower before supper, deliberately washing her hair, and leaving it loose about her shoulders. She refused to accept that this was a futile attempt to appear attractive in James's eyes, but she had to admit she wished she had been able to buy herself something more appealing than the cream silk shirt and brown velvet trousers she was obliged to wear. He had seen them before and, although they were not unattractive, she would have preferred a cotton dress.

But she needn't have worried. As she had half expected, Mrs Hayes informed her that Mr Bentley was dining at Bickersley, and once again she and Leonie were forced to eat alone. But at least Leonie was more cheerful, regaling Jessica with Bekahra's pedigree, and inviting her to ride him when she had mastered the art.

'I don't know what I'd do if I couldn't ride,' Leonie mused, serving herself with another helping of the creamy *coq au vin* Mrs Hayes had provided for their supper. 'You know, Daddy taught me to ride when I was just a baby. And I was never scared, not ever. Not even when my pony threw me, and I landed in the ditch.' She grinned. 'Honestly, I was covered in mud! Mrs Broderick—she was the nanny I had then—she was absolutely horrified! I was a much tidier little girl in those days. Mrs Broderick saw to that. I guess a psychiatrist might say that that was why I've rebelled against being tidy ever since. Do you know, she used to put me in the bath twice a day? I sometimes think that's why my hair is such a mess—because Mrs Broderick's shampooing took all the body out of it.'

Jessica let her go on. It was easier to listen to Leonie's chatter than to suffer the anguish of her own thoughts. Besides, it was good to know she trusted her and was treating her as a real member of the family at last.

However, later that night, in the silence of her own room, there was no distraction from the uneasy tenor of her thoughts. All day she had been coping with the possible after-effects of what had happened between her and James, and she had deliberately avoided thinking about what had actually happened. The night before, when she might have expected to lie awake for hours worrying about the future, she had simply tumbled into bed, too exhausted by what had occurred to think coherently about anything. She had slept, albeit fitfully, and in that way had escaped her own recriminations. But tonight she was wide awake and restless, and no amount of self-discipline could prevent her from reliving those moments in James's arms.

*How had it happened?* Even now, with the benefit of hindsight, she was still not totally conversant with the actual realities. Of course, James had been drinking, and it was possible he had mistaken her for Laura. Certainly, when he had been kissing her there had been a certain desperation in his touch, as if he was acting against his beliefs, or perhaps simply against his will. And yet there had been no sign of restraint, no holding back. He had kissed her with a genuine urgency, which had found an answering urgency in her. And she knew she had not wanted him to stop. She had wanted him to go on making love to her until they were both beyond the ability to turn back. It was crazy, she thought bitterly. She didn't even know if she was a virgin, and here she was fretting over something that ought to have filled her with alarm.

But he had stopped. She had stopped him. Though not in the way she might have wished. He said she had called him a name: *Larry*. But she didn't remember using it, and she had only his word that she had actually said it. Yet what would have been the point of his lying to her? She could have sworn he had been as mindless in his lovemaking as she was. So once again a tentative memory of the past had surfaced from the shadowed pool of her subconscious. A memory as remote and isolated as the rest. Who was Larry? Was it someone she had really cared about? And if it was, why hadn't he come looking for her when the crash was first reported?

But, in spite of these misgivings, the sensuous feel of James's hands upon her body and the indelible memory of his hard body against hers were her strongest recollections. They had fitted together so well, she thought treacherously. Her father's daughter and the man who was having an affair with his wife.

She eventually went to bed, but not to sleep. She tossed and turned for most of the night, waking once with the distinct impression that something had awakened her. But the only sound she could hear, as she lay there in the semi-darkness, was the sound of the wind sighing through the trees, and she wondered if it had been James's car she had heard or simply the unsteady beating of her own heart.

In the morning she was up at half-past six, determined that today James would not avoid her. It was galling, but she had to see him before she made any decision. Apart from anything else, he was the only one who could give her the address of her father's solicitors, and on top of that she had no money. She hadn't yet decided what she ought to do about her own future, but now that the terms of her father's will were known to her there were certain plans she wanted to set in operation. To begin with she intended to find out how she could transfer the ownership of her father's house back to Laura. She didn't want it, she didn't even have any desire to see it. Something told her that any place Laura had lived would have an atmosphere she would not take to. Besides, what did she want with a big house? She was still convinced she had once lived in a bed-sitter, and although after living at Aspen she had no particular desire to go back to a single room, a small flat sounded infinitely more appealing. She would miss this place, of course, but it had never been her home. She had always known her time here was limited. And, no matter what James had said in the past, he was unlikely to argue with her now.

It was a fine morning, but overcast, and Jessica thought it reflected her mood. She would miss waking up at Aspen; she would miss the sound of the birds and the occasional whinny from the horses in the paddock. She would miss the dogs barking and the sound of someone whistling as they cleaned out the stables. So many country sounds she had become accustomed to. And instead there would just be the roar of the traffic and the occasional squeal of brakes as someone stepped unwarily into the road.

It was a quarter to seven when she went downstairs. She hadn't bothered to put on any make-up, and she was unaware that in her T-shirt and jeans, with her streaky blonde hair tied back carelessly with a ribbon, she looked little more than a teenager. But, to her annoyance, when she entered the morning-room, it was to find that James had already been and gone. That was evident from the crumpled napkin thrown down beside his plate, and the coffee-pot cooling on its stand.

'Damn!'

Jessica swung about as the door opened behind her, and Mrs Hayes heard her involuntary exclamation. 'I beg your pardon,' the housekeeper said, arching her brows, and Jessica made a rueful gesture as she swiftly offered an apology.

'I just thought James—that is—Mr Bentley would still be here,' she explained, expelling her breath on a sigh. 'He must have had breakfast awfully early.' Probably to avoid her, she acknowledged silently.

'As a matter of fact, Mr Bentley said to tell you that he would see you later,' replied Mrs Hayes surprisingly. 'I believe he's got some news for you. Something to do with the accident, I think.'

Jessica swallowed. 'The accident?' she echoed. What could he have to tell her about the accident? Unless—unless someone had come forward who knew her!

'Yes,' said Mrs Hayes now, unaware of Jessica's consternation. 'He said he would be back about nine o'clock. I don't suppose he realised you'd be getting up this early.'

'No.' Jessica was non-committal. But her brain was working furiously, and she realised the time between now and nine o'clock was going to go very slowly indeed.

'I'll get your breakfast, then, shall I?' Mrs Hayes suggested, collecting the dirty plates and brushing the crumbs off the table. 'Just toast and coffee as usual? Or would you like something more substantial?'

'Just coffee, thank you,' said Jessica, dropping down into one of the chairs by the table rather weakly. She wasn't hungry. And her veins were so full of adrenalin, she doubted that coffee was such a good idea. But she had to have something. If only to give her something to do to fill the time.

'Just coffee?' said Mrs Hayes. 'That's no breakfast for a convalescent!'

'It's all I want this morning, thank you,' said Jessica firmly. 'And—I'll wait for Mr Bentley on the patio. If I'm not there, I'll just be in the garden.'

'Very well, miss,' said Mrs Hayes grudgingly, and left to bring fresh coffee. But, after she had gone, Jessica couldn't help wondering what the housekeeper must think of her behaviour. However, like the good employee she was, Mrs Hayes kept her opinions to herself.

Leonie appeared later, and shared the table briefly before leaving for school.

'Just four more weeks and it's the summer break,' she exclaimed, when Jessica commented that she looked more cheerful this morning. 'Will you still be here for the holidays?'

'I doubt it,' said Jessica quietly, and Leonie frowned.

'Why not?' she demanded. 'Dad says you're no nearer to recovering your memory than you ever were. I thought you were going to stay here until you were better.'

There was a certain proprietary tone in her voice as she spoke, and Jessica was heartened at the thought that James's daughter, at least, would not be glad to see her go. But, although she knew that she might be upsetting Leonie by leaving, there was nothing she could do about it. And, while she hated the idea of losing the girl's confidence, she couldn't pretend that things were likely to go on as they were indefinitely.

'Well, anyway, you won't be leaving for ages yet, will you?' Leonie declared, as she looped the strap of her bag over one shoulder. Clearly, she was doing her best to cope with Jessica's intention to leave, and she departed for school quite cheerfully.

By the time nine o'clock came round, Jessica's nerves were stretched to screaming pitch. It had taken some courage to come down here and confront him this morning, and after learning that he wanted to see her, albeit about the accident, her apprehensions were rife. Perhaps she'd got it wrong; perhaps Mrs Hayes had got it wrong; perhaps James had only told the housekeeper he wanted to talk to her about the accident to disguise his real intentions. After all, he too had had more than twenty-four hours to think about what had happened, and it wasn't inconceiveable that he should come to the same conclusion that she had. All that he probably intended to tell her was that he had made some new arrangements for her, or was that a totally wrong assumption?

She had left the terrace and was wandering along the path beside the lily pond when James found her. Although she didn't immediately turn in his direction, she heard the sound of his footsteps on the path, and took a moment to school her features before she swung round to face him. In an open-necked black shirt and a pair of black corduroy trousers, he looked lean and powerful and disturbingly handsome. Evidently their encounter had not given him sleepless nights, for, although there was a certain tenseness about his features, the silvery light eyes were clear and alert.

'Good morning,' he greeted her evenly, and she wondered if she imagined a certain clipped quality to the words. Was he as conscious as she was of the awkwardness of their situation, or was it simply her imagination that gave credence to her uncertainty?

'Good morning,' she responded, making an effort to equal his detachment. 'Um—Mrs Hayes said you wanted to see me. That's rather apt, because I wanted to see you.'

'Really?' One dark brow lifted. 'Well, I'm here now. Do you want to tell me what it was?'

Jessica hesitated. 'It can wait,' she said, consoling herself with the thought that what James had to say might make her speech unnecessary. 'Er—Mrs Hayes said you had some news about the accident. Is that right? Has something happened?'

Now James hesitated, pushing his hands into the pockets of his pants and staring down into the still waters of the lily pond. 'Well, I was at a dinner in Leeds last night, and I did have a few words with the chief inspector who had been handling the details of the crash,' he admitted at last. He shrugged. 'They've apparently found some papers in a field, near the site of the crash. Some kids found them, and took them home. And, apparently, their parents decided they were worth taking to the police station. They guessed they were obviously of some importance to someone.'

'Papers?' echoed Jessica frowning. 'What kind of papers?'

'Well, I believe they're drawings; sketches, anyway. The kind of thing an art student might produce. You know.' He frowned. 'Or perhaps you don't,' he admitted. 'They look like pages from a drawing pad; designs for wool or textiles.'

Jessica blinked. For some reason her mouth was dry, and it wasn't just because of his nearness, although she had to admit she had not realised how traumatic it would be to see him again. The last time she had seen him, before she had walked out of the sitting-room and determinedly shut her mind to any attraction between them, she had been able to temper her attraction towards him with the anger she had felt at his betrayal. But now the awareness of how vulnerable she was in his presence was undeniable, and it was incredibly difficult to concentrate on what he was saying when the memory of how it had felt to be in his arms was still so sharp in her mind.

Even so, his words had brought their own sense of unease, and she forced herself to remember what James had told her about the other girl who had been on the train. Cecily, he had said her name was. Cecily Chambers. And she had been an art student, hadn't she?

Which meant the drawings must have belonged to her. But that still didn't explain why he should be telling her about them.

'I—I don't see what significance these drawings have, so far as I'm concerned,' she ventured when James said nothing more, and he gave her a sideways glance.

'Don't you?'

'No.' Jessica was confused. 'You told me yourself that the other girl sitting at my table was a student. Obviously these drawings were hers.'

James inclined his head. 'Yes, that's what the inspector thought.'

Jessica shook her head. 'So?'

'I still think you ought to see them,' said James, astonishing her. He took a deep breath. 'I told the inspector so.'

Jessica stared at him, her earlier anxieties forgotten as she absorbed this totally unexpected development. Why did James want her to see the drawings? What did she know about art sketches? Unless he was grasping at any chance of alleviating his own responsibility for her. Yes, that had to be the reason. He was uncomfortable with her after what had happened. It wouldn't have happened if he hadn't been drinking. Until that evening, his behaviour towards her had always been predictable. Oh, he had got angry with her from time to time, and there had been that occasion in the morning-room, for which she could only blame herself. But what had happened two nights ago could not be dismissed, and she was sure now he was trying to avoid its complications.

'Very well,' she said then, not prepared to argue with him. If he had some crazy idea that looking at these drawings might jog her memory, she would go along with it. After all, he could be right. She was in no position to decide one way or the other.

'Good.' James took a deep breath. 'I told Hanning—that's the inspector—that I'd probably bring you in this afternoon.'

Jessica twisted. 'Bring me in?' she echoed wryly. 'How appropriate!'

James sighed. 'What is that supposed to mean?' he asked impatiently. 'You know perfectly well what I'm saying.'

'Oh, yes.' Jessica nodded in assent. 'You're hoping these drawings will provide a miracle cure, aren't you? Anything to get me out of your hair. Have I become such a source of embarrassment to you?'

It was not what she had intended to say, but the words were out and she had to live with them. And, anyway, why should she feel ashamed? She might have provoked him the other night, but she hadn't encouraged him to touch her.

James turned to regard her dourly. 'Is that what you wanted to talk to me about?' he enquired flatly.

Jessica frowned. 'I don't understand——'

'I think you do.' James didn't let her finish. 'You're referring to my behaviour the other night. Well, believe me, you don't regret it any more than I do.'

Jessica made a concerted effort to still the sudden unsteadiness of her legs. 'As a matter of fact, I wasn't even thinking about what happened the other night,' she retorted, not altogether truthfully.

'No?'

'No.' Jessica held up her head. 'Is that why you've avoided speaking to me until today? Because you were afraid I was going to tax you with what had happened?'

James's face darkened. 'I haven't been avoiding you.'

'Haven't you?' Jessica hung on to her advantage. 'Well, it certainly looked that way to me. But then, I've had no experience in these matters, have I?'

James lifted his hand and, for a heart-stopping moment, Jessica thought he was going to strike her. But he didn't. Instead, he ran frustrated fingers through the dark vitality of his hair, resting his hand at the back of his neck and loosening the buttons of his shirt across his broad chest. 'Look,' he said, 'let's stop playing games, shall we? If you're not here to tell me what a bastard I am for taking advantage of you, then why did you want to see me? What new flaw in my character have you discovered? I dare say I'm already branded in your eyes as a man who sleeps with other men's wives, and tries to seduce innocent young girls. So go on, surprise me!'

Now Jessica felt chastened. 'Don't be silly,' she said awkwardly. 'I'm not a child. What happened—happened. It—it was probably as much my fault as yours.'

'You'd better believe it,' said James harshly. 'And all to make a somewhat futile gesture!'

'What futile gesture?' Jessica blinked.

'The idea that you could give Bickersley to Laura,' retorted James. 'Do you honestly think your father wouldn't have made damn sure you couldn't do any such thing?'

Jessica was taken aback. 'Do you mean——' Her voice was husky. 'Do you mean I can't?'

'I think it's highly unlikely,' said James, his hand dropping to his side again as he turned away. 'I've got to go. If I'm going into Leeds this afternoon, I've got work to do this morning.'

'Oh, but——' exclaimed Jessica, putting out an unwary hand, so that when he turned to face her, her fingers brushed his chest. And immediately his hand came up to remove hers, but instead of pushing her away, his fingers gripped hers with unknowing strength.

'Not now, Jess,' he grated in a strange voice, and before she could formulate any protest, he turned and strode away.

At lunch time Mrs Hayes informed her that James would take her into Leeds at half-past two. Evidently he had thought it wiser not to join her for lunch, and her intention to tell him she was leaving was delayed yet again. This afternoon, she thought, she would advise him of what she planned to do. He must know she could not stay here now. And, after the way he had behaved this morning, she was sure he would be relieved to see her go. At least then he could continue his relationship with Laura undeterred, she acknowledged bitterly. So long as she was here, she was obviously a deterrent to both of them.

It was a hot afternoon, and Jessica threaded her hair into a single braid before securing it with an elasticated band. It was the way she had worn her hair in the hospital, and it seemed to be quite familiar to her, even though in her passport photograph she was wearing it loose. On impulse, she pulled the blue passport out of her handbag, and studied the rather unflattering picture she found inside. Sometimes, she thought it was a good likeness, and other times, as now, she doubted its veracity. Of course, it was her, it had to be, but it was strange how unfamiliar it seemed to her. It was her image, after all. It should mean something. But it didn't. It was just the picture of a girl with streaky blonde hair and blue eyes, who was staring back at the camera with a look of satisfaction on her face. Had she ever been that satisfied? she asked herself. She supposed she must have been. But the smugness of her expression was not appealing, and she put the passport away without any sense of identification.

Deciding against wearing the jeans when she was going to the police station, Jessica was compelled to wear one of the dresses which had been in the case. It was one she hadn't worn before, a coral pink linen shift, with narrow straps at the shoulder and a swirl of pleats flaring from the hip. It wasn't short, but it wasn't quite as long as some of the dresses she had evidently bought with her new-found wealth, and she wasn't dissatisfied with her appearance, as she went down the curving staircase. The time she had spent outdoors had added a thin coating of honey-brown tan to her previously pale skin, and she wondered how long it would take her to get used to living in the city again after these weeks in the healthy atmosphere of the country.

James was waiting for her in the hall. In deference to the day, he was not wearing a jacket either, and the darkness of his clothes enhanced his sombre expression. But he made an effort to lighten his mood when he saw her, and she was aware of his gaze moving over her.

'Sorry to keep you waiting,' she said, realising her words were trite, but unable to think of anything more intelligent.

'No problem,' he replied, opening the front door, and allowing her to precede him outside. 'The car's over here.' He led the way towards the Range Rover parked at the side of the house. 'I've told Mrs Hayes we're leaving.'

The drive into Leeds was accomplished almost in silence. Several times Jessica made an effort to initiate a conversation, hoping to find a way to articulate her own plans. But James was evidently engrossed with his own thoughts, and his responses to her efforts were monosyllabic to say the least. Although she knew she was being cowardly, Jessica decided she could afford to wait. There would be time enough to talk on their way home from the police station. Perhaps James, like herself, was anticipating the coming interview, and wondering if once again it would produce no results. Nothing had to date, and if her own belongings aroused no sense of identity in her, how could someone else's drawings be of any use at all?

Chief Inspector Hanning was a man in his late forties, with thinning brown hair and a wispy moustache. But for all his unprepossessing appearance his smile was warm and welcoming, and he didn't seem at all put out with James for insisting on this interview. He wasn't the policeman Jessica had seen in the hospital. But then, he wouldn't be, would he? Her contribution to the inquiry into the accident had not been considered of any great importance, for, although she had been in the coach that had overturned, she had known very little about it. Less than most, Jessica reflected ruefully. She couldn't even tell them what she had been doing at the time of the accident.

'Won't you sit down, Miss Devlin?' the inspector suggested now, indicating one of the two chairs situated in front of his desk. The smile he directed towards James indicated that he should take the other, and after his guests were seated Hanning subsided into his own chair. 'So,' he continued, 'can I get you both some coffee? Or would you rather get down to business? I have the sketches here.'

Jessica exchanged a look with James and, sensing his desire to proceed, she turned to the inspector. 'I think I'd rather see the sketches,' she said, aware of her own unexpected feeling of urgency. 'I don't know if they'll do any good. But—but Mr Bentley thinks I ought to see them, anyway.'

'Yes.' Chief Inspector Hanning nodded. He glanced at James. 'I should tell you, someone else enquired about the sketches this morning. Isn't that amazing? So far as I was aware, no one else knew about them; except the kids that found them, of course, and their parents. But apparently the local press had got wind of the story and some ambitious reporter had the foresight to pass the news on to one of the national papers in London. So, as I was saying, this chap turned up here this morning claiming that the sketches didn't belong to anyone on the train at all. That they're his.'

'Who is he?' It was James who asked the question.

'I'd rather not say at this moment,' replied the inspector. 'Not until Miss Devlin has had the chance to look at the sketches, anyway.' He put the file in front of him aside. 'Here they are.'

The sheets of paper he passed across the desk to Jessica were about three feet square. The paper was thick and creamy, Jessica saw, and evidently someone had valued its contents. Once again she experienced that curious feeling of familiarity as she handled the thick pages. She couldn't imagine why, but she had the nerve-shattering feeling that she had seen these pages before, though how that could be so when the inspector had just said they had belonged to someone else, someone who hadn't even been on the train, she couldn't imagine. With trembling fingers, she turned the pages, gazing with bewildered eyes at the designs they contained. Someone had taken a great deal of trouble to produce the work in intricate detail, and their colour and artistry could not be denied. Some of the designs were in bold, primary colours, producing patterns for fabrics that were almost Byzantine in composition. Other were in softer shades, flowery mosaics, more suitable for dress-making materials, with a delicate imagery she could almost feel. Looking at them, Jessica felt her heart quickening its beat and sensed a ridiculous surge of panic growing inside her. It was as if her body knew that something momentous was happening, but its reactions were totally involuntary. She didn't really recognise the designs. Like everything else that had happened to her since the accident, this was just another example of her body's weakness. Yet, as she continued to look through the sketches, it was borne in on her, ever more strongly, that these patterns did mean something to her. But what? Notwithstanding what Chief Inspector Hanning had said, had she seen them on the train? Had that other girl, Cecily Chambers, shown them to her? She put both hands to her head suddenly. If only she could remember!

As if perceiving her feelings of desperation, James laid a curiously reassuring hand upon her knee. His touch was unfamiliar, as unfamiliar as these drawings she was trying so hard to identify, yet like the drawings it aroused a strange feeling of identification. His hand, like the drawings, was real; it was something she could hold on to in this world of shifting images, it was strong and warm and comforting. She darted a look at him, meeting his steady gaze with helpless consternation, and pressing down upon her flesh he held her gaze with his. 'Do you recognise them?' he asked gently, and Jessica hesitated a moment before she gave an involuntary shake of her head.

'How can I?' she cried, aware that the inspector was watching her reactions with an intense gaze. 'Do you think I should?'

'That's for you to tell us,' replied James. He seemed to realise what he was doing, and withdrew his hand from her knee. 'If what Mr Hanning says is correct, you shouldn't recognise them. But it's not that simple, is it?'

Jessica pressed her lips together in an effort to control their tremor. James was right, of course. He was always right. The drawings had upset her, more than could reasonably be accounted for by the simple remembrance of having once looked at them on the train. But what did it mean? What was he trying to tell her? Was she not Jessica Devlin, after all? Her head swam. So many questions, and she couldn't answer any of them.

Taking a deep breath, she swept all the drawings together and pushed them back across the desk towards the police inspector. 'Shouldn't they be in a folder?' she asked, taking a deep breath and sitting back in her chair.

Hanning frowned. 'A folder?' He tilted his head. 'What kind of a folder?'

'Oh, you know, one of those binders, with ties to keep the drawings in place,' said Jessica impatiently. And then, realising James was looking at her again, she grimaced. 'Well, I would imagine those designs belong in someone's portfolio. They look like a collection to me.'

James inclined his head. 'Do they?' He spoke consideringly. 'I wonder how you would know a thing like that.'

Jessica could feel herself trembling. 'That's something anyone would know, surely?'

'Maybe.' James was doubtful. 'But would Jessica Devlin have known it?'

Jessica stared at him. 'Are you trying to frighten me?'

'No. Just to get at the truth,' replied James evenly. He turned to the inspector. 'Well, what do you think?'

Hanning lifted the drawings and set them down in front of him again. 'I don't know what to think, Mr Bentley,' he admitted honestly. 'But perhaps this is the moment to introduce you to the gentleman who says the drawings are his.' He got up from his desk and opened the door into the outer office. 'Griffiths, fetch Mr Arnott in here, would you?'

Jessica's mouth was dry as they waited. The name Arnott meant nothing to her. But then, it shouldn't, should it? If she really was Jessica Devlin...

What was James trying to do to her? Having been forced to reveal that she was her father's heiress, was he now trying to protect Laura by pretending she was not Jessica Devlin after all?

The sound of footsteps echoed on the floor of the outer office, and they all turned as Sergeant Griffiths ushered another man into the room. He was a broad man, of medium height, with light blue eyes and fairly regular appearance. Dressed in grey trousers and green cotton anorak, he had no particular distinguishing features at all. And yet, as soon as Jessica saw him, she broke out in a cold sweat. With a sense of panic worse than anything she had felt thus far, she got unsteadily to her feet, aware of a totally unreasonable need to get out of the room. She couldn't think; she couldn't breathe; the room, whose temperature had been perfectly acceptable a few moments ago, was suddenly stifling. She was aware of James getting up too, and of the inspector's sudden apprehension. But they were only minor distractions. She had to get out of there...

But she couldn't leave. Sergeant Griffiths and the man with him were blocking her way, and short of barging past them there was nothing she could do. Then, as the man saw her, she saw the recognition in his face. It was as if he was seeing a ghost, and the pallor of her cheeks was matched by the draining paleness of his.

'Ceci!' he exclaimed in a disbelieving voice.

And she heard her own whispered, 'Larry!' before she slipped into welcome unconsciousness.

## CHAPTER FOURTEEN

'PHONE, Ceci,' called Sharon Gauge from across the office, and the older girl drew a breath.

'I'm busy,' she said, biting the end of her pencil. 'Who is it?' But she thought she already knew.

'It's some girl,' replied Sharon, pulling a face. She put her hand over the mouthpiece so that her words could not be overheard by whoever was at the other end of the line. 'Come on. You've got to answer it. I can't say you're not here again.'

Ceci frowned. 'A girl?' she echoed, wondering who it could be. Apart from her colleagues in the office, she knew few other people in Leeds, and no one who she could think of who could be described as a girl. 'Didn't she give a name?'

Sharon looked aggrieved. 'I think she said Leigh, or something like that,' she answered shortly. 'Look, are you coming? I do have other things to do.'

Ceci got up from her desk. Leigh, or *Leonie*, she guessed unwillingly. What was Leonie doing, ringing her here? She had hoped that episode in her life was over and done with.

Sharon handed over the receiver with ill grace, and Ceci put it to her ear. 'Hello?' she ventured tautly. 'Leonie? Is that you?'

'Who else?' Leonie's voice was amazingly familiar. 'It's good to speak to you again, Jess—*Jess!* I mean, *Ceci,*' she fumbled. 'How have you been? It's been ages since we heard from you.'

Ceci took a calming breath before replying. The last time James had rung, she had thought she had made it plain that she didn't wish to speak to him again, but obviously he had not relayed that information to his daughter. 'I'm fine,' she said now, realising she could hardly blame Leonie for her father's shortcomings. All the same, the girl had to understand that there was no point in trying to keep alive a relationship that at best had never been more than tenuous, and which had proved to be as unreal as Ceci had secretly suspected.

'That's good,' said Leonie now. 'Because I've got an invitation for you.'

'An invitation?' Ceci stiffened.

'Yes,' said Leonie, apparently unaware of the lack of enthusiasm in Ceci's voice. 'Dad's away at the moment, and I wondered if you'd like to come and have supper at the house tomorrow evening.'

Ceci was nonplussed. It had been easy enough refusing any invitations James offered her, knowing as she did that they were only issued because he still felt some responsibility for her. It was foolish, and unnecessary, that he should feel obliged to sustain any communication between them, and she particularly hated the sense of weakness his sympathy aroused in her. She didn't want him to feel sorry for her; she didn't want him to feel he had to maintain the fiction of caring what happened to her. And, in consequence, she got a certain amount of satisfaction out of turning down his efforts to keep in touch. But Leonie—Leonie was another matter, and she couldn't hurt the girl's feelings, not when her confidence was still so fragile.

Playing for time, she asked, 'Um—when is your father coming back?' and Leonie sighed.

'Oh—on Friday, I think,' she replied cautiously. 'Does it matter? Did you want to see him?'

'Oh, no.' Ceci licked her dry lips. Today was Wednesday. James's timing was excellent. 'It's just that—well, I have to work late tomorrow evening. I'd have loved to have supper with you, but I'm afraid it's impossible.'

'Are you working late tonight?' asked Leonie at once, and Ceci immediately recognised her mistake.

'Well—no,' she admitted, realising that if she wasn't careful Leonie was going to suggest she have supper with them on Friday evening. 'No, not tonight,' she added, resigning herself to the fact. 'Why? Would tonight do instead?'

'Of course,' Leonie acceded, as Ceci had known she would. 'If you'll give me your address, Mr Hayes will pick you up at about half-past six.'

'Lovely,' said Ceci, trying to sound as if she was anticipating the evening with pleasure. 'I'll see you later, then,' she appended. 'Thanks for ringing. 'Bye.'

Sharon, the typist who had answered the call, looked up as Ceci passed her desk. 'Bad news?' she enquired sarcastically, having listened to the call and come to her own conclusions.

Ceci shrugged. 'What makes you think that?' she parried, continuing on her way to her own desk. 'As a matter of fact, things couldn't be better. I've been invited out to supper. What could be nicer than that?'

Sharon pulled a face. 'I knew you'd give in to him sooner or later,' she declared, inserting a clean sheet of paper into her typewriter. 'I mean, even if he is old, he does have oodles of money, doesn't he? And that's some compensation.'

Ceci refused to dignify Sharon's remarks with a reply. The girl was only fishing, after all. Everyone who worked at Ripley's was intensely curious about her relationship with James Bentley, and it was hardly surprising considering the story of her misplaced identity had been emblazoned over every newspaper's front page. It was news, and she couldn't really blame anyone for being intrigued. It wasn't every day that an out-of-work student was mistaken for an heiress. And if she was growing a little tired of being treated as an oddity, she could hardly blame her colleagues for that.

It had been such an unlikely coincidence, that she and Jessica Devlin should have looked so alike—enough for her to be mistaken for Jessica. And losing her memory like that had been so convenient—or at least, that was probably how an outsider might see it. She was sure that opinion was fairly equally divided between those who sympathised with her and those who thought she had taken advantage of the situation. It was no use arguing that, if that had been the case, she would hardly have betrayed herself by recognising Larry Arnott. But then again, some might say she had felt obliged to do so before he identified her and destroyed her credibility.

It had been—and still was—a source of some discomfort to her. And the fact that James had rung the office several times in the six weeks since she had recovered her memory had only added fuel to the stories circulating about her. That she had refused all his invitations to Aspen, and evaded his attempts to see her, had made no difference. The cynics around her still thought it was only a matter of time before she gave in to his invitations, and, no matter how many times she tried to explain that her association with James Bentley had never been a personal one, speculating about a possible affair had proved too juicy a topic to dismiss.

And accepting Leonie's invitation now was not exactly sensible, either. But as she had decided that as soon as she could find an alternative position she was going to leave Ripley's, she refused to be daunted by the covert looks she was getting from Sharon and her fellow typists.

Seating herself at her desk, Ceci expelled a sigh. What a tangled web it all was. To think she had actually believed she was Jessica Devlin! What strange tricks the mind could play, particularly if you had no recollection of your past. Instead of which, Jessica Devlin was dead and she was alive, her identity as the other girl having hinged on that calamitous sable coat. Of course, if they had had two bodies to identify... Ceci shivered. But they hadn't. They had only had the one. And because she had looked a little like Jessica, no one had troubled to find out what Cecily Chambers had looked like.

There was another reason why the story had made headlines, though. It had been revealed to her by Toby Langley, the Bentleys' solicitor. Apparently the real Jessica Devlin had been coming north to arrange the sale of her father's property. The mills, which had been in the Bentley family for generations, had faced a bleak future because of Jessica's plans, and in an area where unemployment was still quite a problem there had been a general feeling of relief when the truth had been revealed. Now Laura Bentley, as next-of-kin, had inherited everything, and while Ceci had no love for the other woman she had to admit it was probably all for the best. Laura would maintain her position as mistress of Bickersley, and the house and the textile mills would remain in Bentley hands.

Remembering suddenly the way Jessica had spoken of her late father's wife on the train, Ceci couldn't help a secret pang of regret that the two women had never met. She was sure Jessica would have been more than a match for Ceci's adversary, and Laura might have got more than she bargained for.

Ceci pulled the design she had been working on before Leonie's call towards her now, and tried to concentrate on her work. But it wasn't easy. The idea of going back to Aspen, albeit only for one evening, was activating memories she would rather not remember, and she thought how ironic it was that now there were things she would rather forget.

But, of course, she couldn't. For instance, nothing could prevent her from remembering that scene in Chief Inspector Hanning's office when Larry Arnott had appeared in the doorway. Until that moment, she had been groping in the dark, touching on familiar things here and there, but always conscious of the blankness around her. Then Larry had appeared, and like a streak of lightning his presence had illuminated all the half-formed memories she had been struggling to recall.

It had been a painful illumination, she remembered tensely. So painful, she had lost consciousness for several minutes, and given Larry time to think up some new story to justify himself. *Larry Arnott*, she thought contemptuously. The only man—apart from James Bentley—she had ever allowed to get close to her. And he had betrayed her once again, just as he had done before.

She had still been at art college when she first met Larry. He had been one of the tutors, and she had been flattered when he had shown an unusual amount of interest in her. In those days, she had little confidence in her work, and to have someone like him complimenting her and offering to help her had seemed a marvellous opportunity. She had been infatuated with him, and had foolishly imagined he felt the same. But in fact he had been using her attraction to him to pirate her designs, and when she had discovered what he was doing she had been utterly devastated.

That was probably why seeing him again and realising why he was there had had such a traumatic effect on her. By the time she came round, he had disappeared, and although the inspector had been angry with his sergeant for letting him go, Ceci had had no heart to suggest pressing charges.

She had recovered consciousness to find herself lying on a daybed in one of the cells of the police station. James had been with her, and so had Chief Inspector Hanning. She remembered now how relieved she had been that James was still there, though she could tell from his expression that he had guessed what had happened. But initially the relief and amazement she had felt in discovering herself again had overshadowed all other considerations. She wasn't Jessica Devlin at all. She was Cecily Chambers. She hadn't been on that train intent on some mission of revenge. She had been on her way to an interview with the personnel manager at Ripley's, and, because everyone had believed it was her charred body that had been found in the burned-out toilet compartment of the train, no one, not even her friends in London, had had any reason to question her disappearance.

Ceci caught her lower lip between her teeth. She supposed she ought to be feeling grateful that Ripley's hadn't appointed anyone else when she failed to turn up for her interview. But the fact was, the personnel manager had been taken ill the day after the crash, and all other interviews had been put off indefinitely. Another coincidence, thought Ceci wryly, wondering, as she had done so many times in recent weeks, whether she had been altogether sensible in accepting this job when it was offered to her. But she had had to inform Ripley's of what had happened, and almost by return of post, it seemed, they had offered her employment.

James had said that a probably less charitable reason for their generosity was the amount of free publicity the firm gained by associating themselves with the mix-up. The local press particularly were loud in their praise for the company who had offered her a chance to take up her life where it had left off. But, in all honesty, Ceci had jumped at the chance it had given her to get away from Aspen. The salary Ripley's were paying her was more than enough to afford a small furnished flat in Leeds, and in spite of James's misgivings and Leonie's protestations she had moved into her own home just ten days after remembering who she was.

Of course, her reasons for moving away from Aspen had been more complicated than she was prepared to admit to anyone else. In spite of the fact that the evening James had drunk too much and behaved with such an uncharacteristic lack of control had never been mentioned again, by either of them, it remained in her thoughts, like a troublesome ache that wouldn't go away. And staying on in James's house had only been exacerbating her condition. No matter how kind James was, and he had been excessively kind since it had been revealed that she was not his cousin's illegitimate daughter, his motives for bringing her to Aspen had not changed, and she had no longer been able to claim a family kinship as a reason for continuing to accept his hospitality. On top of which, she was better; even Dr Patel had had to admit there seemed no earthly reason why she shouldn't try to pick up the threads of her life again, and in the month since she left Aspen she had travelled to London and visited her grandmother's grave, as well as arranging for the transfer of her few personal belongings to the flat in Leeds.

And now, she reflected, she was about to tie up the last loose ends of the life she had led as Jessica Devlin. By seeing Leonie, she intended to show James that he need feel no further sense of responsibility for her. She knew that anything she said to Leonie would find its way back to her father, and she was determined to sever that connection completely. As Jessica Devlin, the chances of James ever seeing her as anything more than a poor substitute for Laura had been slim; as Cecily Chambers, they were non-existent; and because she now knew she was in love with the man, she could not allow that discovery to become public knowledge. How Laura would enjoy learning something like that, thought Ceci bitterly. And no matter how understanding James might be, she didn't want his sympathy, either.

It felt distinctly strange that evening, driving through the gates of the Aspen stud. A little deceitful, too, Ceci thought uneasily, acknowledging the reasons why she had chosen to come here in James's absence. But Leonie, at least, deserved some explanations from her, she consoled herself, as the estate car swung in an arc across the gravelled forecourt. And it might be the last opportunity she had to speak to the girl. If she did decide to return to London, it was unlikely she would ever see Leonie again.

Mr Hayes brought the vehicle to a standstill, and Ceci offered a perfunctory word of thanks before thrusting open the door nearest to her and getting out. She didn't wait for his assistance. Mr Hayes, unlike his garrulous wife, was not inclined to indulge in small talk, and in consequence the journey had been something of an ordeal. Ceci had wished Leonie had decided to accompany him. As it was, she had had far too much time to dwell on past mistakes. Nevertheless, she had been glad of the lift, and summoning a polite smile of gratitude she turned towards the house.

But the smile froze on her lips as she did so. Instead of Leonie descending the steps to greet her, James waited in the shadow of the porch, and the overpowering scent of the roses that rioted over the doorway would forever be associated in her memory with this pregnant moment. It was such a beautiful evening; what a pity it had to be spoiled.

For a moment, she didn't know what to do. She was torn between the desire to go on and speak to him, and the equally strong desire to rush back to the car and ask

Mr Hayes to take her away. What was he doing here? How had he discovered what Leonie had planned to do? And what would be his reaction to her accepting this invitation in his absence?

Taking a deep breath, she endeavoured to remain calm. It wasn't the end of the world, after all. All she had done was respond to his daughter's kindness. If he didn't approve, he could always send her home. At least she felt reasonably assured by her appearance, she thought, clutching at that small encouragement. Instead of one of Jessica's flowery dresses, she was wearing a narrow-fitting cotton tunic, whose flared hem ended some inches above her knee. The colour, a kind of honey brown, complimented her creamy skin, and although she was still a little too slim time would deal with that.

James started towards her, and when Ceci cast an involuntary look behind her it was to discover Mr Hayes had disappeared. He had evidently decided to leave her to it, she reflected, trying not to feel betrayed. And where the devil was Leonie? Surely she hadn't deserted her, too?

Realising that by standing there, waiting for James to come to her, she was behaving like a scared rabbit, Ceci gathered her composure. She wasn't afraid of him, for heaven's sake! *No, just terrified that she might betray her feelings,* she added silently. Dear God, it was so *good* to see him again. She had forgotten how attractive he was. And whether he was going to be angry with her or not, she was here now and she had to make the best of it.

'Hi,' he said, when at last they confronted one another at the foot of the steps. 'I'm so glad you could come.'

Ceci swallowed, licked her dry lips, and then permitted herself a brief glance up at him. 'It—it was kind of Leonie to invite me,' she got out awkwardly. 'Um—where is she?'

'Not here,' replied James astonishingly, and, gesturing towards the house, he indicated that she should precede him indoors. 'Shall we go inside?'

But Ceci was still having some trouble with his first statement. 'Not—not here?' she stammered. 'What do you mean, she's not here? Is—is something wrong?'

'Not that I know of,' responded James evenly, his light gaze gliding somewhat disturbingly over the now slightly flushed curve of her cheek. 'She's spending the night with a friend in Harrogate. I'm afraid she isn't going to be joining us. You're going to have to make do with me.'

Ceci, who had started up the steps almost involuntarily, now halted and blinked. 'You mean—you mean, you *knew* I was coming?'

'*I* invited you,' essayed James smoothly, his hand in the small of her back urging her insistently ahead of him. 'You wouldn't accept my invitations, so we had to think of another way to get you here. But don't be alarmed. No one's going to force you to stay if you really don't want to.'

Ceci halted again in the open doorway. 'You can't be serious!' she exclaimed, gazing up at him with disbelieving eyes.

'Regrettably, I am,' James responded, a flicker of impatience crossing his face when she resisted his efforts to move her onward. 'My dear girl, what was I supposed to do? You shied away from any contact with me. I wanted to see you, to talk to you, to find out for myself how you really are. How the hell was I supposed to do that, when you wouldn't even accept an invitation to lunch?'

Ceci drew a steadying breath. 'Well, it's very kind of you, of course,' she murmured stiffly, 'but you really don't have to worry about me. I'm quite all right, honestly. I'm not your responsibility——'

'Damn you, I know that!' James's response this time was a little less controlled, and abandoning his efforts to have her precede him into the house he walked on into the hall, pushing his hands into the pockets of his cream cotton trousers as he did so. 'Look,' he said, halting in the middle of the floor and spreading his legs indicatively, 'we've got the place to ourselves. Mrs Hayes prepared us a cold supper before I gave her the night off, and if you get bored, you can always call a cab to take you home. Or, alternatively I'll take you, after we've had a chance to talk. What do you say?'

Ceci hesitated. 'I—don't see what we have to talk about,' she ventured, and he controlled his temper with evident difficulty.

'Well, let's at least find out, hmm?' he suggested, with a definite edge to his voice, and, subsiding abruptly, Ceci stepped across the threshold.

Mrs Hayes had laid the buffet supper in the family dining-room, where Cecily had eaten so many lonely meals in the past. Cold ham and chicken, a couple of creamy quiches and a juicy pork pie were flanked by plates of vegetables and salad, with a rosy salmon mousse to start the meal, and a dish of fresh fruit salad to finish. There was wine, too, cooling over ice, and deliciously frosted glasses, to add a touch of luxury.

James, having persuaded Ceci to join him, now seemed strangely ill at ease as he offered her a cocktail. 'We can eat now, or later,' he remarked, pacing somewhat restlessly about the room. 'Are you hungry, or would you rather go for a walk? You might like to see our latest foal. Or perhaps not. This place can't have many good associations for you.'

'Of course it does.' Ceci could not let him believe something like that. She coloured. 'Believe it or not, there were times when I was happy here. I certainly didn't look forward to leaving; not when I didn't know who I was.'

James regarded her somewhat dourly. 'But you didn't want to come back,' he reminded her shortly. 'Or was it only me you didn't want to see? Not everyone else?'

Ceci sighed. 'You don't understand——'

'No, I don't.' James set down his glass abruptly and walked towards the door. 'Come on, I may be able to handle this better outside. Will you be warm enough, or do you want to borrow a jacket?'

'I'm fine,' Ceci assured him, setting down her own glass and following him rather less assuredly out of the dining-room, through the hall and the sitting-room, and out on to the terrace that opened from the morning-room.

She was immediately reminded of the first time she had stepped on to this terrace, the afternoon she had been awoken by Leonie arguing with her father. She had been so unsure of herself then, so nervous, she remembered with a shiver. And was she so much improved now? James still had the ability to rob her of all confidence.

He had paused now, and he turned to look at her as she came out of the house. The sun was low and it provided an excuse for her not to return his gaze, though she was conscious of his eyes moving over her with an intensity of purpose she couldn't begin to understand.

'How have you been?' he asked suddenly, his voice soft and unexpectedly gentle, and for a moment she was too choked to answer him.

Then, brushing the treacherous tears aside, as if the low-lying sun was responsible for her eyes' sudden weakness, she murmured, 'Fine. Hmm—just fine. I—er—I'd forgotten what a beautiful view this was. You're—you're very lucky to live here. I—I think I said that once before——'

*'Jess!'* His emotive use of the name she had once thought to be hers briefly silenced her. But then, when he changed it to a tentative, 'I mean—Cecily,' she amended it to *Ceci* in a breathless little voice. 'All right, Ceci,' he agreed huskily, taking his hands out of his pockets and smoothing the palms down the seams of his trousers. 'God—I've missed you,' he added. 'Have you really not missed me?'

Ceci caught her breath. 'James——'

'All right, all right.' He turned away again, and she was presented with the sight of his broad shoulders, taut beneath the fine material of his silk shirt. 'I'm going too fast, I know that. Come on. We'll walk down to the stables. The boys should have finished for the evening, and I can show you Moonlight's new foal.'

Ceci followed him, but it was more an automatic reaction than a conscious effort of will. What did he mean? she was asking herself incredulously. How could he have missed her? He had Leonie—and Laura. And why should he care if she had missed him? It was all too much for her to comprehend.

Although Ceci had been in the stables before, it was the first time she had been there alone with James. Inside the long barn that housed the foaling box, the scent of oats and freshly turned straw was aromatic and strangely intimate, hinting as it did of warmth, and soft bedding, and the close, earthy atmosphere of the animals. It made Ceci instantly aware of their sudden isolation, and although she was enchanted by the mare's new foal she was overwhelmingly conscious of other, more significant feelings.

'Is something wrong?' James asked, coming back to join her at the rail after she had avoided his invitation to come and stroke the highly nervous little colt. She managed to shake her head.

'No, of course not,' she retorted, very much aware of James's arm only inches away from hers on the rough wood. 'Hmm—it's rather hot in here, isn't it? Do you think we could go outside again now?'

James sighed then, but instead of moving aside so that she could precede him out of the barn he turned to rest his side against the fence. 'In a minute,' he said, his face curiously strained in the shaft of light from overhead. 'Cecily—*Ceci*—I've got to talk to you. And first of all, I want to know why you've been avoiding me.'

Ceci gulped. 'I haven't been avoiding you.'

'What would you call it, then?' James was not appeased. 'You've refused to see me. You haven't accepted any of my invitations. I even had to resort to getting my own daughter to invite you here, because I knew if I did so, you wouldn't come.'

Ceci could feel her heartbeat quickening, and if she had felt hot before, she felt stifled now. 'I—I should have thought you'd have been relieved that I didn't try to take advantage of our—er—association,' she replied, a little unsteadily. 'I know I should feel grateful that you take your responsibilities so seriously, but I really am capable of looking after myself now. So please don't worry about me any more.'

James straightened away from the fence, but his solid bulk still stood between her and any means of escape. 'Is that what you think this is all about?' he demanded, a note of bitterness in his voice. 'That my reasons for getting in touch with you are solely because I feel some lingering sense of responsibility for you? My God, if only that were so!'

Ceci swallowed, desperately trying to control her breathing. She wanted to believe what she was hearing, but she was still convinced she must be making a mistake. Somewhere along the line she had missed the point of all this. What was James saying? What did he want of her?

'I—I don't think I understand,' she ventured after a moment, and James uttered a short, mirthless laugh.

'I'd say that was the understatement of the year,' he retorted, raking back his hair with long, agitated fingers. 'Look, this isn't easy for me, Ceci. I'm not a boy any longer. I'm too old to play games. If you didn't want to see me again, just tell me. I'd prefer you to be honest. I can stand the truth. I guess.'

Ceci didn't know what to say. 'I—well, it's not that I didn't want to see you again——'

'No?'

'No.' She moistened her dry lips. 'I did. At least, well—oh, you know I did.'

'Do I?' James did not sound convinced, but the eyes that bored into hers had gained a little warmth. 'Go on.'

Ceci lifted her slim shoulders. 'What more do you want me to say?' she protested. 'It's so difficult for me to—to say anything. I don't know what you want to hear.'

James took a deep breath. 'You could tell me the real reason you've been avoiding me,' he remarked, and she bent her head.

'I thought—I—*would* have thought—you'd have been glad to see the back of me,' she ventured after a moment. 'After all, you were the only one who thought those drawings might mean something to me. I thought that was because you were sick of me.'

'Don't be stupid!' James was impatient. 'I just wanted you to get better, that's all. So long as you didn't know who you were, I couldn't be sure of anything. Anyway, it was just a hunch I had, based on what Doctor Patel had said about you drawing pictures for the kids at the hospital.'

'I see.' Ceci bent her head. 'Well, it worked, didn't it?' She paused. 'I—I bet Laura didn't shed any tears when I left Aspen.'

'Laura?' James sighed. 'Laura has nothing to do with us. It may interest you to know, I haven't seen Laura in weeks.'

Ceci stared at him disbelievingly. 'But—I thought—that is, I understood you were going to—to marry her eventually.'

'Ah!' James inclined his head. 'Well, I guess that's reasonable. Until a few months ago, I suppose that was my understanding, too.'

Ceci held her breath. 'And now?'

'Now?' James stretched out a hand and looped his fingers round the back of her neck. 'Now you should know better than to ask.'

Ceci quivered, still finding it difficult to believe that this was actually happening. 'Are—are you sure you know what you're doing?' she breathed, and James made a rueful sound.

'I'm not sure at all,' he admitted unsteadily. 'But if you don't mean for me to touch you, then you shouldn't look at me like that. I'm not very experienced in these matters, I'm afraid. It's twenty years since I felt anything remotely resembling the way I feel now.'

Ceci was trembling. No matter what he said, she couldn't imagine James being inexperienced at anything. Just the feel of his fingers at the nape of her neck was enough to send waves of excitement down every inch of her spine, and the bones of her legs felt decidedly wobbly.

'Twenty—twenty years?' she echoed at last, unable to think of anything else to say, and he nodded.

'Even then, my feelings for Laura were never like this,' he declared huskily. 'Am I too old for you? Is that a problem?'

Ceci shook her head. 'But—your wife——'

James sighed. 'I loved Irene. But not in the way you mean. She was—well, she was very sweet, and very kind, and very gentle. Everything Laura was not.' He stroked her neck ever so gently. 'Do you understand?'

Ceci swallowed. 'I'm beginning to.'

'And?'

'And?' She was so perplexed by the touch of his fingers, she couldn't even think straight.

'And what are we going to do about this?' James explained softly. 'Do you think we have a future?'

'A future?' Ceci felt incredibly stupid, but she couldn't divert her thoughts from the emotions he was so carelessly arousing.

'Yes, a future,' he repeated, his thumbs brushing the soft underside of her jaw. 'Like you and me: together.'

'Oh, James!'

Ceci could hardly breathe now, and sensing her involuntary submission James used both hands to bring her closer. Then, tipping her chin with one hand, he brushed his lips lightly against hers. Almost instinctively, her lips parted, but although the moist aperture was a heady invitation James restrained any impulse to explore its sweetness further.

Instead, he said unevenly, 'Do you trust me?'

Ceci gulped. 'Yes. I think so.' And then, rather anxiously, 'Shouldn't I?'

'Probably not,' he murmured, his own breathing evidently giving him some difficulty now. 'Oh, Ceci, are you sure *you* know what you're doing? I'm never going to let you go, you know.'

Any resistance Ceci had still nurtured was abruptly severed. For whatever reason, she finally accepted that James did care about her, and whether it lasted a lifetime, or only a month, she was willing to accept the risks as well as the excitement.

'I love you,' she whispered, lifting her arms to wind them around his neck, and with a groan of satisfaction James pulled her closer.

Her limbs clung to his body, as if they had been made for that purpose. It was not the first time she had been close to him, and the hard strength of his pelvic muscles was achingly familiar. And this time there was no reason for him to push her away. On the contrary, he couldn't get her close enough, and she was scarcely aware of the hard bars of the stall behind her pressing into her back until James drew her away.

There was a pile of fresh straw to one side of the foaling box, and without taking his mouth from hers James drew her down on to the soft bedding. Then, pressing her back against the spiky stalks of corn, he thrust his tongue into her mouth, filling her with the taste of him as her body welcomed his weight.

'I love you,' he groaned, leaving her mouth to deposit hot, wet kisses all along the curve of her jawline. 'I think I have ever since I saw you in the hospital. That was why I brought you to Aspen. Not to make things easy for anyone else.'

Ceci turned her lips against his cheek, trembling uncontrollably as his hands slid possessively down her body. The skirt of her dress was hiked up somewhere around her thighs, and when his hands encountered the bare length of her legs she arched convulsively against him.

'God,' he muttered, seeking her mouth again, his kisses deep now and completely abandoned, drawing every atom of response from her, so that she was lost and vulnerable. 'I want you,' he added, moving so that she could feel the undoubted truth of that statement. 'Hell, I'm like a bloody kid again! This wasn't what I intended at all.'

Ceci pulled his face back to hers, gazing at him with adoring eyes. 'Are you complaining?' she whispered, feeling the stirring length of him against her, and he closed his eyes against the unconscious provocation of her bruised mouth.

'No,' he conceded. 'But I've no intention of making love to you here, where anyone could see us.' He rubbed his thumb over her lower lip. 'Will you come back to the house with me?'

Ceci struggled up on to her elbows. 'If that's what you want,' she admitted huskily, and he paused a moment to bestow a lingering kiss at the corner of her mouth.

'It's what I want,' he agreed, getting to his feet and looking down rather ruefully at his unmistakable arousal. 'If I can wait that long!'

Ceci had never seen James's bedroom before. On her occasional explorations of the house, she had always stopped short at the actual idea of entering his suite of rooms. Besides, Mrs Hayes would have probably had a fit if she had discovered her poking around in the master bedroom, so it was strange now seeing it all under James's decidedly possessive gaze. Besides which, she had felt distinctly nervous since they came back to the house, and, although she had no doubts about what she was doing, it was not something with which she had any experience.

James had closed the door behind them, and now he came across to where she was standing and ran his cool brown fingers along the length of her bare arms. 'Having second thoughts?' he probed, his eyes searching her expressive face, and with a definite shake of her head, she went into his arms.

'Are you?'

'Me?' The word was its own denial. 'Oh, no,' he assured her huskily. 'You're the best thing that ever happened to me. The wonder is I've lived so long without you.'

'Oh, James...' Her choked response was made against his mouth, and this time it was she whose hands sought his body, tearing his shirt out of his trousers and spreading her palms against the silky smooth skin covering his spine.

'God, Ceci,' he groaned, as the touch of her hands exposed his weakness to her caress. 'You have no idea what you're doing to me!'

'I know what you're doing to me,' she retorted, arching herself against him. Picking her up, he carried her across to his big, comfortable bed.

The buttons that kept the straps of her dress in place were soon disposed of, and Ceci held her breath as he tugged the cotton tunic away from her. Although she was not a total innocent, it was the first time she had made love in broad daylight, and her heart caught in her throat at the look in James's eyes.

'You're beautiful,' he breathed, refusing to let her cling to the small amount of dignity the scrap of bra and her panties would have given her. 'Let me look at you. Take your hands away. That's right. Oh, yes, that's right...'

James swiftly shed his own trousers, but Ceci looked away when he stepped out of his shorts. She had never looked at a man in such a blatant state of arousal before, and she realised that what little experience she had, had not prepared her for James's solid masculinity. He was beautiful, too, she realised, and when he slid on to the bed beside her she gave in to her natural curiosity.

'What's the matter? Did I scare you?' he demanded, burying his face in the warm hollow between her breasts, and Ceci nodded. 'Well, don't worry. I won't hurt you,' he appended, as his fingers stroked her nipples to a hard awareness. 'I have the feeling we were made for each other.'

Ceci had that feeling, too, and when James took one of the swollen peaks into his mouth she nearly went wild with excitement. Then his hands were moving down her body, finding the quivering flatness of her stomach, where her navel ached for his touch, and finally the moist core of her, that throbbed with a life of its own.

'Now?' he breathed, levering himself above her, and, dry-mouthed, she could only nod.

'Now,' she got out at last, and with a sound of satisfaction he lowered himself between her legs, the blunt spear of his maleness seeking and finding its silken sheath.

'Oh, Ceci,' he groaned, cupping her small buttocks and bringing her even closer, so that his pulsing length swelled and filled her with a mounting sense of excitement. 'I was so right...'

Ceci was incapable of coherent thought. Her senses had taken over completely, and she couldn't think of anything but James and what he was doing to her. And, as she had suspected, there was nothing amateurish about his performance. He knew exactly what he was doing and how to please her, and the steady rhythm he was building was building an answering need inside her. She had never felt like this; certainly never with Larry Arnott, and he was the only other man she had ever allowed to touch her.

But it wasn't over yet. The excitement James was generating was feeding on itself, and she found herself clutching at him spasmodically, digging her nails into his taut shoulders. She was urging him on, but she didn't know to what until it happened, and then the full extent of what they were sharing exploded inside her. As she uttered an ecstatic little cry, James's full weight came down upon her, and she felt the fluid strength of his manhood flood into her.

Ceci opened her eyes a few minutes later to find James's eyes were open, too, watching her. But this time she felt no sense of embarrassment at his steady appraisal. Instead, she stretched luxuriously beneath his gaze and he reluctantly rolled on to his back beside her.

Ceci turned on to her side to look at him now, propping herself up on one elbow and running delightedly possessive hands over the hair-roughened skin of his chest. His nipples tautened beneath that sensuous caress and, acting purely on instinct, Ceci bent and took one aroused peak between her teeth. She bit him, ever so gently, and James was forced to grasp a handful of her hair and bring her head up again.

'Not yet,' he muttered, but there was a promise for later in his eyes. 'We have to talk.'

'Do we?' Ceci pulled a face. 'What about?'

'Us,' said James huskily. 'And the future.'

'Oh.' Ceci drew an unsteady breath. She didn't want to think about the future. Not yet. It was enough that they were together. She didn't want to think about some nebulous time when they might not be.

'Yes.' James ran caressing fingers along her jawline. 'I realise I may be rushing things, but I don't subscribe to the current code of ethics that cleaves to an open relationship. I don't. Maybe I'm too old, or maybe having a daughter of my own——'

'Oh, yes. Leonie.' Ceci had briefly forgotten James's daughter. 'You think—she may not approve?'

'Are you kidding?' James's response was violent. As Ceci drew back in alarm, he pushed himself up to look down at her with disbelieving eyes. 'You can't think that!'

'No?'

'No.' Calming himself, he cupped the column of her neck between his fingers. 'Are we talking at cross purposes here?'

Ceci trembled. 'I don't know.'

'So tell me, why does talking about our future fill you with such alarm? I thought what happened just now was as good for you as it was for me.'

Ceci avoided his eyes. 'You know it was.'

'Well, then?'

'Well, then, what?'

'Well, then—when are you going to make an honest man of me?'

Ceci's eyes darted upward. 'Are you—are you asking me to marry you?'

James's mouth turned down at the corners. 'Whatever gives you that idea?' he asked roughly. 'For pity's sake, of course I am. What did you think?'

Ceci caught her breath. 'I—but—are you sure?'

James's eyes narrowed. 'Aren't you?'

'Oh, of course.' Ceci gazed at him with her heart in her eyes. 'I love you. I'd marry you tomorrow if I could.'

'Good.' James's expression relaxed. 'My God, I thought you were having second thoughts.'

Ceci shook her head. 'But—what about Leonie?'

James leaned over her. 'She arranged this meeting, didn't she?' he reminded her gently. 'Which reminds me, as she's spending the night with her friend in Harrogate, could I interest you in staying the night?'

Six months later, Ceci was out riding with her husband when her mare caught its foot in a rabbit hole, and she was pitched abruptly over its head. It was the first time she had had a fall, and James came galloping back to her, swinging down from his own mount, and rushing across to where she was lying.

'God, Ceci, are you OK?' he exhorted, gathering her shaken form into his arms, and although she felt perfectly all right Ceci couldn't resist playing a little trick on him.

'Where am I?' she asked, blinking innocently about her, and James groaned at the thought that she might have done some permanent damage to herself.

'You're here, at Aspen,' he said, removing her helmet and running gentle fingers through her thick swirl of honey-blonde hair. 'With me—James. Oh, darling, say you remember who you are!'

Ceci gazed at him blankly for a moment, and then, taking pity on him, she collapsed into giggles. 'I'm sorry,' she said, seeing comprehension dawning in his dark-skinned face. 'I couldn't resist it. I'm fine, honestly. Is Angel all right?'

James subdued the impulse to shake her, and helped her to her feet. 'I'll exact compensation later,' he told her huskily, and she dimpled.

'Promises, promises,' she taunted him, and then swayed a little as a wave of dizziness swept over her. 'Oh, dear!'

'What now?' James was suspicious this time, and Ceci realised that perhaps she had been premature in pretending all was well.

'Just a little giddiness,' she confessed, and seeing that she wasn't teasing this time, James took the initiative and lifted her into his arms.

'You can ride back with me,' he declared, hiding his concern beneath a show of disapproval, and when they got back to the house he insisted on calling his own doctor.

'Well, it's nothing to worry about,' declared Dr Taylforth, after examining her, and Ceci gazed up at him anxiously.

'Are you sure? You're not going to tell James something you're not telling me?' she asked, still a little troubled, and he smiled.

'I'll let you tell James yourself,' declared the doctor, folding his stethoscope back into his bag. 'He may find the idea that he's going to be a father again after all these years something of a novelty.'

Ceci propped herself up on her elbows. 'I'm pregnant!'

'About two months, I should think,' agreed Dr Taylforth cheerfully. 'And I'd curtail your riding activities if I were you. We wouldn't want another little accident, would we?'

Ceci was still in a state of some bemusement when James came into the room. 'Well?' he said, sitting down on the side of the bed next to her. 'What did he say? The old devil refused to discuss it with me. He said something about it being a *female* condition.'

'Yes, it is.' Ceci licked her lips, wondering a little anxiously now whether James would be as pleased as she was at the news. 'Um—do you think Leonie will mind if she suddenly finds she has a baby brother or sister?

I mean, there will be at least sixteen years between them, and—'

But James cut her off there. 'You're telling me you're expecting a baby?' he demanded, gazing at her with incredulous eyes.

'Hmm.' Ceci smiled a little tremulously. 'Do you mind?'

'Mind?' James leant over her, covering her doubtful lips with his mouth, and proving in no uncertain terms that his feelings were all positive. 'For Christ's sake! A baby!' he muttered. 'So long as you're happy, I couldn't be more pleased.'

'Oh!' Ceci linked her arms around his neck and hugged him. 'And Leonie?'

'What about Leonie?' enquired a sardonic voice behind them, and James drew reluctantly away from his wife as his daughter came to prop her shoulder against the door-frame. She had obviously just got home from school, for she was still wearing her uniform. 'Is Ceci OK? Mrs Hayes told me she had a fall this afternoon.'

Ceci swung her legs off the bed and sat up. 'I'm fine,' she said. Then, glancing at James, she added, 'Just pregnant, that's all.'

'Pregnant!' Leonie was obviously amazed at the news. She looked at her father. 'Really?'

'Did you think I was too old?' suggested James drily. Then, 'What do you think?'

Leonie shook her head. 'I don't know. I—think I like the idea.' She grimaced. 'Imagine! I'm going to have a brother at last!'

'Or a sister,' amended Ceci ruefully. 'I can't promise you what sex it will be.'

'Hmm . . .' Leonie considered. 'When will it be born?'

Ceci frowned. 'Well, it's December now. I suppose it will be born in June or July next year.' She hesitated. 'You'll have plenty of time to get used to the idea.'

'Yes.' Leonie was obviously beginning to approve. She looked at her father. 'Maybe, now you're going to have another son or daughter to follow in your footsteps, you won't be so adamant about me staying on at school, hmm?'

James regarded his daughter wryly. 'I'll think about it,' he remarked. 'And if that's all you have to say...'

Leonie grinned. 'I can't wait to see Laura's face when she finds out,' she gurgled. Since her father's marriage, the other woman had been forced to swallow her pride and acknowledge them. If only because it would have looked like sour grapes if she hadn't. 'Can I be the one to tell her?'

James sighed. 'I'll think about that, too.' He looked at her expectantly. 'Don't you have to get changed, or something?'

'OK, I'm going.' Leonie turned, but before she left she smiled at them. 'You're really happy together, aren't you?'

'We *all* are,' said Ceci firmly, and Leonie nodded.

'See you,' she appended, sauntering off to her own room, and James expelled a sigh.

'Kids,' he muttered, getting up to close the door. 'Do I really want any more?'

Ceci looked up at him doubtfully as he came back to her. 'Do you?' she asked anxiously, and he grinned.

'I like the idea of having children with you,' he told her huskily. 'And I'll do anything I can to make *you* happy.'

## INDULGE A LITTLE SWEEPSTAKES

# OFFICIAL RULES

### SWEEPSTAKES RULES AND REGULATIONS. NO PURCHASE NECESSARY.

1. NO PURCHASE NECESSARY. To enter complete the official entry form and return with the invoice in the envelope provided. Or you may enter by printing your name, complete address and your daytime phone number on a 3 x 5 piece of paper. Include with your entry the hand printed words "Indulge A Little Sweepstakes." Mail your entry to: Indulge A Little Sweepstakes, P.O. Box 1397, Buffalo, NY 14269-1397. No mechanically reproduced entries accepted. Not responsible for late, lost, misdirected mail, or printing errors.

2. Three winners, one per month (Sept. 30, 1989, October 31, 1989 and November 30, 1989), will be selected in random drawings. All entries received prior to the drawing date will be eligible for that month's prize. This sweepstakes is under the supervision of MARDEN-KANE, INC. an independent judging organization whose decisions are final and binding. Winners will be notified by telephone and may be required to execute an affidavit of eligibility and release which must be returned within 14 days, or an alternate winner will be selected.

3. Prizes: 1st Grand Prize (1) a trip for two to Disneyworld in Orlando, Florida. Trip includes round trip air transportation, hotel accommodations for seven days and six nights, plus up to $700 expense money (ARV $3,500). 2nd Grand Prize (1) a seven-night Chandris Caribbean Cruise for two includes transportation from nearest major airport, accommodations, meals plus up to $1,000 in expense money (ARV $4,300). 3rd Grand Prize (1) a ten-day Hawaiian holiday for two includes round trip air transportation for two, hotel accommodations, sightseeing, plus up to $1,200 in spending money (ARV $7,700). All trips subject to availability and must be taken as outlined on the entry form.

4. Sweepstakes open to residents of the U.S. and Canada 18 years or older except employees and the families of Torstar Corp., its affiliates, subsidiaries and Marden-Kane, Inc. and all other agencies and persons connected with conducting this sweepstakes. All Federal, State and local laws and regulations apply. Void wherever prohibited or restricted by law. Taxes, if any are the sole responsibility of the prize winners. Canadian winners will be required to answer a skill testing question. Winners consent to the use of their name, photograph and/or likeness for publicity purposes without additional compensation.

5. For a list of prize winners, send a stamped, self-addressed envelope to Indulge A Little Sweepstakes Winners, P.O. Box 701, Sayreville, NJ 08871.



DL-SWPS

INDULGE A LITTLE SWEEPSTAKES

OFFICIAL RULES

SWEEPSTAKES RULES AND REGULATIONS. NO PURCHASE NECESSARY.

1. NO PURCHASE NECESSARY. To enter complete the official entry form and return with the invoice in the envelope provided. Or you may enter by printing your name, complete address and your daytime phone number on a 3 x 5 piece of paper. Include with your entry the hand printed words "Indulge A Little Sweepstakes." Mail your entry to: Indulge A Little Sweepstakes, P.O. Box 1397, Buffalo, NY 14269-1397. No mechanically reproduced entries accepted. Not responsible for late, lost, misdirected mail, or printing errors.

2. Three winners, one per month (Sept. 30, 1989, October 31, 1989 and November 30, 1989), will be selected in random drawings. All entries received prior to the drawing date will be eligible for that month's prize. This sweepstakes is under the supervision of MARDEN-KANE, INC. an independent judging organization whose decisions are final and binding. Winners will be notified by telephone and may be required to execute an affidavit of eligibility and release which must be returned within 14 days, or an alternate winner will be selected.

3. Prizes: 1st Grand Prize (1) a trip for two to Disneyworld in Orlando, Florida. Trip includes round trip air transportation, hotel accommodations for seven days and six nights, plus up to $700 expense money (ARV $3,500). 2nd Grand Prize (1) a seven-night Chandris Caribbean Cruise for two includes transportation from nearest major airport, accommodations, meals plus up to $1,000 in expense money (ARV $4,300). 3rd Grand Prize (1) a ten-day Hawaiian holiday for two includes round trip air transportation for two, hotel accommodations, sightseeing, plus up to $1,200 in spending money (ARV $7,700). All trips subject to availability and must be taken as outlined on the entry form.

4. Sweepstakes open to residents of the U.S. and Canada 18 years or older except employees and the families of Torstar Corp., its affiliates, subsidiaries and Marden-Kane, Inc. and all other agencies and persons connected with conducting this sweepstakes. All Federal, State and local laws and regulations apply. Void wherever prohibited or restricted by law. Taxes, if any are the sole responsibility of the prize winners. Canadian winners will be required to answer a skill testing question. Winners consent to the use of their name, photograph and/or likeness for publicity purposes without additional compensation.

5. For a list of prize winners, send a stamped, self-addressed envelope to Indulge A Little Sweepstakes Winners, P.O. Box 701, Sayreville, NJ 08871.

© 1989 HARLEQUIN ENTERPRISES LTD.

DL-SWPS

## INDULGE A LITTLE—WIN A LOT!

Summer of '89 Subscribers-Only Sweepstakes

# OFFICIAL ENTRY FORM

This entry must be received by: Sept. 30, 1989
This month's winner will be notified by: October 7, 1989
Trip must be taken between: Nov. 7, 1989–Nov. 7, 1990

YES, I want to win the Walt Disney World® vacation for two! I understand the prize includes round-trip airfare, first-class hotel, and a daily allowance as revealed on the "Wallet" scratch-off card.

Name ________________________________

Address ________________________________

City ____________ State/Prov. ________ Zip/Postal Code ________

Daytime phone number ________________________________
Area code

Return entries with invoice in envelope provided. Each book in this shipment has two entry coupons — and the more coupons you enter, the better your chances of winning!



DINDL-1

## INDULGE A LITTLE—WIN A LOT!

Summer of '89 Subscribers-Only Sweepstakes

# OFFICIAL ENTRY FORM

This entry must be received by: Sept. 30, 1989
This month's winner will be notified by: October 7, 1989
Trip must be taken between: Nov. 7, 1989–Nov. 7, 1990

YES, I want to win the Walt Disney World® vacation for two! I understand the prize includes round-trip airfare, first-class hotel, and a daily allowance as revealed on the "Wallet" scratch-off card.

Name ________________________________

Address ________________________________

City ____________ State/Prov. ________ Zip/Postal Code ________

Daytime phone number ________________________________
Area code

Return entries with invoice in envelope provided. Each book in this shipment has two entry coupons — and the more coupons you enter, the better your chances of winning!

© 1989 HARLEQUIN ENTERPRISES LTD.

DINDL-1